SEX AND OTHER SACRED GAMES

SEX

and Other

SACRED
GAMES

Love, Desire, Power,
and Possession

KIM CHERNIN
AND
RENATE STENDHAL

Fawcett Columbine • New York

A Fawcett Columbine Book
Published by Ballantine Books
Copyright © 1989 by Kim Chernin and Renate Stendhal
Foreword copyright © 1990 by Shana Penn

Library of Congress Catalog Card Number: 89-91510

ISBN: 0-449-90463-6

This edition published by arrangement with Times Books, a division of
Random House, Inc., New York.

Cover design by William Geller

Cover photo by Ian Miles—The Image Bank. Sculpture: Barberini Hera,
Vatican, Museo Pio Clementino, courtesy of Scala/Art Resource.

Manufactured in the United States of America

First Ballantine Books Edition: June 1990

10   9   8   7   6   5   4   3   2   1

ACKNOWLEDGMENTS

For their reading and their friendship, our thanks to: Alice Abarbanel, Elizabeth Abel, Marcia Angus, Michael Bader, Sandy Boucher and the writing group, Diane Cleaver, Tobey Hiller, Louise Kollenbaum, Roz Parenti, Amy Rennert, Rena Rosenwasser, Elisabeth Scharlatt, Ute Schiran, Gillian Stewart, Gail Theller, Alice Walker, and Phillip Ziegler and especially Joyce Lindenbaum—to all of whom this book is dedicated.

Our thanks also to Beth Pearson, Amy Robbins, Karen Watts, and Margaret Wolf.

Socrates: Let us turn aside and go by the Ilissus; we will sit down at some quiet spot.

Phaedrus: I am fortunate in not having my sandals, and as you never have any, I think that we may go along the brook and cool our feet in the water; this will be the easiest way, and at midday and in the summer is far from being unpleasant.

Socrates: Lead on, and look out for a place in which we can sit down.

Phaedrus: Do you see that tallest plane tree in the distance?

Socrates: Yes.

Phaedrus: There are shade and gentle breezes, and grass on which we may either sit or lie down.

—Plato

CONTENTS*

*Alma Runau's parts written by Renate Stendhal
Claire Heller's sections written by Kim Chernin

FOREWORD

"Truth is the most powerful aphrodisiac of all."

Sex and Other Sacred Games is the story of a friendship between two women. Kim Chernin and Renate Stendhal portray two women—one straight, one gay—grappling with the questions that drive us all: sex, love, power, intimacy. One of the characters, Claire Heller, is an American novelist who believes that women are an elemental sexual force, more powerful than men. The other, Alma Runau, poet and translator, is a European feminist who thinks that women have not yet invented sexuality. We initially encounter the two women in a Paris café—a romantic setting, très femme. Over large, steaming cups of café au lait they discover that they disagree over every question they raise: Does intimacy kill passion? Is sex a return to the mother–infant bond? Are women victims? Is there anything a feminist can learn from a femme fatale?

Provocation fuels a mutual chase: "You envy the power you imagine in men," taunts Claire, "because you are afraid of your own." "How many men do you know," Alma retorts, "who could deal with a woman's power?" Worthy opponents, they each assume the challenge that difference poses. We follow Alma's and Claire's theoretical battle through the course of letter writing, storytelling, surprise visits, journal entries—even through everyday activities like flirting in cafés and changing shoes. Theory spills into storyline and story leaps into theory. The book's experimental form is provocative and puzzling, like a lover. Desire defies form as well as category. In the spirit of fiction disguised as nonfiction (or is it nonfiction disguised as fiction?), the authors depict theory as inextricably bound to experience.

It is refreshing to find a book devoted entirely to a friendship (and more) between women, especially a friendship based on the tension between disagreement and acceptance. A relationship in which confrontation ignites transformation. Chernin and Stendhal have invented a contemporary feminist dialogue recreating Plato's classic discourse between Socrates and Phaedrus on eros and beauty. In *Sex and Other Sacred Games*, too, characters talk and cruise one another. It is impossible to read about this cleverly crafted courtship without also being lured into its erotic labyrinth—and thus entangled and sometimes lost. One is always lost when traversing new territory; being lost is where the new story begins.

Alma and Claire are very real modern women with sharp, curious minds and healthy appetites for adventure, ideas, and romance. Their self-reliant outlooks have been clearly influenced by feminism, even though Claire claims she figured it all out on her own. Both are in transition when they meet. Alma has been analyzing why her affairs end unhappily.

My relationships [with women] *became a cradle . . . anything that could separate us from each other had to stay out. We protected each other like mothers protect their children from the world. From too much adventure, challenge, unequalness, competition. In short, from life. And thus from our truth. Sex in such a cradle can come to be felt as part of the danger of life. How can one be totally naked and open if there's a need for protection from some truth?*

Claire is a self-mocking seductress who has always pursued sex as sport. She easily short-circuits Alma's feminist wiring with her brash coming-of-age stories and her audacious sexual conquests. Claire dresses sexuality in myth and metaphor. She wears the costumes of whore as artist, Aphrodite, priestess in a temple of sacred sex. But Alma sees through her game: Claire's bravado conceals loneliness and despair. Her sexuality, in the absence of love or intimacy, is not as satisfying as Claire claims.

By guessing each other's games, both begin to sense the ways they sexually trap themselves, lose their way, repeat patterns, burn out. Each presents to the other the possibility of a next step in her own becoming, the possibility of a new sacred game. As separate characters representing two aspects of the female psyche, we observe the magnetic lure between them as they grope toward integration.

What gradually emerges, as we follow Alma and Claire, is how polemical differences between a lesbian and a heterosexual woman mask a secret longing for the unexplored parts of self—how difference attracts the unknown truths of what a person can be. The possibility that a lesbian can recognize herself in a "hetera" (and vice-versa) calls up a surrender to the unknown.

What is sex? Do I mean: whatever has to do with the body? Its need for the other, earliest knowledge? Sex: this groping, from one stone solitude to another. Do I mean: this confession? Taken up, tasted afresh, in the arms of one who can be trusted? An act, the most hazardous, let us say, of recollection? But worth the risk. A possibility. And above all, in case you have not understood: An invitation.

Sex, according to *Sex and Other Sacred Games*, is an invitation to absorb what eludes us in everyday reality, to capture momentarily the subtleties that slip through our fingers like childhood, like dreams. All that slips from the surface and turns into memory recorded in our bodies. Revealed through touch.

In many ways the characters in *Sex and Other Sacred Games* are drawn from the authors' own experiences. Stendhal and Chernin originally met in a Paris café, entered into years of dialogue, disappeared from, and suddenly reappeared in, each others' lives. In a recent radio interview, they revealed that much of the story developed spontaneously. They sent each other their characters' letters from which both authors then created the next narrative moves. In some sections of the book, each author developed both characters. The literary techniques and form are thus as playful as the picture the authors paint.

In each of her books—*The Obsession, In My Mother's House, The Hungry Self, The Hunger Song, The Flame Bearers,* and *Reinventing Eve*—Kim Chernin has pursued an idea, "The Woman Who Is Not Yet," the woman who cracks through layers of cultural obstacles and retrieves memories lost in early childhood under the pressure of family and social taboo. Claire Heller is an intriguing addition to Chernin's cast of characters, because she is the first to defy sexual taboo, not only patriarchal but feminist as well. *You feminists imagine you've invented the liaison between eros and the sacred. I want to remind you the idea is more than two thousand years old.*

Renate Stendhal was born in Germany and lived in Paris for twenty years before moving to California. As a translator, she introduced German readers to many American feminist authors, including Gertrude Stein, Audre Lorde, Adrienne Rich, and Susan Griffin. Her theoretical focus, in articles and multimedia performances, has probed the female versions of eros. Renate Stendhal has also explored our cultural splits, particularly the ways in which feminists enact them—for example, splitting spirituality from politics, while all the time splitting off sexuality. Her lesbian character, Alma, is a witty, honest, and courageous contribution to American feminist writing.

Readers of mystery novels may enjoy this book more than feminist theorists. One probably has to let oneself lean toward the nonlinear, nonliteral aspects of life to appreciate it. As Claire herself says: *That way she has of never telling you anything directly. She says, about the literal: it often contains a profound lie. By stressing what is, what has happened, you are allowed to hide what is meant. That kind of hiding does not appeal to her. On the other hand, to understand her meaning, it may be necessary to decipher her code.*

Claire and Alma decipher each other's codes and invent new ones. That is the beauty of any form of sexual exploration, theory or praxis. They keep us guessing. The outcome is veiled. This mystery lures us into an answer—an erotic fantasy of our own.

When reality is not enough—or maybe too good to be true—one needs a story. Writing oneself into the other's story, writing the other into one's own. Isn't that what is called falling in love?

Shana Penn is presently writing a collection of memoirs and short stories and is editor for the Elmwood Institute, an international ecology think tank in Berkeley, California.

Part One

ALMA RUNAU:
A MEETING, A DIALOGUE

SCENE: A PARIS CAFÉ

1

Alma leaned out of her window to search the sky for swallows. It was the first warm day and already she pined for the birds. Their screams, their plunges along wind-curves. Their shrill chases over the edge of her house, swifter than sudden held-in breath. Last spring Solveig had been standing in front of her in the wide-open window, the birds screaming, her body frail in the high frame.

She stepped back and contemplated the frame. Even empty, the windows in this country had body-shape. The proportions of a human figure. This she loved about Paris, the windows, the swifts. And the gray. Next to the faded slate of the roofs the clouds and smog always appeared warm, slightly yellow, a promise of sun. The houses had the same color as the sky. But on a day like this the gray lit up. The old sandstone of the city revealed the secret warmth of the earth. Stone desert, Solveig called it. Compared to her lush green North, she found Paris sad and oppressive.

Alma turned away from the window. She ought to go to her café and start work. She grabbed a stack of paper from her desk, took an opened chocolate bar from her bedside, and threw it all into a bag. It would be easier to work in the café. Easier to start. When there was no editorial deadline forcing her into excitement, she needed another strategy. Her self-criticism had to be distracted. She needed a big, busy café.

On the way to the door she caught herself in the mirror, about to walk out in her baggy house pants. Should she

show herself in her harem look? She resented having to
give up her comfort. Still, this first spring day anybody in
the world might pass by her café opposite the only park
in the neighborhood. Maybe she had better squeeze into
her washed-out jeans. Her gaze questioned her old tennis
shoes, updated by Solveig in bluish tiger stripes. But to
sit through hours of tightness—for whom? She didn't
even want to be seen. Nor to see anyone. All she wanted
was to dive into the café crowd, make herself a nest in
the sunwarmth behind the panes, and let her thoughts
roam.

Sun . . . She cast a glance through her shadowy rooms.
It was getting late. Already coffee time. She wouldn't get
hold of a big table at the window to work at. On the left
side the cup, the two white jars with coffee and hot milk,
the ashtray. On the other her papers, books, and elbow.
The tables in the second row were second class, round
and so small that one was practically forced to write on
one's lap. The "voyeur row," she called it. People sat
there shoulder to shoulder, staring at the privileged tables, into each other's papers and notebooks . . .

It wasn't worth it. She dropped her bag and returned to
the window. Mountains of clouds sailing eastward. Atlantic clouds. Paris by the ocean. Always in a hurry, as if they
had an unfailing aim. Never a doubt as to the direction.
Why couldn't she and Solveig decide about a direction?
Why couldn't she decide and put pressure on Solveig to
come south?

This incapacity to decide. She shook her head. Typically female. I can't even decide whether to stay in or go
out! This obviously is what the French feminists call
being "colonized." Man has invaded woman and cleverly
exploited his "colony." Now the poor thing is exhausted,
doesn't have a mind of her own left to make up. Always
waiting for the other to make a decision, take a step.

And yet it was her decision to be where she was. She

didn't want to leave again. Paris inspired her. She had always felt that the culture sitting in these gray stones held a promise. Of being left in peace. Of being free—from the weight of her own culture. She came from small windows, dark rooms, thick walls. From a north German climate where one couldn't help cowering inside, stuck there to get some warmth. Doubting life thoroughly and feeling slowly.

Here, the windows let in light. A well-tempered transition between inner and outer world. Adorned with cast-iron flourishes, stretching almost from floor to ceiling, each window was a celebration of transparency. Solveig would say she exaggerated. But something was sheltered and something could freely breathe through. The world inside was strictly private, shielded by massive doors and mischievous concierges. The windows, however, were an uncurtained invitation, a generosity toward those who were excluded or preferred to stay outside.

Thank heaven I live alone, Alma recited her daily prayer. Far from my country, my family, in this city of gray and gentle indifference. This culture doesn't care about strangers, exiles, outsiders. Lets them be, lets them have their salons, movements, whatever. Anonymous and sociable at the same time. Thanks for the cafés!

This then was *Kultur der Mitte,* the culture of the center, she decided. Simultaneity of extremes. Or rather no extremes, no either-or. A moderate balance. This was why she loved France. She needed its balance. It wasn't that she could not decide. She hated having to choose between extremes. It went against her grain to exclude one for the other.

The formulation pleased her. It was right to be here. She slipped into her café clothes, brushed her fingers through her curly wisps, took her bag, snatched half an apple from her table, and slammed the door.

2

Biking the last yards over the sidewalk, Alma arrived at the crowded café and immediately caught sight of an empty double table at the window. She threw her bike against the pane of the next boutique, grateful that the large straw basket cushioned the blow. She pressed down the combination lock and stormed into the café. She would defend her table against the tip-greedy waiter who wouldn't let a single person spread over four places at the rush hour. "I'm not alone," she would tell him, "I'm expecting someone." Fortunately she wasn't.

She kept an eye on her table, marking time behind two old ladies who ceremoniously took off their coats in order to join two more old ladies—*dames du quartier*—for their neighborhood chat. Alma wished she could take them by their plump behinds and shove them into their chairs. She saw a dark-haired woman with a pageboy dart out from a side passage, eager as Alma to reach the empty table. The woman reached it first. She threw herself down at it without stopping, spread her jacket over the chair next to her, and blocked a third chair opposite with her bag.

Alma cursed silently. She was sure the woman had seen her and taken advantage of her consideration for the old ladies. People were rising up in the smoky back corner. No empty cups on the tables nearby, no one fumbling with money in order to leave. Better stay up front, ready to jump at any better opportunity, Alma decided, settling at a tiny table in the second row. Besides, she was curious how the woman at her royal table would stand up against the waiter. This she wanted to see. It would be her sole consolation to see someone else be chased off in her place. She knew it was impossible to get by this unwritten café rule. There would be fight, and defeat. If not from the waiter, then from the *patronne,* a bleached-blond bulldog who barked. Being obstinate was a temptation that carried the risk of not being served. And what good would it do to sit in a café without coffee?

Better the voyeur row, Alma sighed. At least she didn't have a man's knee under her table. On her left, a young punk woman reading *Libération,* on her right a woman as motionless and old as a stone. Alma kept a curious, hostile eye on her table rival, who was comfortably leaning over two chairs, gazing out at the Luxembourg Gardens.

Proud carriage of the head, she noted. Expensive neat-and-proper haircut. Silky hair. Ferrari-red sweater, silky too, with knitted-in leather bands. Fashion doll. Alma could not see her hands, but she imagined the fingernails. She bent over sideways as far as she could to catch a glimpse around the corner, curious if the lipstick would match. She caught sight of a Ferrari-red lady's boot from which a faded jeans leg rose. Fashionable attempt at understatement, Alma analyzed. Fake, not to be taken seriously.

She looked up. Someone was staring at her while she was staring at the woman. She fell into the wetness of a dark gaze fixed upon her with unconcealed interest. Oh no, she moaned, not you again! He came to the café as regularly as she did, sitting alone or with male friends. Alone or not, he would make eyes at any unaccompanied woman at the neighboring tables.

With deliberate contempt Alma sat up straight and focused her eyes precisely past him at the window. She'd chosen the wrong place after all. The cruiser! He was never the least impressed by her icy negations. Probably he was a foreigner, poor devil. Never getting a French woman. His only chance could be tourists, solidarity between strangers. He certainly took her for a stranger. Well, that's what she was, wasn't she? A blond stranger sitting in the voyeur row, caught by a voyeur as a voyeur.

Damned table, she muttered. At the other one I could have simply changed sides, turned my back on him—as the red doll does. She would be the right target for him. Nothing helps me. Short hair, no makeup, jeans, tennis shoes—nothing makes me invisible!

She pulled her papers out of her bag and banged them onto the table. Her rival turned her head and Alma flashed a furious glance at her. Naturally the lipstick was a perfect match. It definitely wasn't Alma's day. She could as well have stayed home.

"Are you alone, *Mademoiselle*?"

Finally the waiter. Alma leaned her chin expectantly into her fists. Justice was close.

The woman looked at the waiter, unmoved. He repeated his question. Her answer was a dignified order: "A caffay oh lay, please." With this she turned back to the window.

Not bad, Alma grinned into her fists, American. Melodious voice, not a "sweet" Minnie Mouse. The waiter came an impatient step closer. "*Mademoiselle,* if you are alone I must ask you to sit at a single table." He gestured away from the window.

"Pardon?" Indulgently she turned back to him.

"This table is for four, *Mademoiselle. Four.*" He made use of his fingers. "*S'il vous plaît.*" He waved both his hands invitingly toward the back of the café.

"Excusay." She lifted her chin with dignity. "Me not alone. Me three."

She drew three fingers—with Ferrari-red nails, Alma noted, drawing in her breath—and almost touched the waiter's chest. Her poppy mouth drew into the most innocent smile.

"*Three*. A caffay oh lay, sill voo play."

Peevishly the waiter veered off. *Chapeau*, hats off, Alma thought. Quite a style. Her appreciation made her forget her grudge for a moment. But she remembered it when the American suddenly looked at her. Her look was everything but innocent. It was all cunning and triumph.

Don't rejoice too soon, Alma muttered into her papers, fiercely turning the pages. This is only the first round. We'll see how long you'll last. In case you don't turn into three after all . . .

The American in turn pulled writing stuff out of her bag, opened a checkered notebook and, without a pause, began to write. The waiter placed the cup and the two white jars with coffee and milk on her table. She thanked him without looking up and immediately moved everything over to the left side. Just what I would have done, Alma marveled.

"I'd like the same!" she shouted after the waiter. All of it, the table included!

The waiter stopped.

"*Un p'tit crème*," Alma specified in colloquial French in order to stand out as a Parisian. She noticed from the corner of her eyes that the woman looked at her again. Alma ignored her. She plunged back into her papers with an air of importance, giving the cruiser's table a quick, suspicious look. Sure enough, they were putting their heads together, looking over at her, then staring at the red back of the American as if the answer to some intriguing question was hidden there.

One day I would like to have the insolence of men, Alma brooded. To sit around all day staring at women. Well, isn't that what I am doing? And right away the guys are alarmed. If this isn't my subject! A woman can do the same as a man, but it doesn't mean the same. My staring at another woman is an intrusion into their territory. Women are theirs, and women don't look. If a woman looks back at a man, it's complicity. No matter how—her look is perceived as an invitation. He moves right in. Another second of looking, and he is at her table. Alma shuddered.

We have two different codes. No matter if I stare at men like a man—in their eyes I'll never turn into a subject. That's why this cruiser puts me in such a rage. There he is staring again. Wet glue. Nauseating. Why can't I break his code? I ignore him, I look at another woman instead. Indeed, that breaks his code. But it's not enough. He just gets alarmed and simply tries harder. And I can't concentrate. There sits the American writing in heavenly peace. The words literally flow from her pen. It can't be true!

Impatiently Alma looked around. People were getting up at the windows farther down, but others were already waiting in line. It had become more crowded. Now the waiter was working his way again through the passage between the tables, shouting: *"Pardon, messieurs-dames!"*

And there he was bending menacingly over the table of the American. *"Mademoiselle!"*

She looked up.

"Would you please leave the table? I have clients waiting. As I told you, this is a table for four." He shook four yellowish fingers over her.

She graciously spread her arms as if to say: But is this my fault? Then she looked at her watch in utter disbelief, lifted her white hand with the red nails once more and repeated: "I am—we are three. *Three.* I am waiting."

"Alors, non!" the waiter snarled. "We'll see to this in a minute."

Alma jubilated. Now the *patronne* would have her

entry. All heads had turned to watch the scene. The American gave Alma a questioning, slightly disconcerted look. Alma felt embarrassed for her own pleased grin. This beauty queen thinks she can get away with anything, in her painted and manicured grace. Slender, of course, her breasts too high for her age (how old could she be—thirty-five, forty?)—signals a man would hardly resist. And a woman not either. Alma had to admit she was beautiful, not just a dumb doll. She had more weapons to her arsenal than war paint. But even these wouldn't help against the *patronne*. She was doomed. The wonderful table would be lost. It was a shame. Even here, in one of the rare literary cafés the solitary writer had to give way to the consumer-crowd. Alma regretted her all too visible triumph. So what? she told herself. How could she know what I was grinning about?

But the cruiser seemed to know. He smiled at Alma, made a mocking sign with his head at the American, and winked encouragingly as if he were already looking forward to the climax of Alma's satisfaction. I see, Alma thought, her defeat is supposed to unite us, you and me, in victory. What next, old fool?

She grabbed her papers, bag, and jacket, crossed over the passage, and gestured at the two chairs at the opposite side of the American's table. "May I?" she asked in English. The woman looked at her surprised and, Alma thought, not unpleased. "You will be chased away any minute by the owner, you know. The waiter has gone to fetch her. But if there is a second person at the table, they can't do anything about it."

"Thank you," the red mouth said and smiled. The dark eyes stayed reserved. Alma had the impression they were checking her out. She went to get her cup, suddenly relieved that she was wearing her jeans. She liked the contrast. The tightly fitted pants and her ample grayish-blue cardigan. She knew her movements looked as casual and relaxed as her clothes. She couldn't resist sneering at the cruiser's flat, incredulous face. She saw the *patronne* approach with billowing sails, the waiter in tow. When she caught sight of Alma at the American's table, she stopped with a frown. The waiter flapped his arms. They both turned back again.

"That's it." Alma was pleased with herself. "She's veered off. Saved!"

The American who had turned to follow the scene, looked back at Alma.

"Both of us . . . " she remarked, and Alma was surprised by her sly smile. "Both saved."

Alma laughed. She liked it.

3

"I wanted this table from the start."

The American lifted her eyebrows in pity and drew her·
mouth down like a clown's: "And I snatched it!"

"Indeed," Alma answered with a mocking frown. "I
hate to write at those toy tables."

"Excellent observation posts, aren't they?"

Alma searched the black eyes that appeared even
blacker with their fine contour of kohl. She recognized an
amused spark in them and accepted the challenge:
"Meek consolation, isn't it?"

"You would have been welcome to share this one
sooner. So, you write?"

"Hm-m," Alma made as if this really wasn't worth a
comment. The question sounded too eager for her taste.
The woman had closed her notebook. Americans, she
marveled. Americans can always afford to move in. They
always feel welcome. They think their intrusion is interest. You smile back at them once, and they have already
told you their first name and invited you home. Are they
naïve? Or simply open? Is it a way of not losing time—
time being money? Or an urge to get right to the heart of
the matter? A French woman would have been too proud
and discreet to even notice you. Let alone ask you intimate questions. A French woman would have compro-
mised herself with any sign of interest.

"Tell me—" Alma leaned in—"were you really expecting two more or was it simply a trick?"

"You know the trick yourself, I gather."

Alma couldn't resist the amused smile, the attentive

eyes. There was something brooding in this face with its pouting mouth and slightly drooping eyes. No, it was only the lashes. The eyes were dark like sadness. But every smile brightened them up with tiny sparks of fire.

"You really don't speak French?"

"I exaggerated a bit . . . for the occasion."

" 'Me three,' right?"

They laughed. Alma swiftly looked over to the cruiser's table. She wished he had seen this. Two women strangers laughing together.

"It's been a while since I've spoken a word of French," the American explained. "I spent some months here six years ago. Always writing in this café . . ."

"At precisely this table, no? I had the funny impression you were an *habituée*, yet I'd never seen you here."

"Excellent observation indeed. You don't miss a thing, do you?" Again the sparkle in these eyes.

"You bet," Alma replied wantonly. "I rarely miss people [women, she thought] who write. But six years ago was before my time. My café writing time, I mean."

"How do you come to speak English so well? You can't be French."

Alma grinned at the assumption. "I am kind of an *exilée*," she said. "From Germany. I left an eternity ago. Couldn't stand my constipated country with its Nazi past. Unspoken, of course. Everyone competing to be the good, clean German—a washing-powder nation. Suffocating!" She stopped, surprised by her sudden talkative mood.

"I imagine Paris must feel excitingly dirty to you."

"You're not kidding. The paradise of the exiles! I love Paris. Paris, France . . . The balanced, nonextremist culture in the heart of Europe."

"An old, well-ripened wine, isn't it? Well-ripened values too. I've always been fascinated by a culture that gives *l'art de vivre* such a high place among the arts."

Alma hadn't expected an answer to her remark about culture. And certainly not a *raffiné* one by a woman in red, painted, and signaled out for hunters. If she was an intellectual, why all this feminine fashion attire? Was she sexually frustrated? Or the opposite—an oversexed intellectual? It challenged Alma's sense of style, her own well-ripened values. What was hidden behind this red façade?

"*L'art de vivre*," Alma took up the thread, "how do you say: live and let live? That's really a great art. Consider the French rituals of food, for example. Each food, each taste served and appreciated by itself. Wine to heighten the sense of taste . . . and the sense of conversation. Bread that is baked at least twice a day. Finally cheese, desserts, and coffee to round up the experience. What an experience!"

The woman watched and listened, her mouth curving a smile. Alma couldn't stop talking. Sharing her love for France with a stranger was like talking down Solveig's doubts.

"The whole ritual doesn't feel rigid," she went on, "at least not to me. I don't sense the moralistic attitude that forces pleasure into duty. The French just seem to know what is good. They don't care if you also know it. They'll despise you if you don't. If you don't partake in the natural blessing of being cultivated French."

"Or if you don't speak their grand language perfectly."

"*Mon Dieu, mon Dieu*, 'me three'! Such a barbarian could never hold a big table in the *Grande Culture* . . . "

The woman laughed, and Alma tried again to determine her age. The melancholy of her face gave her something of a wise old clown, and yet every facial expression made her immediately look young and very much alive.

It was fascinating to watch such an uncontrived face under its perfect mask of makeup.

"Anyway," Alma tried to come to a conclusion. "I think, the French *laissez faire* is saying: 'We may ignore you, but please, be as you please!' It's at least not the missionary mentality of the Germans, who constantly educate the world to be the way *they* are."

"It's a pleasure to analyze the differences between cultures. Trying to define . . . A writer's pleasure, isn't it?" She gave Alma a look from the corner of her eyes. "I imagine"—she leaned her face into one hand, the fingers with the striking nails delicately spread over her cheek—"the reason for this *laissez faire* is the French sense that individualism is something quasi sacred. They protect their privacy, their *caprices* so well that they don't have to control or even care much about somebody else's idiosyncracies."

Alma was impressed. How long had it been since she had had a conversation like this? Solveig was more of a visionary; a spaced-out artist, less of an intellectual. This was a treat.

"The sacred individual . . . " Alma repeated with appreciation. "The French credo *par excellence*. Somehow there seems to be enough trust in the culture as a whole and in the cultivated individual to create a principle of pleasure. Well-tempered pleasure, of course—like this way of serving the coffee, have you noticed? They don't force their taste upon you. They serve you two well-measured amounts of coffee and milk, and *voilà*, you are free to mix your own individual taste. If you're poor you can hang out with the rest of your milk all day."

"What an elegant symbol—the individual freedom linked to pleasure. Or is it always?"

"I guess it is." Alma shrugged. She let the expression 'elegant symbol' roll over her tongue. Was this outfit really meant to trap a man? Couldn't it simply reflect this woman's sense of elegance?

"Do you suppose," the American went on, "this 'pleasure principle,' as you call it, also colors the human relations?"

"What do you mean?"

"The relation between men and women, for example?"

"Uhh, that's hard to tell when you're an outsider. . . . " Alma added: " . . . to a culture," realizing the ambiguity of the phrase. She didn't have much intimate knowledge of French men. The little she had was firmly tucked back into oblivion by her maxims of woman-loving. So, was this what the "cultural" interest of the American came down to after all?

"Doesn't everyone agree that French sex is more exciting, more passionate?"

"It's hard to know," Alma said reluctantly. "How should 'more' be measured to begin with? With a little passion thermometer? I doubt it anyway. It's a myth."

She sounded a little more acidic than she would have liked. The word *French* flashed through her mind from sex ads. "I don't think the achievements of individual freedom extend to women." She decided to keep the discussion cultural and her voice cool. "It's a men's culture. Women are not really included. France is no better in that. On the contrary: the roles may be even more tricky. Trapping French women more . . ."

"French women trapped? Next you are going to say: 'by the famous charm and sex appeal that haunts the rest of the world!' "

"Have you studied mind reading? I think they are indeed haunted by their femininity. Because French men have already so much of it."

The woman had raised one eyebrow, whether in expectation or doubt, Alma couldn't tell.

"They are delicate and refined," Alma went on. "Even the old men—right there in the Luxembourg—playing *boules* in their dark blue suits and neat Basque hats. They have their own gallant notion of *charme*. Or think of the movie stars: Gérard Philippe, Barrault, today even the bully Gérard Dépardieu. So emotional, so unafraid of showing his vulnerability . . . There seems to be an underlying freedom for French men to be delicate, esthetic, even romantic. Feminine in short."

The American listened, her eyebrow still raised, her fingers stroking her cheek. She seemed to contemplate images inside herself.

How can anybody make love with such nails? Alma mused. But she doesn't make love, of course, she's made love to. *Voilà la différence.*

Alma looked around for a convincing example of her theory.

"See the blond braid over the black space jacket back there? It's a man. I've seen him enter. Beautiful, no? And he's not at all effeminate. There are more and more men like him. I think they steal the show from women."

"Have French men managed to change roles? Without anybody knowing?"

Alma stared at her. What the hell am I talking about? Maybe she's tried them all—even men with braids. There's certainly only one expert in these matters at this table!

"What I was saying," Alma corrected herself, "next to such feminine men French women have to make gigantic efforts to stand out as the 'other,' the attractive opposite. That's what traps them. That's what makes up the myth, if you ask me. These efforts of superfemininity, this stress. I find French women contrived."

"Any highly developed style has contrived aspects. I admire their stylish beauty and poise. It's precisely cultivated. Cultivated charm—like French gardens as opposed to the English. One's preference is purely a matter of esthetics. Or of taste. In any case, a clear choice is always liberating, don't you think?"

I can tell you prefer French gardens, Alma thought, all trimmed, shaped up, beautifully unnatural . . . I wonder how clear my own choice is? I want to be invisible to men, but visible to women. I want men's casual elegance and *charme*, but I don't want to be "masculine." As little as I want to be "feminine."

"I hate both extremes of gender imprisonment. I want the best of each," Alma said. "This compromise is certainly liberating to me. I'm glad I don't have to be a 'French garden'!"

"You love French culture, but don't acknowledge it in women?" The American sounded amused. "Don't you miss out on something?"

Alma moored her thumbs in her jeans pockets.

"French women's charm is so refined . . . " The woman let her gaze wander through the café. "Their attraction doesn't diminish with age. What about Jeanne Moreau? Or right here. The four old ladies a few tables behind you: wearing lipstick, of course. Their noses still delicately powdered. Rosy cheeks, chic hairdos . . . What a satisfaction at being a woman this expresses. They are gracious, proud—"

"Grotesque, pathetic," Alma fell in. "The clowns of the race!"

But you can't see it, she thought, watching the woman lean back with a lenient smile. Because you are part of them. You have to believe that you are happy and satisfied. What if you recognized your frustration with men? What if the clowns stopped playing the game? What would appear under your shining mask?

"I bet they are quite unhappy with their powdered

noses," Alma insisted. "How huge most of their noses are. Sharp, bold, dominating the whole face—and even the rosiest dots on their cheeks can't distract from that fact. Poor things. They would have made great men!"

4

The American gave Alma a sidelong glance before she turned around to study the noses in the café.

"See the one with the hair bomb and the eagle beak over her pinched mouth? She would have made a great general, don't you think? And the big one over there, with the little feather hat and the energetic potato nose: a great agricultural minister . . ."

"You have the evil eye." The American gave her a pouting look. "And now I've caught it. I found them so charming a minute ago."

Alma knew she was only pretending to play Alma's game. Alma felt a devilish joy: "And their legs! Made in fact to walk right up to the top—another reason to be unhappy. Short, strong, stout French legs which they still shave . . . *hélas*—" She heaved a sigh. "They don't get peace even in their old days!"

"Peace? From?"

"From being female impersonators!"

She read in the other's face that she was considered an amusing but hopeless case. She enjoyed the fool's freedom: "They have to come up with constant extra charm in order to prove they aren't men. Naturally this eats up constant extra energies—which they then lack for the important matters. And can they ever prove they aren't men?"

"Poor French women!" There was the clown's face again, all ironic pity. "Their charm is the most exhausting and obstructive thing in the world! Yes, I see that you can't be French. You seem so unexhausted—" Her gaze brushed over Alma's face, hair, cardigan. "With all your *charme . . .*"

It was Alma's turn to lift her eyebrows.

"So relaxed," the woman persisted, and Alma perceived a note of appreciation mixed with her irony. "At ease . . . with being a woman."

Right, Alma thought, but you get it wrong anyhow. I'm at ease with women. I've stepped out. None of your corsets anymore, your beauty aids and extra efforts to please. Not even a ring, she added, aware that the woman's eyes were resting on her hands. How are you going to figure this out?

She started playing with her empty cup, unsure if she wanted the woman to figure it out and stop her inspection. She wasn't at ease with her hands. They suggested no elegant understatement. They were big and muscular. When they did not move they appeared naked, like a man's, revealing a naked greed to grip.

A gracious hand wave made Alma aware of how the woman kept her hands in sight, just as she kept her whole self in sight.

"Sure. French men are also at ease. An interesting aspect of cultural balance. This naturally allows women to express their sexuality more freely. The myth—like all myths—is grounded in reality. French women or—" she smiled a cryptic smile—"women in France, are more liberated, fulfilled, and sexy."

Alma couldn't come up with anything more than a half-embarrassed grin. To find herself aligned with "sexy" women . . . This American had a way of coming up with something unexpected. Was she one of those seductresses who can't help flirting with everyone, even a woman?

She didn't seem to be flirting. Flirtation wants something, wants to please, to seduce, to get. This woman didn't give away what she wanted. If she wanted any-thing. Her eyes didn't tell. It was hard to reach such dark eyes. You couldn't make out what was surface and what was depth. They didn't let you in. They were playful, ironic, always watching, always on the watch.

"Liberated, fulfilled, and sexy" kept ringing in Alma's head. She was tempted to reply that she was indeed lib-erated. How could this remarkable woman stick to men? A woman's intelligence seemed so much more appealing than a man's. More connected, she went through her list, more wholesome, warm, humorous, human . . .

"I'd better get some work done," she said, stretching her arms. "What a day! Not exactly meant for work-ing . . ."

The late afternoon sun had entered the café unhin-dered by the budding trees. It was pleasantly warm. Peo-ple had settled at the tables on the sidewalk. Some women were already lifting their faces to the sun, their eyes closed in devotion. There was almost summer in the air. Summer would now come in a leap, maybe bring Solveig back . . .

"If this isn't café culture," Alma gave the conversation a polite conclusion. "The ease of strangers talking . . ." She signaled to the waiter.

"The best of it, I agree. And of course writing."

"I normally write best in a café."

"Me too. But why?"

Alma picked up her bill. "The same reason one can talk in a café. It's a cultural space. Ideas seem to be hanging in the air. Like apples. One picks them up or is hit by them . . . No, I don't really know. It inspires me." She counted her coins, leaving them next to her cup. "You'll have to fight for your table again." She stood up.

"Yes, the apples! And the constant movement and noise. Especially in a place where I don't understand what's actually said. I'm in the middle of a thought or just drifting. A noise, a word, or a sudden movement enters my mind and subtly shakes it. Like a kaleidoscope." Her hand performed a delicate twist of the tube. "Another picture appears. I suddenly get an idea."

"So much for impeccable observation!" Alma sat down again. The sharpness of this woman! Here she held up the key to a riddle that had puzzled Alma for years. Since the very first day she had sat down at a café table with her notebook.

"You know what it does to me?" Alma supported her elbow on the chair next to her and dug her fingers into her short curls. "Something is silenced inside me. The voice of my own demands, I guess. This kaleidoscope of happenings puts me into a more playful mood. I'm distracted—from myself!"

A warm smile held Alma's searching eyes. "I am a perfectionist too."

"Isn't it a dread? Stage fright every time I have to start! I hate it. Let's have another coffee, *d'accord*?" She put her arm out to stop the waiter. *"Encore deux crèmes, s'il vous plaît*. . . . He tries to overlook us, little bastard. That's our punishment."

Alma grinned, still pleased to have tricked out the cruiser and moved out of his direct line of view. She put both her elbows on the table: "What do you write?"

"Novels mostly."

Said without the least sign of discomfort, Alma noted with slight envy.

"I wrote most of them in a coffeeshop," the American added. "A Berkeley coffeeshop . . . where I lived. I mean, I lived in the coffeeshop as well!"

She laughed. Alma realized that she had been fascinated from the start by the woman's brilliant white teeth. American teeth. Too perfect not to make you wonder if they were real.

"Are you writing a novel in Paris?"

"Essays."

"On what? Culture?"

"How did you know?"

"I have X-ray eyes. Couldn't you tell?" Alma immediately felt self-conscious. Solveig had told her that her grayish eyes could be frighteningly green, sharp, and penetrating. She tried a half-ironic smile.

The American bent forward and playfully stared into Alma's eyes: "And you? Let's see. Oh yes, lots of essays in there . . ."

Alma laughed and shook her head. "I wish there were. It's mostly poems in there. Lots of journalist stuff. And countless diaries . . ."

Normally she would feel she hadn't much to show. She had "only" poems. This time it felt as if altogether there were a neat little mountain of writing piled up inside her.

5

"Have you published?"

"Yes."

How much? Alma wanted to ask. The question felt too greedy.

"What's your name?"

"Claire Heller."

Funny, Alma mused. I've been indiscreet enough to ask about her writing. Now it's also I who first asked her name. Am I already under American influence? Or is it some other influence? Will I next invite her home? And why not if I wanted to? Claire Heller—it didn't sound American. It sounded French, Jewish, German even. The name didn't ring a bell.

"My name is Alma," she bridged the silence. "Not Mahler-Werfel, however . . ."

The American smiled: "And not a musician, a poet."

Alma couldn't deny it went down like honey. "And not married," she presented herself with a reverential bow: "Alma Runau."

"Alma Runau. Beautiful name. Have you published anything?"

"Apart from my journalist stuff I only published some poems in . . . magazines." Alma wondered why she didn't say, feminist magazines. Was she trying to impress this woman who would certainly give more credibility to magazines published by men? Or would she? It was hard to tell what would impress her. She kept herself remote while making you come strangely close. Too close perhaps. She had already told this woman she wasn't married. Adding the word *feminist* might scare the stranger away. It was the outlaw's paranoia, Alma decided.

"Can you survive from your books?" She was eager to avoid further questions.

"Oh no."

"How did you manage to write them?"

"Marriage." She looked straight at Alma.

"Oh."

What else, Alma thought, flashing her eyes over the matching mouth, sweater, nails. She tried to keep a poker face. A kept woman, even though productive. Too bad.

"And a successful divorce," the American added, closely observing her.

Alma refused to brighten up. A woman using men instead of being used—this was at least something. What had she expected anyway? She wondered if it was true. It sounded too easy to be true. Certainly things always sounded easy once they were accomplished. She also sensed the ease of strangers talking in a café. Telling each other whatever they pleased. Telling stories. Leaving out certain truths. The truth was she was suspicious of married women, or even ex-married women who still appeared married. Their loyalty could never be trusted.

"I am a trickster," the American explained.

Perhaps the words of this woman had a false bottom. Like magicians' boxes hiding their secrets beneath the glittering tricks . . . She visibly enjoyed Alma's confusion.

"What I got I deserved," she added with a note of arrogance.

"You deserved to marry?" Alma asked, trying to get a peek into the dark box.

"Why not? Men have so much to learn from women."

"Learn what?"

"Sex, passion—everything."

"And how do you suppose women learn it if men have to learn it from them?"

Alma was facing a sphinx:

"A woman knows."

"Why do you say you are a trickster?"

"How would a man know that I know he knows nothing?"

"Yes, how would he?" Alma echoed, puzzled. "What did you deserve then?"

The woman's eyes seemed to be lit by a gleam of triumph, the corners of her mouth played with a temptation downward into scorn: "All he had to give."

Alma couldn't tell if the scorn was addressed to her question or to the man. She saw something in the woman's face she had not yet seen: a luster of sensuous self-satisfaction, a superior pride, royal and wicked at the same time. There was suddenly a scene of sexual domination—a woman clothed, pushing a man to his knees in front of her, the man naked.

Alma looked away. "I wouldn't trade my freedom for anything!"

"Not even for love?" The challenging glance returned, wiping the luster off the stranger's face.

"Love meaning marriage?" Alma laughed dryly. "I never deserved it! I was always too suspicious, you know. Marrying meant being bought: sixty camels, some trunks of embroidered sheets and nightgowns—it's all the same. You end up with pocket money for nonstop service."

"Service sacred to old Babylon . . ."

"Sorry?"

There it was again. Pandora's box. The woman had lifted her chin, stroking her throat, her eyes lost in the distance. Old Whore Babylon, flashed through Alma's mind. Sodom and Gomorrha. Sexual debauches abhorred by the patriarchs of the Old Testament . . . What did it mean? She carefully swept her glance back over the woman's face. Was there a connection to the sexual scene she had envisioned?

"Are we still speaking about marriage?" Alma resented being cut off in the middle of her marriage diatribe.

The woman shifted her eyes back to Alma: "It's mutual service, isn't it?"

"When one buys and the other is bought, what's mutual in that?"

"The interest."

"You mean, it's your interest to be bought?"

"If you like. It's my interest to sell books, for instance. Books, the body . . . of my work."

Alma fell silent. It was no use discussing marriage with a partisan. It was probably no use either to want to know what she was writing about. She could tell by now that it must be slick romances, set in prehistoric times and spiced with modern sexual license. The best-seller stuff of an ever-frustrated heterosexual society. It filled her with contempt as much as with envy.

"How do *you* manage to write?" the American said.

"I don't, *justement*," Alma said somberly. "Or rather, it just takes longer. But I couldn't write a line if I wasn't totally independent."

"I have always felt free."

"How did you do that? Even in your marriage? No demands, no restrictions? No kids?"

"No kids." She seemed to study Alma's bewilderment.

"Funny," Alma pondered, "as a teenager, this would have been my dream. To pick a Prince Charming who would pay for everything and ask for nothing, protect me, but stay out of my way. My only duty, to be present and beautiful at his cocktail parties. Charming dream, isn't it?"

"One has the deepest dreams when one is young."

She said it without irony and again Alma got the impression they were not talking about the same thing.

"You did not find him?" the woman asked.

"I gave up looking. It would have been too expensive after all."

"For him?"

"For me!" Alma enjoyed that for once the other seemed lost. "It would have been too expensive a compromise." She was proud of her formulation. "I luckily realized in time that a woman would always have to pay everything back."

"That depends."

It sounded equally proud. The woman straightened up and supported one hand on her thigh, her shoulder slightly advanced. She looked provocative, Alma thought, like a tango dancer.

"It all depends on how you go about it. A woman who knows her power can get whatever she wants." Her gaze insisted as if she wanted to fix this thought in Alma's head.

Alma was unsure what to think. The authority of the other suggested that she was speaking from experience. How could she handle men like that? It made her feel like a schoolgirl, curious to know what this woman knew. But she wouldn't ask questions revealing herself. After all, she, too, was convinced a woman could get what she wanted—especially a strong, conscious feminist. One who had looked behind the cards men played. But when it came to intimacy she was convinced a woman would always end up the loser. She would never be detached enough. She would end up the giver, the nurturer, the loving nurse of his delicate ego, the lonely hunter of his distant heart. If, however, a woman turned the tables and became herself the distant-hearted egoist . . . If a woman chose weak men and in turn exploited them . . .

"Are you so dominant?" she heard herself ask.

"Dominant?" The full red lips tasted the word. "I just think, as long as you know what you really want, it's natural to get it."

"Natural—for a woman?" Alma gasped. "You can't mean that. You sound like a man!"

"And you sound like a feminist."

Their mutual disbelief carved out a moment of utter silence. They started to laugh.

"Big secret!" Alma was relieved. "But what are you? You aren't a transvestite, are you?"

"And you don't believe in women, do you?"

Alma caught her breath: "Would feminism be necessary if one did?"

The woman paid her a mock compliment with a bow of her head: "How ironic. Feminism needs an enemy. The patriarchal overlord. You only see woman's oppression, her weakness. Never her power?"

" 'Needs an enemy'?"

"Like any political movement. It only sees in black and white."

"*Au contraire*. We see red."

"A feminist with a sense of humor?" Her eyes were again watching attentively.

"What are you?" Alma insisted. "A man, a woman in disguise?"

The clown's face reappeared: "They have not invented a category for me yet . . ."

That's probably true, Alma thought. One category to fit that many contradictions would be hard to find. Fashion doll, oversexed intellectual, French garden, Babylonian domina, clown . . . She would have liked to fit the pieces of this puzzle into one coherent image, but they resisted, or rather the woman resisted. She dressed like an alarm signal but refused to be seen. It was even difficult to define what she looked like.

Then Alma knew. It wasn't really a clown's face, it was

31

out of a cabaret. Lulu, of course. Pandora . . . The recognition pleased her. She imagined the woman with a bop cut—a face in the Berlin crowd of the twenties or thirties, at the Romanisches Café, where in the upper section typewriters used to stand on the tables. The porter, separating the world into artists and *bourgeois,* would of course know that this intriguing woman in red or black belonged to the typewriters—or to one of the artists up there . . .

The waiter, still looking grumpy, set down their fresh coffees without taking the empty jars away. The table looked as though they had been there for quite a while. This time only one jar of hot milk accompanied the two pots of coffee. This was the disadvantage of sharing a table and the same taste: one had to share the milk. Again the American thanked him with a nod of her proud head, not granting him a look. Who was she? Alma mused. How could any intelligent woman (or man, for that matter) not be a feminist? It was one of those things she could never figure out. To her it seemed like choosing obscurity while living in an era of enlightenment.

"I remember when I was about twelve," the woman said, serving herself the coffee. "My mother took me to see *All About Eve.* Do you know the movie?"

Alma nodded. She grabbed the milk jar and offered the woman a helping: "Say stop . . ." With her spoon she added a neat little island of white foam to the cream-colored coffee. The woman watched her, sparks of surprise in her eyes. For a second Alma felt her choice of living in Paris deeply confirmed.

6

"My mother said: If you want to get anything in life, you have to go for it! I always remembered. She approved of Eve."

"Evil Eve!" Alma shook her head. "Ambitious like a man . . ."

"In love with her work. Putting her own desires first."

"Using the love of others for her career. My mother would have heavily disapproved. My mother used to say: 'If you want to be happy, you have to learn to compromise!' She spoke about marriage, of course, not about art."

"Did she succeed?"

"And how! She hates to admit any mistakes in her compromises. What she doesn't like, doesn't exist. Her world is once and for all happy, hygienic, and rosy."

"You speak of your mother the way you speak of your country."

"I ran from both."

"Your mother sounds scared and powerless to me."

"True . . . " Alma felt a stop in her flow. Her mother-rage could make her forget her feminism. Her empathy with all women could dwindle away in her anger with this single one.

"And yet she was powerful." She sought for a balance. "She shaped the family with iron energy into a *heile Welt*, you know—a safe cotton-candy world. When her kids had gone she had no self left."

"Did she have one to begin with?"

Alma looked at her in surprise. "How would one know?

She was bright, and so willful, and gifted. But all she wanted was a man and a family—to sacrifice herself to this traditional role. I find it maddening, but she probably never really had a choice."

"That's one of those feminist ideas? That women don't have a choice? That they are victims? Innocent? Don't overestimate this self-sacrifice. It can be quite a relief—especially when there is no self. The delight of surrender when someone else is in control . . . It's comfortable. It allows women to avoid their sexual destiny."

Alma frowned. "It's not comfortable not to have a self, don't you know that? It's a torture for any human being—whether it's conscious or not. Who would freely choose that?"

The woman stretched out her hand toward Alma's arm on the table. She placed three fingers lightly upon her wrist for a second: "You have a way of avoiding what I say."

Her touch was light and yet amazingly warm. Alma fought a temptation to blush. "And you have a way of speaking in riddles!"

The woman said nothing. She stared at her, smiling. Alma wanted to pull out of this gaze. "Well, Mona Lisa," she said, "what is it? What have I avoided?"

The woman shrugged, opening her fingers like a fan. Alma read the message: Why don't you ask yourself?

"Women's sexual destiny? Is that it? It sounds like 'biological destiny': it rings a Pavlovian bell. Rape, defloration, menstrual curse, PMS, involuntary pregnancy . . . and frigidity, needless to say. That's a woman's sexual destiny. My mouth waters when I hear it! It means not having a sexuality at all—at least not one's own."

"If women didn't evade their own sexuality, they would have it, that's the point."

"How on earth would they?"

"I don't say it's easy. The art of loving is demanding

like any other art. Unfortunately most women avoid it, as I said."

"It's not a question of avoidance! They don't realize their sexual power exists because men won't let them. Men do everything imaginable to castrate women. How many men do you know who could deal with a woman's power?!"

There was a silence. Alma returned the woman's scrutinizing gaze flatly, holding up a banner with a single question mark.

"Anyone can be taught."

It was said with such conviction it made Alma suspicious. The Diotima-Syndrome! she thought. To go and teach not only one Socrates, but every man you meet . . . Good luck!

"Avoidance doesn't enlighten anyone." The woman flashed a spark of contempt at Alma. She shifted her eyes and folded her arms. Her gaze brushed past the café crowd.

Is it true that I avoid her? Alma lined up the jars on the table in a straight row. Have I hurt her feelings? Maybe I don't want to be enlightened? I don't know. I am curious about her. But talking about the art of loving is different from talking about the art of living. Why should I share my sexual secrets—especially with a stranger whose knowledge is limited to men? I am not interested in the art of loving my oppressor. I am as uninterested in a woman overpowering a man as in a man overpowering a woman. That's precisely what I can't stand—the inequality of power. Between women just the same. No, I don't need her enlightenment. I know all about it, and it makes me sad. It reminds me of Solveig and me. The one who loves less and refuses has the power. The one who desires is powerless. I don't want to talk about it. She is right. I do avoid it. And that's what I want to do.

7

Alma was aware that she, too, had folded her arms. Now there were two body fortresses facing each other. One Mediterranean with little red-tiled towers and flags, so graceful you could easily mistake its strength. The other a northern citadel relying on the very functionality of its crenellated sandstone façade for beauty, showing off a self-assurance that could easily be taken for strength. The contrast couldn't be greater and yet . . . It tickled Alma's mouth into a smirk. She didn't move. The southern castle let down its bridge first. The woman kept one hand loosely wrapped around her hip, the other came back to the table to glide slowly and pensively along the edge of the spoon.

"It's a question of personal choice," she said, watching her fingers on the spoon, "That's a far more fascinating thought than the abstract blaming of society . . . or of men. Everybody follows his desire. It's simply less visible if it's a conformist desire. Like your mother's. You seem to have gone in the opposite direction. How? Were there no social pressures on you to conform and be like her? No pressures from your mother? Are you telling me you had a choice?"

Alma hesitated; then, with a little grin, she gave in. She liked to get this woman to talk. To get her on a common ground where her words did not have their false bottom.

"There is no answer to your question. Whether you perceive choice or not is almost a question of taste. As with French and English gardens! Was it my choice to rebel and be different from my mother? What if my mother had a secret impulse to have a daughter who would rebel and have the life that she herself had sacrificed? If I fulfilled my mother's unknown dream, wouldn't my opposition to her be solidarity, in fact? So— is it a choice, and whose choice is it? I think there is no simple either-or . . . "

The woman had pursed her poppy mouth as if trying words on the tip of her tongue: "I prefer French gardens."

"Why not?" Alma shrugged. "But why choose? Why not embrace the paradox, two things being true simultaneously?"

Like with her mother? She had just declared that her mother had not had a choice. She tried to consider the opposite: that her mother had sacrificed herself for her own reasons, her own desires even—not only, as she used to claim, for her children's sake. If both were true, it would certainly shake some of the guilt off a daughter's shoulders. Miserable shoulders—she lifted her hands to knead them—hurting like her mother's used to hurt. Had she shouldered her mother's burdens—out of guilt? Out of love? This guilty love that, instead of relieving burdens, doubles them?

No more fortresses at this table, Alma noted. The American was watching something outside. Following her gaze Alma saw a couple with a young girl in front of the café. The girl was dressed for Sunday, in pink, with black patent-leather shoes, her hair neatly combed, tied back with a pink ribbon. She was holding a Hula Hoop around her waist. Her mother directed her to a tree. Her father was getting a Super-8 camera ready.

The little girl gave the hoop an energetic swing and followed it with eager movements. "Stop, wait!" the father yelled. He was not ready. The girl dropped the hoop, stood and waited for his command. Everyone stopped to watch. The girl was getting tense and anxious. "Now—go!" She pushed the hoop and with a nervous smile started to wiggle around. She pushed her hips upward and her belly forward. Her pink *volant* dress crept up. Her thin little body looked exposed, a precocious, awkward sex object. It only lasted a moment. The hoop landed at her feet. Her unhappy face waited for her father's signal before she picked it up. She didn't look at anybody. She gave her mother the hoop to carry. Her parents did not comment. She walked off beside them, controlled like an adult.

Alma and the American followed the girl with their eyes.

"That's how a girl learns . . . " Alma said.

The expectant gaze of the other invited her.

"It's all for someone else's pleasure. She learns to give up her own."

"Did you notice how she began? Her body knew the swing. A woman's erotic knowing . . . They may stop her because they can't bear it, but it's hers. It's there to be remembered."

"You see her pleasure, to be remembered. I see that it's not hers from the start. She imitates a movement she's already seen. Women swing their hips for men's eyes wherever you look. She simply repeats it, sensing this is what she's supposed to do. Men's eyes are everywhere. Didn't you see her embarrassment? She has no idea, of course, why she should feel embarrassed. She can't read this gaze. But something creeps into her innocent pleasure that makes her feel naked, dirty somehow. She wants to forget this pleasure. She can forget it in order to protect herself. Or she can learn to please this gaze. She can act the part expected from her. Pretend it's her own pleasure."

"What a pathetic story . . . " The woman gave Alma an inquisitive look. "Is it yours?"

"How could any girl escape it?"

"One sees what one knows."

"True. And what one doesn't want to know one doesn't see."

They exchanged a knowing smile.

"Are you saying you escaped it?" Alma asked. "In high heels?"

The American stuck her leg out from under the table: "You mean, in my ten-league boots?"

"Another version of Cinderella's glass slippers, aren't they? There's no running away in those!"

The woman's eyebrows went up: "Me, caught?"

"At first glance one might think so . . . "

"Did you think so?"

"This Ferrari-red invitation?"

The American tipped her head, amused. Alma's questions visibly fulfilled her expectations: "Might be a red light?"

"A red light?"

"I'll show you."

The woman pushed up her left sleeve and put her fist on her hip. Pumping up her shoulders, she leaned in, right elbow on the table, her pen between her teeth. Eyes narrowed, a dangerous glare. A boy-pirate holding his knife?

"You look like you've just tried your mother's lipstick for the first time!"

The posture collapsed. The woman sat back, putting up her regretful smile: "You've just missed a meeting. With the loud-mouth girl I used to be. Can't you imagine a girl too tough to be taken?"

"You? I would have said, *sophistiquée, raffinée, cultivée*. Anything but tough."

"You? Stuck with an either-or? Either vulgar or *raffinée*? Something else you avoid?"

"Vulgarity was my mother's bête noire, I'm afraid."

"Vulgarity, meaning pleasure. I grew up with a woman who never forgot her own pleasure."

"Were you really a tomboy?"

"My mother's law was: everything for herself. As a feminist, you should be delighted. Vulgar or not, you would probably call it strength, achievement. I wouldn't agree. Her desires wrought ravages. Every attractive man had to be hers."

"And she got them, all those attractive men?"

"She never got enough of them."

"What did she do? What did the men do?"

"The men knew she would give everything she had in order to get them. They took it and took off."

"And your father?"

"He was one of those who took off."

"So you didn't really have a father."

"I had many and none. I didn't really have a mother either. My mother was a sailor, moving restlessly from dream to dream. What would a sailor need children for?"

"Maybe she did need you for something?" Alma felt uneasy with the haunting, poetic image bestowed on a careless mother. "Maybe she needed the reassurance of something traditional? In order to end up as a 'good' woman?"

The other listened, her cheek resting in her hand, her eyes guarded.

"Maybe that's why your mother liked Eve so much? Eve never tried to be good. Your mother tried. Even women with passionate, rebellious desires end up with bound feet . . . "

"And torture everyone around them!"

Did she suddenly agree? There was an unexpected nakedness in her face.

"It's always a chain reaction," Alma rushed for solidarity. "The selfless mothers have to suck on their children in return. The ideal family: a chain suck instead of separate selves!"

"A chain suck!" The American rewarded Alma with a delighted shudder. "But you sound like you got some blood left in your veins."

"I sound like a feminist." Alma grinned. "I guess I was lucky. But I was also a fighter. I was in a terrible battle with my mother when I was growing up. I loved her and felt so guilty. I had such pity for her. Endless compromises. Until I left, left her, the motherland, and went to England, France. It's not the panacea, but it helped."

"I left early, too."

The American shrugged without clowning, took up her cup and drank in small pensive sips.

She must have felt unwanted, Alma speculated. That's why she put up this tough act. Now she uses men. Lots of men, I bet, to prove that she's wanted. . . . It was sad to see every woman she could think of struggling to save her damaged self. She remembered some joke about a fly drowning in milk, beating its legs and wings so desperately it turned the milk to butter. How long would it take?

The silence didn't seem uncomfortable this time. The woman was looking out of the window, looking at nothing. A pathetic shadow was cast over her bright red. Her mouth still had a rebellious pout, but her eyes drooped with bleakness. She seemed to feel Alma's gaze. Like a glove pulled over a cut fist her challenging look reappeared. Her mouth assumed its familiar expression of self-mocking regret.

"All about Eve . . . " she said. "It can't be all, can it?" Her sidelong glance hid a gleam of childish hope.

"No." Alma pulled herself together to give the right answer. "We'll get what we need, we'll be needed." It sounded too good to be true. She opened her hands in exaggerated acceptance.

"I could do with a cognac," the woman smiled. "What about you? My treat."

"With pleasure!" Alma put her hand on her heart. "Let's have a toast to our mothers!"

8

"Would you order? He can't pretend not to understand French when you shout after him . . . "

"He can't?" Alma realized she had been successful in her earlier attempt to stand out as a Parisian. "What kind of cognac?"

"What about a Hennessey?"

"I'll go and tell him. It'll take hours otherwise."

Alma went to the counter and cornered the waiter. What an order! "You know where . . . " she added with a naughty grin and went downstairs. She combed her fingers through her hair and decided she liked the way she looked. Her eyes had the greenish glow that always hinted at an erotic stir. Her mouth didn't show the frustrated tension that often narrowed her lips. Her face was radiant. She was pleased after all with this afternoon.

Making her way back through the tables, across legs, umbrellas, coats, she again caught sight of the cruiser. He must have been chased from the table by the window after his friends had left. She gloated over the tiny table at the far end of the passage that had become his hunting ground. From that place his eyes could only pierce her back. She made sure he noticed her saucy look before she turned around to her table.

The American was scribbling into her notebook. A true professional, Alma thought with awe. Not losing a minute! I wish I knew if she has noted any of my observations—on culture perhaps, or French women. . . . She received a questioning look and drew up her eyebrows to signal joyful expectation.

"Thank you." The woman closed her pen and notebook with an edge of weariness, a reluctance, Alma felt. She wondered if her presence at the table had come to disturb the other. She waited.

"Well, Alma Runau . . ." The woman inclined her head, her eyes probing. Alma was struck by the thought: She's written down my name! "Why don't you tell me all you think about Eve. As a feminist."

Alma buried her fists between her thighs, raising her shoulders in a sheepish shrug. The suggestion sounded artificial, as if the woman wanted to divert attention from some personal matter. Alma felt a touch of disappointment. It broke their intimacy. Was it time to quit?

She looked out at the Luxembourg Gardens. The sun was low, pouring its rays in thick bundles through the clouds. Fewer clouds were traveling, their edges transparent. The sky had calmed down for sunset. At the tables outside people were leaving, soon the park would close. Inside, the noise had settled into a cozy buzzing. The café crowd was drawn together into a community as the day sank. It would be a pity to leave. But she could profit from the last sunlight for her ride home.

She cast a careful glance across the table. The woman was holding one of her enigmatic smiles. Had the awkward suggestion simply been another trap? Of course, the spell had been broken on purpose. Most women like this stranger couldn't bear intimacy with another woman, at least not for long. You had to expect it. They would always take themselves back precisely when one was settling in. They would come up with a comment or a question just like this, pointing out their difference, their indifference. Pinning down some unbridgeable gap with a lacquered fingernail. "You as a feminist . . . " Was it an unconscious slap in the face?

This woman, however, was neither unconscious nor

mean. She had said she was a trickster. She had closed her notebook twice, invited Alma for a drink. It probably was just one of her games to make you stumble with surprise. Why be offended? Why not take it as an invitation to play? You just needed to stay cool in order to stay in step. Well then, she squinted her eyes, how much provocation was this Claire Heller asking for in return?

"You know what I liked best about *Eve*?" Alma gave her shoulders a nonchalant stretch. "The sexy three minutes with the young Marilyn Monroe. I liked what was going on between the women—the adoration of each other."

"I remember the admiration . . . "

" 'Admiration'—indeed! Apart from that, it's the typical after-war movie with the message: now women, this is enough. You are strong, independent, artistic, etcetera— but you need a man. You aren't *real* women without a man."

"I see. You think they shouldn't have a man."

"No, Claire Heller, they can have hundreds of men if they like. The correct answer has always been, a fish without a bicycle isn't a *real* fish!"

After a second of surprise the woman laughed: "What if you made it, 'a woman without love'?"

"Well, what about it? Couldn't she have a dog, for example?"

"Oh yes, I forgot." The woman smiled her unoffended smile. "Why does a woman need a man if she is in fact a man herself?"

Alma clicked her tongue: "Wrong again. A man is a man is a man—no matter if he has a woman or a bicycle. But a woman's reality is reduced to her love or sex life. Revolting!"

"Reduced to love . . . Does this go together with charm being exhausting? Could it be that you stick to the old rules? Why not turn them around and declare that a man without love isn't a human being?"

"Men believe they are human beings *par excellence,* no matter what I declare."

"Why adopt what they believe?"

"It's a world belief—in case you haven't noticed. How can one change that? Men and women, masters and slaves. The slaves believe it, too. It's maddening for me . . . as a feminist!"

"Getting mad is an interesting way of participating in the same belief."

Alma stared at her. "But you have to acknowledge the facts before you can change them! Rage is the basic step of any revolt."

"Maybe. It's a gesture of impotence rather than power, however."

Alma stopped, suddenly unsure what this was all about.

"Listen. The question is, how do you reveal a lie everyone believes in? The emperor's new clothes, remember? You cry: But he is naked! Only it doesn't change a thing. He believes in his clothes. He calmly stays the little macho god ruling over a universe of women on their knees!"

The American had buried her cheeks in her hands. She watched Alma from below, the red dots of her nails underlining her gaze, the black gaze of a child who knows better games. But Alma wanted to get her point across: "Like this guy right here, sitting in the passage behind me." She signaled backward with her thumb. "A notorious cruiser. No matter what I do, he has to appropriate me. Gluing his wet eyes to me, forever unshaken in his belief that I must be in need of him. Simply refusing to take the message! He has carried on in this café for ages —maybe he's already tried it on you in your time?"

As soon as Alma mentioned the cruiser, the woman's

eyes sparked interest. Alma had a vague sense of making a mistake, bringing up the wrong example. What was the remark the other had dropped about rage and impotence? Too late . . .

"The one with the dark suit and curly hair? I see. Intense eyes indeed. No, I don't think I've had the pleasure."

Alma was alarmed at how she took her time studying him. He might notice. He would take it as a massive invitation. What would happen then?

"I have the pleasure every time!" she said angrily.

"What do you do about it?"

"Do about it? What would *you* do?" She was not sure who irritated her more at that moment, the man or the woman who was *solidaire* with men. "I'm afraid I have not yet discovered the trick to make myself invisible!"

The woman gave her the same embracing look that had tested her *charme*. It bothered Alma that something in this look flattered her.

"You have also not yet discovered the trick of making yourself visible—as a warning. Anyway, how can he appropriate you?" She seemed to enjoy the idea. "You are free, aren't you?"

Alma frowned. Why on earth had she brought up this topic? She wished she were debating with a man. Her feminist discussions with men used to be easy victories.

"Indeed, he can't appropriate me. But it's irritating enough that he keeps fantasizing he does."

"Don't you ever do that with someone you find attractive?"

Alma swallowed. "And if I did, do you think it would be the same?"

"What would it be, let's see . . . observation?"

"You bet." Alma had a moment of relief. She was able after all to control this game. She took a deliberate step ahead: "I'm not a man. But if I were, and put my sticky looks all over you, what would you do?"

The woman laughed in surprise: "Like this guy? You?" There was a nervous edge to her laughter. She shook her head. "I don't know—I'd have to see it . . . "

She's at least honest in her games, Alma noted. A serious player. "Try to imagine," she insisted. "A man always tries to hunt down a prey. You are the prey. Try."

The woman searched Alma's eyes. "I'd become a hunter myself, you know." A catlike pride spread over her face. For a second Alma caught the naughty girl's defiance. A sly, brash, deliberate look from under her lashes. "I'd look back in a way that would make him drop his gun."

"Lucky if you can stand the sight!"

"I usually get what I want."

"But I as the guy will alway interpret what *I* want."

The woman leaned forward, amused: "What if we want the same?"

"So you can stand the sight?"

Alma felt ridden by a sudden demon to defeat her. She shoved a bunch of curls into her forehead, narrowed her eyes into a brooding stare, stuck out her neck, advanced a resolute jaw, and let her stare wander over the woman's face, down the line of her neck to her breasts and greedily back to her face. Making her nostrils heave with heavy breathing, she glued an imploring gaze to the poppy mouth—which opened in amazement and horror into resounding laughter.

Alma profited from her role and went on staring at the laughing face in front of her. The woman threw her head back. Her perfect white teeth shone. She laughed like a child in blissful terror, gave quick peeks to make sure Alma was still playing, and threw her head back again. Alma couldn't get enough of this beautiful, relaxed laughter. She fell in with it.

The woman sighed, shaking her head at Alma in delighted disbelief.

Alma slipped back into her brooding man's face. She moored her eyes in the woman's. Then, in a slow, dramatic turn, with a voluptuous sense of victory, she gazed over her shoulder at the cruiser. Of course he looked. Everybody looked.

—

Part Two

CLAIRE HELLER:
A LETTER, A PROVOCATION

TIME: SEVERAL MONTHS AFTER THE MEETING
   AT THE CAFÉ

CLAIRE'S FIRST LETTER

Bonjour Alma Runau,

Remember the stranger who stole your table at the café?

Back then, when I promised to write, I did not anticipate a confession. A question of theory it seemed then. Are we a private choice, a social constriction? Have our mothers made us? Has our childhood?

You recall the day. The teahouse closed in the garden near the café. South wind in the city. A small boy in a red cap on his way to the fountain. Lilac in blossom. The two of us, have we walked together before?

At the gate, on the far side, where we parted. You to ride home on your heavy bike, I to return across the garden. I watched you. There was something, a sense, maybe: I could have called out, called you back, run after. Did you know? I lifted my hand, was it regret? A possibility, squandered?

Something, that might have been said. Between coffee and cognac, finally spoken. Stories, told to no one before.

Do you remember me? I, who have been writing you letters. Have found the courage to deliver them, finally.

You are on the way out, I imagine. The concierge, let's say, drops an envelope into the wicker basket on your bicycle. Perhaps you know, immediately. The woman from the café has written. She has kept her promise.

The envelope is old, has been used before. Was sent and received long ago in some other country.

The concierge returns your gaze. Curious, indifferent. The brown envelope? *Mais non,* she knows nothing about it.

You hesitate, glance at your watch. Of course, you can take the envelope with you, wheel your bike, manage more or less to read as you walk. Or open it now, glance over it quickly, save it for later. For tonight, when you return home, pour a glass of red wine, sit down at the kitchen table.

The concierge keeps an eye on you discreetly. Picks up her striped cloth, pads off down the hall, wipes vigorously at the black iron bars of the elevator door.

The letter has arrived when you no longer were expecting it. This makes you smile. Why should you care, after a silence like that, what this stranger has to tell you?

The boy from the apartment next to yours swings into the hall. Takes it all in with a glance. You in your gray leather jacket, leaning against the handlebars, bent over the basket, reading:

Alma, try to imagine this girl. (You almost met her in the café.) She is tall for her age, slender, ferocious. Wide eyed, but she is constantly narrowing her eyes. She is ashamed of her hands, the tapering nails, the long fingers. Her mouth looks old to her, the mouth of a girl who has almost been kissed.

Add to this: she is wearing a white sailor cap, blue jeans with bell bottoms, someone gave her an old sailor shirt too large for her. She has cut her hair in a ragged bob. These clothes are never away from her; they grow like a skin, she has been wearing them since she was six years old.

She doesn't know. It hasn't occurred to her yet. She is one of those girls innocent until they wake themselves up. Six months from now, seven or eight at the most, she will decide to become a woman. But now she imagines these clothes make the difference. She thinks she can be anything she wants to be: panther, Greek warrior, Phoenician sailor.

She has fights with boys in the schoolyard. She's the talk of the neighborhood. She comes home looking mean, disheveled. They've seen her with blood on her knuckles. A cut above her eye. It is not known how she wins these fights. Sometimes the boys are much older, bullies, swaggering around the schoolyard. This girl, she lies in her bed at night, clenching her fists. "Let me," she prays, "beat the shit out of one of them. Tomorrow."

Those men who watch her in the evenings when she is out with her dog, what did they see then? Tough girl in a sailor suit too large for her, a girl striding. Hands in her pockets. One of them came to her house, climbed over the garden fence from the alley, where she had made a wooden shack for herself. She is a child still, wants a place for her childhood.

He at the window. She naked in her room. Lifting weights. He at the screen door. It is hot, a summer evening, her age is unknowable, she is a girl dancing, lifting weights, growing muscles, what does it matter. For him, for the others, she is an obscene sacredness, cannot disguise it, there are ones who are like that, every gesture shedding veils.

Shall I say we are all, each one of us, in a body we've chosen? The body that matches up with us. Everything else a lie, daydream, mere ambition. What we are, need to be, is that body. She, when the time comes, will pour herself into a new slenderness, hips that ride high, breasts waiting to be devoured.

The man, at the window. Don't think she's afraid. She catches a glimpse of him over her shoulder, laughs, runs to the door, makes a bow, invites him in. Does he think he will ever forget her? Tomorrow, she will beat the shit out of his son, in full sight of everyone, on the school playground. Follow him home from school, calling him names, mama's boy, milk sucker, taunting. Tonight she bites the father's lips, narrows her eyes, stares him down, smirking.

He's no match for her, this girl of the wooden shack from the alley. Where she dreams. Devours poems like broken pomegranates, won't eat, lives on old stories, camped out on the beach at Aulis where the Greek fleet is becalmed.

(You know the story of the Trojan war? Which of the heroes did you fall for? Did you too keep the book under your pillow?)

She is Achilles, she says, training his Myrmidons. Loved Iphigenia, put to the knife by her father, the King Agamemnon, so armies could sail to Troy.

She should be matched against victors, men in their warrior prime. She has seen them, naked on the beach, waiting for the winds. Running the hot sands, killing the deer in the sacred grove, lifting the knife, casting it off, whatever it is that holds them back, doing away with women's softness, bent on the sacrifice. She knows, the man at the window cannot imagine.

She cannot be raped, she will not let them rape her. That man with blood on his lips was not the first. She has done it before, with a sneer, a nasty glint in her eyes, a quick word. That way she has of sizing them up, placing them exactly. They wither, cannot endure the scorn, where does it come from, this knowledge of their impotence, their inadequacy? She cannot be fooled, she knows they cannot run the sands, fight the winds, breach walled cities, prowl the shore with drawn sword.

How will they take what cannot be taken without power sufficient to receive it? This wild one, she is inviolable. When the time comes she will ask to be taken, weep then because no one knows how.

There is no one at home to receive the rumors, the gossip that goes with her wherever she goes. She has a mother and a younger brother. He knows what they say about her, won't believe it. He admires her. He wants to grow up to be just like her, in sailor's cap, lifting barbells in the evening. He wants to smell of sweat, to be an invitation, provocation, memory. She stinks of an old knowledge and cannot disguise it.

Try to imagine this girl. She thinks it her shame this man slinking from her room, a summer evening, has taken her for a woman. She curses him, runs to the door, shouts out insults. She calls him little man, softy, chases him down the alley, throws pebbles, dares him to come back, try her. But it is all still an act, bravado. He has

covered her with blushes, penetrated her disguise,
pierced through, found her.

A few months from now it will happen suddenly one
day. It will occur to her that she is already bigger, taller,
more intelligent, more ferocious. There is nothing to
prove, nothing in that sphere to accomplish. She sees
the lie of them, the swagger, the strut, the preening. She
cracks the code, pierces it, finds them.

There is no one at home. Mother is selling Fuller
brushes. She is combing the neighborhood, looking for
those who will enable her to bring home bruised apples,
yesterday's bread. Tonight, as every night, she will sit
by the phone, waiting for the call. He has not called
since he went out to meet a friend for a hot tip and did
not come back, six years ago. That's the story they tell.
Run over by a car? No I.D. in his pocket? A sudden
fugue state, wandering somewhere, trying to get home to
them like Lassie? Mother is tired. She has long hair, she
braids it in four braids, pins them up on her head. Her
nails are ragged. She wears an old dress, black.

Something wrong with this story? Does this woman go
out selling Fuller brushes, looking like this, unkempt,
ruined, broken? This perhaps is only the way the daughter sees her. A permissible lie, an exaggeration. This
mother, she thinks, would have broken her heart, if she
had one. But she is tall for her age, ferocious.

Her mother. What does she look like, really? Soft face,
eyes of a doe, easily taken. Another possibility: hard as
nails, flagrant, driven. A family story: mother brought
them out here from the East, from the Big City, where a
daughter like her daughter would have made some kind
of sense, maybe. She wanted the children to have green

grass, eat oranges from the tree. She brought them by road, catching rides with cars passing, then not passing, slowing down, stopping.

The little girl dressed in a pinafore, in patent-leather shoes. She and the little boy in his sailor suit stand on the smoldering highway, drinking parched water from the distance. The little boy is worried. What if mother gets a ride and they don't?

Who is this woman, her mother? Perhaps she doesn't go out during the day to sell Fuller brushes. Perhaps she goes out selling something unthinkable.

Yes, I insist. What the mother does, does not do, has nothing to do with the daughter's mysteries. She perhaps doesn't care to remember the streets where she's gone with her dog following one street and another, out beyond the small houses. In those other streets, behind ragged neon lighted at noon. Motels. Beside a tree stunted with car fumes, she imagines her mother. Or the stories she tells herself behind those narrowed eyes. One day she will want you to believe she is sensitive, a dreamer. Even now, she has managed to move her mother to Babylon, has gone to dwell with her in the temple, where once in her life, rich or poor, every woman in worship proudly offers herself to the embrace of a stranger.

Give her a tall, brash woman on high heels, she will give you back a woman laid out in the temple. Give her a street of stone, houses without eyes, money passing from pocket to hand in the backseat of a car. She will tell you these wages are for Ishtar. Forgiver of sins. Lady of ladies. Goddess of desire.

CLAIRE'S SECOND LETTER

There was a magic ointment, she says. If you rubbed it
all over you, you know what would happen? I told you,
didn't I? If you rubbed it all over you nothing could get
you. She tells this to the boy, her brother. She says she
was rubbed with the magic ointment.

Quails migrate across the Mediterranean in a single
night to breed in the marshes and cornfields of Pales-
tine. This girl I'm telling you about, she says she's seen
them.

She has made a shack. Out of wooden boxes from the
supermarket across the alley. Nailed them, tied them,
glued them, gathered them up again after the rain,
smashed them together. She has filled it with whatever
she finds or steals. Blue Tyrian carpet, cracked Egyptian
bowl, golden fleece, Sumerian pillow. The boy believes
her stories. Even the ones she doesn't tell him. Reads
her eyes, sucks up secrets from them.

The garden, wild. But someone who must have lived
there before they did must have worked it, she tells the
boy. They must have loved it. There's good stuff in that
garden, she says. Wild roses, she insists, they have come
down all the way from wild roses of Sharon, carried by
the Hebrew midwife when she traveled to Rome. And
from there to Lesbos, crossing the sea with the Phoenician sailors, arrived among the Celts, carried by a
starving Irishman from the potato famine to Boston.

A *Letter, a Provocation*

There are nightingales, she says, you can hear them
if you wake up exactly at midnight.

The boy leans against her knees. Sometimes he is
afraid. Will she wake up, ask him can he remember, can
he repeat it? It rarely happens. Sometimes, he thinks,
she forgets him, doesn't notice if he scratches or coughs.
Then, he says something stupid, asks a question, inter-
rupts her.

She has dressed him in short pants, a tunic, given him
a lute. She calls him her page. He doesn't recognize her,
doesn't know what happened to her. This girl in a
draped sheet, cut with a scissor, torn into precise holes.
He is a minstrel, she tells him, she his lady.

She's been the warrior sister. Naked, oiled, casting the
javelin. He has seen her in her sailor suit. Never any
other. Bitten nails, ragged fingers. Narrow eyes, fist
ready.

Now she languishes there. That's what she says. She is
covered in lace, wrist touches her forehead, she reclines,
throws back her head, sighs deeply.

These dainty ones, for whom she always had so much
contempt. Sitting on the sidelines next to the baseball
diamond. She keeps an eye on them now. One of
them stumbles into her bed one night. She wakes up
weeping.

"Tell me your secret," she says to the girl, walking her
back from the drugstore and the Cherry Coke on Adams
Avenue. "How did you do it?"

The girl looks at her over her shoulder. She is practicing, doesn't matter on whom. Coyly. It goes with lowered
eyes, long lashes. She has curled them with a gadget

left over from an older sister. The girl in the sailor suit
has seen it, had it explained.

The girl who knows these secrets touches the arm of
the other with her fingertips. "Clae. What secret?"

Breathed softly. She feels the breath, it crosses her
cheek, she wants to feel it again. A way of walking. The
word for it, *mincing*. Using a first name. Bending forward, touching a shoulder. Laughing, head thrown back.
Slow glance from corner of eyes.

It is something one learns. Like lifting weights, throwing a discus, driving a chariot. She's never bothered with
it before. To her they were pale creatures in dresses.
The unembellished. Sacred, needing protection, falling
down in the games. It never occurred to her she was like
them. Or might want to be?

Those who wore pants, those who didn't. Those who
made noise, those who did not have voices. That little
thing between their legs? What did that matter? Who
pushed hardest, yelled loudest, chased who across the
schoolyard? Was there ever anyone more daring than
she?

She has figured it out. Once they were all like her.
The ones in dresses, they weren't always frightened,
shy, like doves, a deer in hiding. It must have been
something they wanted, chose, willed to happen. Took
on because they'd figured it out before she did. There
was something they knew. A question of secrets, giggling
and whispering by themselves, bent over their bag
lunches. They'd seen through the boys sooner? Seen
through the empty swagger?

The girls fall silent when she comes near. For this, she

has respect. What do they whisper? She imagines: it is some kind of power.

She comes home from her walk, lips bruised with artificial cherry. She finds the boy, her brother. When she is not there he sits alone in the shack, waiting.

Look, she tells him, I'm different. Don't close your eyes. Who am I?

Hectir? But he is frightened; he knows, it's clear from her eyes, he won't get it right.

Not Hector, stupid.

She gives him the sailor cap, he's never seen her without it before. Her hair falls into her eyes. Using one finger, slowly, she strokes back her hair, lifts her chin, doesn't get it right, gazes at him. He gets excited, jumps to his feet, clutching the sailor cap, dances a jig.

Who am I? she insists.

He catches the game; laughs, doubles over, rolls on the floor. She is upon him, tickles, won't let him breathe. She puts the sailor shirt over his head, helps him settle it, smooths it over his shoulders.

Odysseus! he shouts, it all comes back to him: Achilles, Agamemnon . . .

He doesn't know what to make of the look in her eyes, the scorn, the contempt. He slumps back, covers his face with his hands. Through his fingers, when he dares, he sees her stepping out of the bell-bottom pants, kick them away from her. She bends down, tears his hands from his face.

I am the lover of Adonis, she says.

She shakes him by the shoulders. Listen, you dreamy thing, she says. Remember. When the Athenian troops, you know who they were, marched down to the harbor to embark for Syracuse, you know what the streets looked like? Those streets were lined with coffins, with women wailing for the dead Adonis.

Adonis? Who's he?

He was born from a myrrh tree. I told you. You know why?

I don't know.

His mother, she got pregnant from her own father. You remember.

I don't remember.

Listen, stupid. This whole mess, it's the doing of Aphrodite. She knows what she's doing. Turns the girl into a myrrh tree. Gets her hands on Adonis when he comes tumbling out of the trunk. Hides him in a chest. She's planning something for herself, you better believe it. She figures: an incest brat, born from a tree, a real beauty, this kid's gonna know something when his time comes. So she takes him down into the underworld to keep him safe. Remember Persephone? You know who she was? Queen of the underworld, that's who. But Persephone wouldn't give him back. She just wouldn't. Even when Aphrodite went back to the underworld to fetch him.

He says: Why did they hide him in a chest?

She says: Stupid. He belonged to Aphrodite, the goddess of love. She wanted to make sure no one else would steal her treasure.

Why didn't Persephone give him back?

She fell in love with him, stupid.

I'm not stupid, he says.

No, you're not, she agrees. She stoops down and touches his hair. You're my clever little monkey. My small egg.

Why don't you lift weights anymore?

That's for me to know and you to find out. Anyways, Persephone wasn't supposed to look into the chest. But she gets curious, peeps inside. What does she see? This beautiful little kid lying there. You already know it's gonna turn out bad. I mean, if you've got a tree for a mother, if you were brought up by the queen of the underworld, there's good odds this guy has learned something about love.

She spreads oak leaves on the floor of the shack. Lies down, reclining. Left arm raised, supporting the head. This time gets it right: the arched back, inconceivable languor.

Wild thyme, she says to the little brother. In a bed of wild thyme. They are lying there, Aphrodite and that boy, Adonis. Beneath the holly oaks. They're smooching.

Smooching? Yuck.

He is balancing on his toes, rocking up and down on the balls of his feet. He's cautious, on guard, might have to get out of there any minute.

What happened to him?

Remember, I told you! The Syrian damsels, they lamented his fate, they wept for the death of Adonis. The red anemone was his flower. It bloomed among the cedars of Lebanon. When he died the rivers ran red with his blood, they really did, I tell you. Down to the sea.

Why did he die?

Since then, she says, putting out her arms to the little

boy. (Since then, if ever you would see this girl look sad, that's the moment.) Since Adonis went hunting and got himself killed by a boar there is no one, she says. No one who has the art to take her.

It's too much for him. He can't figure her out. She, who had camped out on the great plains with Agamemnon's army, coaxed sullen Achilles from his tent. She who had taught him to love the Trojan soliders, carried him on her back when she crossed the lines, went to dwell in the doomed city, what does she want from him now?

He punches the pillow. It's an old rag, he says, destroying her stories. He shoves her away. It's no temple, it's a filthy shack! he shouts. I'll tell our mother.

She hasn't heard a word he's said. Sits there, cutting holes in an old sheet. Listening to the wailing flute, Adonis has died, she tells herself. I am in mourning.

After that he told himself, it's because she cried. After that for three days she didn't come to the shack. He figured it out. The tears, they made her into a girl. He was careful, then, this younger brother. If that's what she wanted. If she changed her mind, gave up the heroes, shaved her head in mourning. Sat with bare breasts, carried the dead god down to the river. What could he do?

Rebellion in the temple. He won't listen to her now, won't be her page, can't remember the word *languish*. He wants her to be what she was, has always been, doesn't want her to go on in front of the mirror. Can't get his eyes off her.

She, naked. He, at the window. She, studying herself, eyes wide, lips pouting, she makes a fist, yells him away,

yells him to leave her alone, let her concentrate. Won't
come out to the shack, fierce again, narrows her eyes,
spends hours in front of the glass. One day she tells him:
Tomorrow, you'll see. By tomorrow I'll do it.

He won't grow up, this small boy. There won't be time
to figure it out. He'll die six months after she leaves
home. She won't hear about it for a year. By then it's too
late to be sorry. He'll never know his sister doesn't come
to the shack because she is choosing her body. Picking it
out of all possible bodies. Reflecting on it, trying it on,
casting it off, inventing another.

Stop this moment. What is happening here?

He watches her, gets chased away, comes back, sneaks
into the room, hides under the bed, is found in the
closet, can't keep away from her. The mother comes
home at night, sometimes she doesn't. Where does she
go, he asks? Now, the sister doesn't invent an answer.

Hard work, nerve-shattering work. What if she gets it
wrong, picks the wrong shape for herself, is stuck with
it, can't get out of it once she chooses? Dangerous enter-
prise. What if she made the mistake of willing a body
like the mother's? Doesn't want pendulous breasts,
doesn't want pendulous breasts pushed out of a dress,
then collapsing. Won't look at the mother when she
comes home. Slams the door to her room. Fears the con-
tamination of vision, wants to keep her sight pure, inner
eye unencumbered. From the infinite clay of childhood
she is selecting. This one possibility. She is creating a
woman.

Mother is tired, takes off her heeled shoes, has dyed
them red; last year they were another color. Puts her feet

up on the couch, falls asleep instantly. Snores loudly. Spittle in the corner of her mouth. Wakes up with a start, wary, on guard, eyes too bright, artifically widened. The girl has seen it all, got it by heart, the skin puckered at the throat; she is afraid, what if she makes a mistake, chooses this body?

Doesn't believe in destiny, this brash girl; pagan, refuses influence, takes her time deciding. Goes calling, buys Cherry Cokes, steals the empty bottles from the wooden boxes in the alley, cashes them in for courtship.

Figures it out. She will not become one or the other. Not man in his striped suit, ogling neighbor's daughter. Not woman of infinite exhaustion, tireless, prowling for a night's living. Not big boy in the schoolyard, stripping the pants from a little boy, howling with derision, pushing him out into the street, naked. Not girl of the Cherry Coke, simpering homeward. No place for her here.

She tells the little brother: Don't you remember? Achilles, the son of Thetis?

He is only too happy to remember Achilles. I know! he shouts, lifting his head: Chiron was his teacher.

You know nothing, stupid boy. I tell you, nothing. Next spring, you'll see me. Then you'll know what I'm talking about. Thetis his mother, she sent him to Scyrus. She wanted to keep him safe. She knew Achilles would die in Troy if he went there, she knew everything before it happened, she was a goddess. So you know what she did? She hid him away. In Scyrus. She had him live with the women. Yes, she did. That's how it was, I tell you. Achilles among the women, dressed like a girl . . .

I don't believe it, he says. He never. Not Achilles.

A *Letter, a Provocation*

Would I lie to you?

He closes his eyes, sees it clearly. Fires on the beach, the oiled bodies, naked soldiers. She lifts him, puts him to bed in the prow of a boat.

Hey, she says, it's like I told you. Odysseus, he goes out to look for Achilles. He looks all over the place. He can't find him. Then he figures it out. He goes to Scyrus and the people there say: Huh? Achilles? Those people, they say they'd never heard of Achilles. But Odysseus, he's crafty. He brings out his gifts. He spreads them out in front of the maidens. He puts out a shield and a spear. He gets someone to blow a trumpet. That's how they call their soldiers to war. What happened? Achilles bit, he took the bait. He leaped out, he grabbed the spear, he grabbed the sword.

She jumps to her feet, she wants to show him. Achilles in that moment, rushing to battle, dressed like a girl.

Try to imagine this girl: tall for her age, slender, ferocious.

CLAIRE'S THIRD LETTER

This girl, she wants to tell her own story. She thinks I won't get it right. She's older here, no trace of the sailor suit, wooden shack, Tyrian lace, the girl languishing. This is the third story, how she put to use the body she made for herself. She wants to tell it in her own words. The Portrait of the Artist as a Young Whore, she calls it.

She's given up pomegranates. Become a loud-mouth kid, living on tacos and french fries. She's moving too fast? Doesn't tell how it happened? How did she go from that dreamy child to this brash, sexual being?

Alma, this girl sets you a challenge. One day, when she's older, you'll meet her in Paris. In a café. She'll make you wonder about man the enemy.

She'll look at you with astonishment. He holds us back? Won't let women be sexual? Curbs, circumscribes, limits, intimidates, confines? Are you kidding?

She doesn't think she will manage to convince you. Nevertheless, she wants to tell you her story. Here it is, in her own words.

"It was a Friday," she says. "Old high noon. Me. I'm thirteen years old. There I am, Miss Plaid Skirt and Saddle Shoes. Miss Always Wears Bobby Sox. Miss Looking Just Like I Oughta. Glad to meet you. And this here's Mr. Polyester, vocational counselor."

It is an artful story. Has been told before, become stylized. She likes it. Telling it, she'd lean forward, put her chin in her hand.

A Letter, a Provocation

She says: "Can you believe it? Mr. Baggy Pants giving up his lunch hour in the faculty lounge? There he is, eating away from his brown paper bag. He fumbles about in my file. He looks over my test scores, looks up at me, wets his thumb. 'Young lady,' says he, 'why, if you'd apply yourself, why, you know it, Claire Hilyard, you could be just about anything in the world you want to be.'

" 'Call me Clae,' I says to him, real sarcastic like. 'Anything in the world I want to be? Hey, you've got it.'

" 'Good,' he says. 'Good.' But you better believe it. That's not what he's thinking."

At this point she'd interrupt herself. She wants a listener who can take it. "Hey you," she'd say, looking you in the eyes, "you sure you want to hear about that time I stopped being a virgin?"

Suspend your questions, Alma Runau. Swallow your doubts. Tell yourself: She passed through the stage of hero worship. She picked the goddess of love for a role model. If she talks tough, that's another way to keep herself hidden. Women, you say, are always in hiding? That's your story.

She sits back in her chair. She's settling in for a good long tell. "So anyway, Mr. Polyester, he says to me, real confidential like, 'Now Clae,' he says, 'let's say I asked you, to close your eyes, you know? And really think about it. I mean, seriously, Clae. What is it you really want to do?'

"Well, I didn't exactly close my eyes. As for considering, did he really think I hadn't lost sleep over the question? There he is, leaning forward on his desk, taking me very seriously with his little pig eyes.

" 'Well?' he says.

" 'Well,' I answer. 'Shall I tell you the truth?' And that's when I got it. That's when I knew for sure. This guy wasn't kidding. I could be anything in the world I wanted to be. I'd gone to Troy. I'd picked quails' feathers out of the sky. I'd made this real cool body for myself. Hey, hadn't I already proved it?

" 'Okay, then,' I says. 'What I really want to do . . . you sure you're ready for this? What I really, really want to do with my life is . . . fuck a lot!' "

Tough kid, hidden behind vulgarity the way once she was hidden in a sailor suit. Why not let her exaggerate a little?

Did I tell you? she says. That there was my thirteenth birthday. Time to enter the tribe. So, I'm thinking. Where I live no one's exactly gonna give you a moonlit bath, smear you with menstrual blood or anything. You want a ceremony? You need the old rite of passage? You're gonna have to make one for yourself, you know what I mean?

A surprise party. That's my mother's idea. So of course I have to pretend I know nothing about it. I have this boyfriend, Warren Vogel, he's that kind of guy, he kisses and fumbles around but only on the outside of the sweater. The kind who never thinks below the waist, he blushes when you catch him with his hands in his pockets. You know the type? So anyway, Warren is going to pick me up and take me somewhere and then oh my god, he's forgotten his wallet at my house, we'll have to go back for it.

That's supposed to happen. But now I start thinking. There's all kinds of careers a girl can set out for. What's to stop us? And don't give me any of that equal-opportunities stuff. Me, equal? Thirteen years old, coming of age in America, all you want is being equal to a man? That's your problem.

The point is: What happens if you decide you want to be a doctor? Or a judge? Or a cop? Or a psychoanalyst? You fill out an application, you put in your time with your books, you get professional training, you take an exam, you get a license. Hey, but what about a girl who wants to master the unmentionable? I mean, really learn it. Like it was something worth knowing, as important as being, let's say, a school nutritionist. Who's going to teach you?

I mean, the whole thing, from the first eye contact, to following him home, walking up the stairs behind him, taking his clothes off, taking off mine. Then what? You think it's nothing to put these bodies together. That takes art. Art is what I wanted to learn. I wanted to enroll myself somewhere, I wanted steps and lessons and stages and degrees and licensing exams. I wanted matriculation and graduation. I'm serious.

I've read a book or two. Courtesan. Hetaera. Temple prostitute. I know all about it. Those dames, and I don't care who you were, they put out in the temple when their time came. Thought it was a sacred act, they did. Like, that was how they worshiped the goddess? Come on, you say: a whore is an artist? Well, if a whore is not a four-letter artist, who is?

Back to Warren. The kind of guy who comes on time,

wearing a suit and tie, comes in to say hello to your
mother, she's putting on her act, believe me. He sits
with his knees sticking out so he's got a place to put his
hands not to put them in his pockets. Holds your jacket
for you, opens the door, walks behind you to the car,
turns back to say, you can count on me, she'll be home
on time, opens the car door for you, leans over when he
gets inside to give you a peck on the cheek. So I start
thinking. She wants this to be a surprise party?

We drive to the movie. Something on Hollywood
Boulevard, far enough from home to give the kids a
chance to arrive. We pull into the parking lot. Poor
Warren, he's not much good at lying; goes through his act,
picks up his jacket from the backseat, shakes it, shakes
his head at me, damn uncomfortable. Well, it's almost
dark. Time for the priests with shaved heads to go light
their fires in the temple.

I say, Warren, listen here. I'll tell you what I'm going
to do. I'm thirteen years old today, you know what I
mean? I'm dying to get you inside me. That's how I talk
to him. I figure, you've got to start with what you've got,
later refine it, make it subtle, develop an art. For now,
what I've got is thirteen years and a bad mouth.

Those stories I used to tell that kid Dennie? I can't get
that stuff out of my mind. There were these holy places.
Sanctuaries, they called them. They had them all over
the place. Here's this temple up on a cliff. You walk out
on the porch. You look down. There's a river there, these
huge rocks, and some of them are carved with Adonis
and Aphrodite. He's humped over, she's in mourning.
He's holding a spear, he's waiting for the boar that's

gonna kill him. It's summer, there are these red anemones blooming all over the place. The river's red. Dyed
with his sacred blood, that what they say. So I keep
seeing that damsel laid out on her pillows in the temple
waiting for the stranger. That stuff turns me on. I mean,
think about it. She's all washed and oiled, they put
perfume in her hair, I mean, this babe is laid out in a
temple.

Okay? It's getting late. There's this guy, maybe he's a
shepherd. He's been walking all day. His sheep are
tired. A bunch of priests goes past him, carrying a bier.
These people, they think their young god has died.
They've hung that dead boy with jasmine, roses of
Sharon. Everyone's weeping. They're playing drums.
The women have shaved their heads. They're in mourning. There's that woman in the temple, waiting for a
stranger.

Well Warren, you can believe me, doesn't know what
to say. "Now, look here honey," he says to me, when I
start to get up on his lap, straddling him, which is not
easy if the guy's trying to stop you. Warren says: "A
joke's a joke." But I'm serious. He's a big hunk of a guy,
thick, muscular thighs the girls drool and gossip about
when it gets late at pajama parties. I've got my skirt
hiked up around my hips, he's still trying to stop me,
lifting me off his lap with those big hands of his, and I
start thinking, if it goes on like this, this guy's gonna go
off any minute.

Did I tell you? The day I got this new body? I was
doing that kid Dennie a favor. Riding "horsy" on a
broomstick. Galloping all over the place shouting

"Giddyap, giddyap" when something started and after that you can believe me I thought that broom handle was a magic wand. I used to hide it under my bed. I made it into a fetish (come on, I told you I read books). I mean, wasn't I jealous when mother used it to sweep up the patio? It took me two whole weeks before I figured out that hot pleasure was in me. So Warren's wand, although I wouldn't of course think of comparing the male member to a broom handle or the pole of a clothesline or the arm of a red couch, didn't have much to offer unless I could get it into some closer proximity.

Old Warren, he really was a nice guy. He was planning for us to get engaged when I graduated from school, he wanted us to go to college together, he kept trying to keep me from dropping out like I was thinking, I got bored, I didn't like to attend classes, especially not Fridays when the football team played games away from home and I, missing the sight of Warren in his tight pants running around on the playfield.

I mean, I'm no Pindar. But I tell you, those Greek boys played their games naked. They sure did. Rubbed shiny with myrtle oil. Sweet muscle bulging all over the place. In that hot sun, can you see it? The crowds eating olives, drinking resin wine. Goatskin for a pillow, they were there for the day, they wanted hot, fleet, naked beauty, I tell you.

Meanwhile, Warren's managed to get me off his lap. He comes to the decision I must have been drinking vodka (Warren has heard vodka doesn't smell on your breath). Warren doesn't smoke or drink, he does what the coach tells him to do, he's off to college on an aca-

demic scholarship and Warren believes that coming saps
a man's vitality. He wants us to be virgins when we get
married.

Now this kind of guy is a real turn-on. Most of the girls
I know are half fainting when Warren walks out of Spanish class in his blue football sweater and tight jeans.

Friday night in the late autumn; a dark corner of the
parking lot off Hollywood Boulevard. Women pass by
with their sheaves of wheat. They're carrying lentils and
canary seed to the temple. This football hero in his best
suit out with his best girl on her birthday, fighting her
off as if she were poison or something, and meanwhile
this guy's so in love if one of his friends stops to talk to
me Warren's there in two seconds, shoving him aside.

So we tussle; I keep trying to put my arms around him
and breathe into his ear, I tell him about the way Adonis
was killed by a wild boar. I use this husky voice I'd been
practicing. Hey, Warren, I say to him, you know what
that means? It means even old Aphrodite can't get this
kid to concentrate on loving. What does that tell you
about men? I mean, not even the goddess of love? Warren, he keeps lifting me off his lap, I wiggle against him
because now I don't really care anymore if Warren lets
himself go, it's a beginning at least and then, not even
thinking about it I happen to push against the seat lever,
the seat slides back, I tumble off his lap and there I am
crouched in front of Warren Vogel on the rubber mat,
between his legs.

You remember that time I told you about? When I
chose my body? So here I was again, a real turning
point. I looked up, this guy's face was troubled. There

were little beads of sweat on his upper lip, two white dots on his nostrils, his lips were white and I tell you this was one unhappy man. Old Mother Nature she got to him, finally. He would have done anything I tell you to let himself go and give himself up to me.

Me, I wanted this guy any way I could get him, but my mind gets real cool when my body's in heat and now it was working overtime and I figured, if this guy unbuttons I'm never gonna be able to lose him. He'll track me everywhere, he's the type would as soon kill you if he can't make you his wife, this guy's a fanatic husband-to-be, pillar of everything respectable. If I make it with Warren it's all over for me.

But this guy is in anguish, he could be maimed for life depending on the outcome of this little encounter. If I pull down my skirt this guy's never going to be able to risk it. I'm gonna leave behind me a case of eternal blue balls. That's what I'm thinking.

On the other hand: suppose I unbutton him. I'll never be able to fight him off. He'll be dragging me down the aisle and filling me with babies, I'll never find out what real sex is about, my whole life will come to an end right here between Warren Vogel's legs and, honey, it's not worth it.

Now all this is not taking a whole lot of time. What I'm talking about must have lasted, five minutes? But that's how it goes. In five minutes I'd got myself into a situation. Warren's sexual future was in my hands, my sexual future pitted against it. I'm a woman, right? I mean, in spite of the fact I chose to put myself in this woman's body, I know I'm supposed to put the man's needs first.

So I think: there's gotta be a way out of this thing, some way that will give Warren what he needs to become someone else's grade-A serviceable husband and leave me free to become a whore. And meanwhile, Warren's in a sweat.

But now old Aphrodite is taking over. Warren's dragging my hand toward him, we get to his Tide-white jockeys. I've got my mouth one-sixteenth of an inch away, there's this beautiful love drop riding at the tip of him and finally I get it. The way out comes to me. I mean, that's what happens when you're really up against it, when nature and art get together to save your skin. Because I mean, I intend to be a whore, I've been called to it, it's my gift. Someday, I am going to be great. A real queen between the sheets. Nothing is going to keep me from that.

So I say, getting my mouth up real close to him, "Warren, I'll make a deal with you." Poor Warren, he groans when my breath touches him, his whole body shudders, but he manages to choke out, "Anything you say, honey." I put my hands on him. Now this, I want you to know, is the first time I've touched a man. And I like it. That soft skin tender as a baby's cheek; that hard throbbing in a piece of flesh that any moment's gonna become soft and cuddly. That's dynamite, I tell you. I want to let go and forget my future and scramble up into Warren's lap. He's got his hands on my waist but this time he's pulling me onto his lap and I put my hands on his shoulders and I say, "Warren, you're not getting anywhere until you promise." "Sure, honey, you know I'm crazy about you," Warren says. I take Warren by the ears, pinching him real hard: "Promise. Promise. When all this is over, it's all over between us."

Poor Warren, he's gone so far he could never get himself out again, he's a virgin, remember. And I've got slim hips and a little round hard belly and high tits (you listening? that there is the body I made for myself) and all I want to do is ride this guy the way I ride the clothesline pole outside my bedroom at night but I lift myself up off his lap and put my hand down and pull him out of me.

Warren, I say, promise me. Promise to let me become a whore. I slip down onto him, he gasps, puts his hands on my shoulders, says it every time I pull at his ears, letting me ride him, he promises to give me my destiny, let me go, let me become what I intend to be. Yeah, thirteen going on four thousand. That's how I put to use the body I made for myself. That there is how I made a temple out of the front seat of his father's Olds in a parking lot off Hollywood Boulevard on the 26th of October, the day the Pleiades set in the morning.

Hey, that's what I call a rite of passage.

CLAIRE'S FOURTH LETTER

Act four. Alma, you still with me? The next time we run into her she is eighteen years old, living at a château in the Dordogne valley. Her bedroom looks down over the river. She has a small Louis XIV writing table pushed up between the shutters. She's writing her memoirs.

I know what you're thinking, she writes.

You think I ran into some rich fellow, some European wasted kid from an old family. In fact, I met a guy like that. He would have married me any day, and you're still wrong. You want me to tell you a story you've heard every time you've heard about a woman that's made it. Let me tell you. How I got here is on my own steam. From my own god-given ability to lie when it's appropriate. Take advantage of a good thing when I see it. Figure out where my interest lies in any situation. You've heard about Hermes, god of thieves? Let me introduce you: Hermes, my protector.

A few minutes ago I came back from my walk. Went past the empty parlor. They'd all gone out for a stroll. They've been traveling about, learning French, studying embroidery. Those girls are my age. So, here's this room: fire burning real low, late afternoon, pack of Indian cigarettes on the table. They left most of the goodies, little round pieces of dried meat, homemade chocolates, tulip-shaped glasses with cognac (for the chaperones, you better believe it).

Any minute now that boy with long legs is coming to clear it away and I have pockets. So, two cigarettes into the shirt pocket. Silver cigarette lighter one of these chicks bought in Venice. Dipped chocolates into the mouth. Down with the cognac and into my left hand the dried-meat open-face sandwiches.

Okay, I'm not claiming it's a big heist, it's how I keep in training. And that boy, one of these days he's going to go out with his gun and his dog, he'll run into me in the woods, coming back along the river. This time I'm not going to let him get away so easy.

This here is a family affair. Madame runs the place, the kid with the tight pants and knee boots is her son, visiting from his school in Switzerland. There's a daughter, who looks after the kitchen and goes into the village to pick up vegetables and fresh eggs, this is a class operation and Madame couldn't be more pleased to have me. She doesn't know what's lying in wait for her son.

I dress the way I should for a place like this. I'm quiet, don't talk to anyone, don't make trouble. The only thing I've asked? Push the old Louis Ex I Vee next to the window, so as I can watch it get dark out there on the river. Hey, I like to imagine this man, see, he's been away for ten years in the Crusades. Coming home again, by this river. You can't see nothing, not even a farmhouse from this place. When it gets dark it just gets totally black. How do you know then you're still in this stinking twentieth century?

Did I tell you? My brother Dennie, that little kid? Yeah, six months after I left home. They didn't know where to write me. I found out one day in the American

Embassy, Rome. Standing there, asking for letters, some
kid from my high school hears my name, tells me old
Dennie's dead. Yeah, old Dennie.

You think I cried?

Must be five thousand years ago now. Took one suitcase of clothes. Got Warren to drive me to the highway,
him cryin' his head off, he really was. He kept apologiz-
ing, promised to marry me, I kept reminding him what
he'd promised, promised leave me alone, let me do what
I wanted.

You know what happened after Warren took his pleasure? He pulls me up into his arms, starts sobbing and
snuffling right into my hair. I've got this long, chestnut
hair, it drives men crazy. I take time making myself look
good, you're gonna be a woman, I think, do a good job of
it. I've got dark eyes, I swagger, don't shake my ass,
wide shoulders, I throw them back, a long neck, I hold
my head high on it. When I walk into a room you'll look
up, believe me.

I got Warren to drive me to the highway. I'm not
trying to tell you it was as easy as that. Warren didn't
think much of his promise. He kept saying I took
advantage of the situation. Yeah, I kept saying, I took
advantage of the situation. I liberated you from a life
of certain sexual disaster. Warren, I says, stop crying.
Patti Jo Can't-Wait-to-Get-Married and Mary Jane
Dying-to-Have-Kids will snap you up the minute I'm
out of the picture. You don't even have to tell them
I've set out to be a whore.

Warren is worried about my reputation.

Warren drops me off near this taco stand. He kisses me

good-bye, gets out of the car to help with my suitcase, takes me into his arms, and then he says, "Well, listen. I mean, you know, we've done it once already . . ."

There's something in Warren's voice. I mean, it's subtle. But I can tell, this guy has put me in a very special category. I'm a girl who "does it." That means I'm a lower kind of a girl. Degraded. He thinks I'm a whore in the sense he means whore, not in the way I mean it.

Ask Warren, he'll tell you. Sex is an instinct. Go on, press him. He'll tell you sex is something that happens to you, not something you choose. It's never occurred to Warren that sex is the desire to get pleasure all over your body. Warren's planning to spend his life engaged in struggle against an urge. Civilizing it, making it proper. Doing it with a woman he loves, or in the marriage bed, for the purpose of begetting. But since I'm his whore, and I'm getting out of there, why not just get back into the car, drive off on some little dirt road and make it together?

That makes me mad. I'm nobody's whore, not in the sense he means it. I'm out to practice the art of body sensation, enlarge my sex capacity, if you know what I mean. It's a hot day, the highway rippling, I'm dressed to the nines, low heels, faded old blue jeans, striped halter, my white shirt open in front and falling down over my ass, hair tied back, smoking a French cigarette, wearing sunglasses, I'm off into my life and no Warren Vogel is going to tell me what I am at that moment.

"Warren," I says to him, giving him a good push against the chest. It takes him by surprise, he stumbles

back a step or two and I close in on him. "Warren, you
want to make it with me? Well, look here. I mean there's
not a soul on the highway."

Warren couldn't help himself, I guess. His head sort of
twitched once to the left and he looked down the road as
if he just had to find out if there really wasn't a soul after
all. You could smell the meat and onions and melted
cheese from the taco stand. Someone had left the radio
on in his truck and there was this country music that
just makes you want to go lie down in the hay and sob.
Warren and I both hear it, I suppose it passes through
his mind he could just do it, take me around to the other
side of the car, he doesn't say a word, doesn't look at me,
he opens the car door from behind him, gets inside, and
peels off down the highway without looking back, leaving me watching him from the side of the road, my
mother's suitcase standing next to me, my best shirt on
my back, three hundred dollars in my pocket, thirteen
years old and off into the world to become an artist.

An artist, you say? Go ahead, call me whatever you
want. At least you know now what I mean by whore.

She sits at the window, writes in her diary. Sips cognac,
stares at the river for signs of the man coming home from
the Crusades.

You've got it all wrong, she writes. You think men are
powerful? You're all worried about their uses and abuses
of power? I tell you, the most powerful thing walking
this earth is a sexual woman. More powerful than a wild
boar, more powerful than a wild crane flying. She's not
packaging sex like it's something else. Hey, she's not

planning marriage, babies, commitment. She's out there,
I tell you, for the body.

She says: she never found a teacher, has grown tired
of her power. Wants someone to deliver her from herself. She says she is Aphrodite's daughter. Wandering
the earth over, weeping for a dead boy, weeping for
Adonis, who was her lover.

Men, she says: they know nothing about sex, they
haven't discovered it yet, haven't invented love's body.
Poor things, you've got to pity them. They think the
body is fishy, they really do. Think some parts of the
body worse than others. Ought to be hidden, kept private, not be touched in public, not be touched at all. Not
one of them, and I ought to know, thinks the sexual
member's got dignity. Not one of them thinks below the
waist civilized as what's above it. Yeah, she says: they
organize the body into zones, some okay for penetration,
others meant to be kept virgin. Not looked at, fondled,
smelled. According to them, it's okay for the lower parts
to get it on with the lower parts. But lips, which are part
of the head, better stay out of it.

She is enjoying herself. Puts her elbow on the desk,
leans head against hand. Yeah, she says: they make up
categories for pleasure, some lawful, some punishable
by law. There's this man, see, he's all dressed up in his
suit and tie, he's sitting in a chamber, there are these
other men in suits and ties and they're making up pun-
ishments for people who put their lips to other people's
private places. They're making up laws, very worried
about pleasures taken in private, behind closed doors.

Take your man in the street. Sure, he wants to do it

with you. He's got his wife at home for the chaste marital embrace. His whore, his mistress, his call girl, his go-go dancer, his little girl of the streets for everything else. Yeah, he's liberated; yeah, he believes in liberated sex. But secretly he's suspicious. Thinks the body will lead him astray, sap his ambition, take him over, make him its slave. Better keep it outside the house, away from the family, away from the kids.

She says: it wouldn't do to take a guy like this too seriously. Make him into an enemy, he'll believe in his power. Tell him he's oppressed you, he'll think he can.

This guy, I tell you, he's real uneasy. Is it big enough, will he get it under control, keep it up for an hour, keep it going?

You ever read Freud? Yeah, that's what he says. To begin with, all little kids, they think there's only one sex. They think everyone's got the male organ. They think the clitoris is a little penis. Then, they grow up a little. They're now maybe four years old, they reach the old oedipal complex. Suddenly everything changes.

What happens? Well, first the boys, they start looking under your dress. They stand by the swings to see what you've got up there. They notice you don't have the same thing they have. Pretty soon, the girls, they start paying attention too. Now they feel they've got something missing.

The boy, of course he starts thinking about the girl's missing penis. Hey, he says to himself, somebody must have cut that thing off. He's scared, you'd better believe it. What if someone did the same to him?

As for the girl, poor thing. She also thinks somebody

came along and cut that thing off. She feels real
deprived. She starts wishing and she starts envying and
pretty soon she's got no other thought in her head. Now
all she wants is be a boy and get back that penis.

Yeah? That so? Didn't anybody ever ask Herr Freud
how come, if the clitoris seems to be a penis, suddenly
overnight it's something missing? I mean, if the girl
thought it was a penis to begin with, what made her
change her mind?

You think maybe she got a peek at her daddy?
Decided that thing between her legs was too little to be
a penis? Hey, but if that's what she decided, why didn't
her little brother? The first time he caught sight of his
dad, his daddy was a whole lot bigger! If that little thing
Sonny's got is a penis why shouldn't her little thing go
on being a penis?

You ask me, to begin with, little girls and boys both
think the one sex is Mommy's. Then they grow up a
little. They start noticing this, start noticing that. Pretty
soon they come to the conclusion, poor Daddy, after all,
he's not like Mommy. He don't have breasts, he don't
make babies. They think Mommy feels sorry for him.
That's why she gave him that thing between his legs.
That's his baby!

Now, this here is the part where little kids get real
scared. There's Mommy with breasts and milk and real
babies. There's Daddy with a penis for a baby. Hey,
what if they grow up to be like Daddy?

That's where you see the difference between girls and
boys. The girls, they get over their fright. Pretty soon
everybody's telling them they're for sure going to grow

up and be like Mommy. But the boys? What happens to them? They gotta face the truth. They ain't never gonna grow up, have real babies. Yup, sooner or later they got to face it. They gonna have to make do with their little dong, only that kind of baby.

You think that makes them happy? No matter how hard they try they're never going to grow breasts, spawn brats, be a mother? So, now they start thinking and pretty soon they figure it out. The only way they can get near all this mother stuff, the only way, I tell you, is get back inside her.

Yeah, they're figuring. Looks like you've got to be a daddy, have a big thing to get hold of a mother. Okay, they'll wait a few years. They'll grow up, they'll be like Daddy. They'll get bigger.

There it is. Right there. That's their problem. Right there they start suffering their inferiority. Right there they get into their envy of the father's penis. Old Freud, he got mixed up. Boys suffer from penis envy, not their sisters. Boys, poor things, never do manage to believe they're big enough. They just keep on worrying, measuring, doubting. You ever seen them looking at one another? How far do they piss? How big is that thing they're pissing out of? Never do get over their doubt. Old puberty comes along, now they're going to be tested. No wonder that guy's frantic. What he calls sex? What's that got to do with the art of sensation? He's tracked you down the alley? He's stalking you to prove he's as big as his father. That guy's nervous, I tell you. How does he know how big that broad is inside? What if he gets in there and starts falling and falling? He's opened his pants? Honey, that's a little boy wondering if he'll ever be big enough to satisfy a mother.

She bends over her desk, loses track of the river, leaves the Indian cigarette burning out in the dish. Those bullies you're so worried about? Those tyrants you want to expose? Honey, that's a nervous creature. Puffing himself up, pretending he's driven by an untamed urge. You want to show him just how controllable his urges are? I tell you, all you've got to do is take him at his word. Try him, look him in the eyes, kick off your jeans. Go on, do it.

A woman who is raped, she says, has been unable to choose to deprive a man of the sad power of depriving another of choice. No rapist, she says, is out to catch an elemental power, let me tell you.

She makes a rendezvous. Decides, that boy with the long legs will come to her room. Yeah, tonight she says, dragging on the dead cigarette, exactly at midnight.

She writes you a letter. Twenty years before she's met you, she writes you a letter.

The master? The dominant one? Who lords it over them? Who calls the shots? Who takes them to bed with him? Are you kidding? Aphrodite's daughter, you know what she's up to? She's trying to teach them how; rope them in, make them surrender, invent them all over again in desire.

Aphrodite's great, failed scheme for Adonis.

We leave her writing.

Take up her story. Follow her from the taco stand, find out where she went when she left home. But first, she wants you to know: she has used herself well. She, who

cannot be raped, cannot be taken as another's possession. She wants you to understand, when she looks at a
man it is he who will follow. Never the reverse. Never.

She thinks you lie to yourself. You imagine their
power because you are unable to imagine your own. You
envy the power you imagine, because you are afraid of
your own. She does not think there is much to fear from
men who fear women. One look in the eyes, she says:
they back down, or they follow.

This brash, dreamy kid, she's got a sex philosophy
between her legs, how long do you think before she got
a ride, she asks you?

Young guy in a gray Ford; strips of black tape where
the seat cover's cracking. He wears a striped shirt, but-
ton-down collar with a missing button, Bermuda shorts, a
few threads frayed out at the cuff.

"You a runaway?" he asks her, offering her a cigarette.

"One thing's sure," she says and moves fast, lighting
his before he can recover. "I ain't gonna have no reason
to be running from you."

They drive up the coast. She sees donkeys tethered to
an olive tree, hears them braying. She notices paper,
blown from the highway, a filthy underbrush beneath fig
trees. He's driving up north for a job interview. She
notices his hand too close to the passenger seat.

"Keep your eyes on the road," she advises. "You pull
over to the side one minute more than I think you
oughta, I'll bite that thing off," she says.

Later, outside of Malibu, catching his eye: "What's
your staying power, mister? How long exactly can you
keep it up?"

Claire Heller

She's turned him to stone, turned the Gorgon's head against him. He doesn't look at her twice, not the whole way, through fields of wild, blossoming thyme, to Santa Barbara.

"Got you," she says. "One quick thrust from old wisdom's tarnished shield."

"We're sure makin' time," he mutters, glad to be rid of her.

"I've put winged sandals on the wheels," she says.

The outskirts of a mid-California Spanish city. She opens the door to the car; takes the Camel from his shirt pocket, brushes ash from the fine lines in her knees, wonders if the stone in his ring is a fake diamond.

"Give my regards to Troy," she shouts, thinking some girl farther down the highway, and it's getting dark now, sure is gonna thank her.

Those days, she's looking for a teacher; she's a sex revolutionist, she says, to the pale boy who doesn't hear her in the pizza window: don't need no other kind of revolution if you've got that one. Hey, she inquires, carrying her high heels by one finger hooked over her shoulder, you hear the one about the girl who thought about nothing but sex?

How she sold violets along the road, to make an easy buck. Tamed nightingales, sold them for a song. About this trip, which takes six hours and three years exactly, she later tells various stories.

Spent a year holed up in a shack with a young kid with pimples. Left him better than she found him. Built a sanctuary for Aphrodite in the vineyards.

It's a fact, she sets it down in her notes. In California,

if you drive a used car out of the lot, and don't come back, just keep driving, it's twenty-four hours before they can make a report.

There are other stories.

Catch her in a good mood, she'll tell you she sold the car to a guy she picked up along the highway. Mercedes, she says: you better believe it. With a stash like that, who couldn't make money in Reno? Don't get me wrong, she'll assure you if you run into her sitting on her leather suitcase in the train station in Barcelona. I'm no gambler.

You figure it, she says. Slick bad boy behind the blackjack table. Does he care? I don't have to take him to bed. The odds are at his fingertips. That means, work it right, the odds are in your favor. For one particular look.

Think about it, she'll advise you. I'm not saying you can do it the first time you try. I've been practicing that look, let's see, for about . . . ten thousand years?

She ticks it off on her fingers, walks through the restaurant car, invites you to dine. Half an hour with the used-car dealer, one ride in a car, she tells you, three days in Reno, leaning across the table to tuck the napkin into your shirt, leastways if you know how to look at them, sister.

Ten minutes before midnight. She takes a bath, drowns herself in myrrh, puts on a silk T-shirt, rayon pants. The boy with long legs, he's got ten minutes before she takes back his opportunity to play Adonis.

About that look, she writes. She leans on the desk, dries her hair between her fingers. That look is all you need, I tell you. Ten seconds, head tipped back, you've got him sighted. You better believe he'll be noticing you. Nine seconds left. You keep on looking; no smile, nothing promised. That look says you know what you're doing; you know things he'd like to know, if you gave him the chance to know you better. Six seconds to go. Nothing seductive. That looks says you've got something he's never gonna know without you. Count down. Hey buddy, you taking the risk?

Did she ever tell you that one? How she gets her clothes? Goes into a store stark naked under her coat, gathers a few choice items into the dressing room. Puts on a silk chemise, over it a purple blouse, over that a hand-knit sweater. Silk skirt, she reminds herself, taking it carefully from its hanger. Big smile for the salesgirl, out she goes, fully attired, beneath her coat.

Another story, she calls it the immortal act of thinking dirty. Having perfected eye contact, she's been practicing mind control. She closes her eyes, counts the strokes of the church clock telling midnight.

It goes like this: you catch sight of the guy in the woods. Or, let's say: lunchtime. Fishing from the terrace. She takes her place at the table. Sips a glass of water. Waits.

He's got his back to her; he pulls in a fish, bends over to ease the hook out of it. She thinks her thoughts.

She says, you can see him blushing. He doesn't turn. Casts the line. Out there, where the river bends, the prow of a ship moves into sight. Odysseus sailing to his rendezvous with Nausicaä. Sunlight rides the river, she casts her thoughts out there.

Last stroke of the clock. She puts a handkerchief over

the bed lamp. Breaks a myrtle blossom, spreads the floor with canary seed.

Maybe this time, she thinks. She's given up long ago the idea of finding a teacher. Maybe this one will be a learner, she thinks, counting his quick steps on the marble stairs.

P.S. Three days later the boy in tight pants goes back to his school in Switzerland. The loud-mouth girl goes with him. She rents an old mill in the country about four kilometers outside of Geneva. Better to start them while they're still in transition, she thinks. Still soft, not yet armored against the body. Sensual, not yet disciplined to defend the tribe.

She puts out her shingle:

SCHOOL FOR BOYS WHO ARE NOT (YET) AFRAID OF THE BODY

One final note: This girl will be thirty-six years old the next time you meet her. She'll set you a riddle. Women are such fools, it begins. If women are so afraid of men's power, what the hell could a woman learn about sex by going to bed with a woman?

CLAIRE'S FIFTH LETTER

That way she has of never telling you anything directly.
She says, about the literal: it often contains a profound
lie. By stressing what is, what has happened, you are
allowed to hide what is meant. That kind of hiding does
not appeal to her.

On the other hand, to understand her meaning, it may
be necessary to decipher her code.

For instance: it is probably already clear that when
she speaks about Adonis, the dead god has something to
do with Dennie, the little brother.

That kid, she's been known to say. He loved blackjack.
Used to play it all night sometimes. The night before I
left? I tied purple ribbons all over his hair.

"Say goodnight, you little insect. Close your eyes, go
on, do it, I'll tell you a story."

But he wants the kissing machine. It starts kissing you
on the head, on the nose, on the cheek. You can't stop it
until you find the right place somewhere to push the
button that turns it off.

He tries, pushes her shoulder. The machine goes on
kissing. Kisses him all over the neck. He can't breathe,
choking on laughter. He pushes another button, on the
top of her head. The machine keeps kissing.

"Button's broken," she says. "Damn thing won't stop,
little bat."

He drags her down onto his pillow, curls up against

her, kisses her on the head, the nose, the cheeks. The war of the kissing machines, he murmurs, cheek damp on her arm, falling to sleep.

What she knows of tenderness, left behind in the temple-shack behind the incinerator. Tied up in purple ribbons. Buried with Adonis.

She found him again, perhaps, in the boy with tight pants. And in his school friends. From them, she may have hoped what Aphrodite had expected from her young lover. A sensitivity, not yet touched by men's aims; a vulnerability of body, not yet hardened by sport, or war. Closing the beautiful babe in a chest, the great goddess of love wished to keep him apart from the fate of men, the progressive hardening, the toughening of sinew, the fatal practice of muscularity. Her failure, which tells us a great deal about the difficulty of this project, our loud-mouth girl must also have known.

Do you remember, Alma, how she looks? The mocking clown's face, eyebrows lifted, corners of the mouth pulled down? Can you imagine her beside you on a dark street, her expression visible as you walk beneath the lamp?

You know how much she wants you to take seriously what she has to say, how carefully she protects herself against misunderstanding. She's in a good mood, let's say, indulges in a brief episode of sexual theology.

She asks you to notice that in the figure of Aphrodite (or even more in Astarte, Ishtar, the mother goddesses, who took their sons as lovers) an image is preserved of the sacred, sexual mother.

Leaning forward, head bowed, she lights the cigarette

from your cupped hands. Those goddess-worshiping
boys, she says, they spent a season in the arms of an
older woman, died a violent death, went underground,
were resurrected, came back to her the following spring.
Aphrodite and Adonis, she says, too lightly: Ishtar and
Tammuz, Isis and Osiris, Attis and Cybele. You think
she is talking to the little brother.

She does not want to go back to your flat. The cold
does not bother her. The rain slides from her white cap,
slides from her shoulders, collects at your feet. Those
modes of power with which you have concerned yourself, analyzing the conditions of women in a culture
where men have power, seem far less significant to her
than they do to you. She does not think much of the
powers men have abrogated to themselves, sees them as
forms that disguise a natural frailty, a haunting sense of
feebleness when set against the perennial potency of
women's sexual endowment.

She follows you into the Métro, moves up close
behind you to pass through the gate with your last ticket,
her face flushed as she sits down close to you on the
wooden bench. In the ancient world, she says, in the
sanctuaries of the mother goddess, the fundamental dis-
parity between the sexes was acknowledged. The son
who is his mother's lover knows this hidden truth of his
sexual situation: she is an elemental power, has given
him birth, suckled him at her breast. He, who can never
become the mother goddess, can only acquire her powers through her embrace. If she takes the man back to
her breast, he returns to her always as the son-lover. And
therefore, each fall, he dies; his sexual powers have

failed, they have been exhausted; the orgiastic force
which in her is constant, inexhaustible, for him rises and
falls. Therefore she pities him, mourns him.

She believes, and has practiced the idea that this
sacred power of sexual love is missing in the modern
world. That it is a revolutionary force. That women
know more about it than men, when they allow themselves to surrender to it. Women, she thinks, have the
historic task of bringing this ancient power back to the
world.

You are silent in the last car, she stares into the darkness beyond the window, stands when you do, wants to
race you up the steps. You walk on, arm in arm, in
silence. In our time she says as you pass the café, closed
now, where you met some time ago, this inequality
between the sexes is hidden, carefully submerged.
Therefore, in our culture, sexuality does not exist. In its
place, one finds merely a muscular effort to reverse the
natural truth of man's sexual condition: this terror of
being a boy in the arms of elemental female power.

Why, she wonders, should this truth not be acknowledged as it was in the ancient world? She tucks her
hands into the sleeves of her coat. She cannot bring
herself to believe that an experience known in ancient
times has entirely vanished from the world. She says
that in those now forgotten sanctuaries of the mother
goddess, if only one could return to them, and study
their sexual lore, women would discover the way to
unleash their innate sexual power. Women, she says,
live sexuality as the hopeless effort to help men forget
women's awesome orgiastic capacity.

The park is closed. You stand outside the iron railing, looking in. What you call sexuality, she says, is a desperate act of forgetting. A lie on the part of both sexes. A sham in which men are allowed to believe that they have returned to the woman in a position of power.

About herself during the years before she met you she is willing to tell this:

There came a time, it was not long after she went to live in Geneva, when she discovered that sexual freedom was not a simple matter of throwing open closed doors to an ancient force. This force, which had appeared in the old world, sometimes carried by Dionysus, the drunken god, who spent his childhood disguised as a girl, sometimes by wild women, his followers, at other times in cults that worshiped a love goddess and her young lover, was likely to prove extremely frightening.

She learned this from the behavior of the boys in her love school. The boys found it difficult to keep away from her. They began to drink, quarreled among themselves, became insolent with their schoolmasters, neglected their studies.

She, who had taught them what she could of sensual surrender, had become a drug to them. One taste, they could not do without her. Were exalted, enslaved, degraded, they felt, in quick succession. Could not get away from her. Were expelled from school, came back, broke with their families. Broke doors, smashed windows, set snares for each other in the woods near the mill where she lived. Enacted, she says, the tedious, brief tale of love in the Western world.

A *Letter, a Provocation*

Why, she asks you, in a voice you have not heard before, should a woman so easily gain power over men? Why does the body's pleasure unsettle them so? Is it possible, she wonders (a note of urgency), that without her they would never have felt sensual joy? Would have known nothing more than the drive to conquer, subdue, tyrannize the body? That sad gathering, into a thrust of force, of the body's widespread capacity to delight in its own sensations?

She has written it down somewhere, will have to look for it, send it to you as well someday: it is men who have deprived themselves of sex, given it up whenever it was they turned the body into an instrument of force. The art of surrender, the cultivation of sensation, she claims, is the sport Aphrodite was teaching Adonis. The art of giving himself back to the body, to the woman who lies at his side, awakening him.

The wind has risen; it throws down on you a shower of rain held captive in a chestnut tree. What men have called instinct, she insists, was once recognized as the voluntary surrender to the happy necessity that brings the sexes together to keep the world sap flowing. The men we know cannot imagine the sexual act as sacred pleasure, sanctified precisely because the goddess and her son enjoy it. Think of it, she sneers. The central religious symbol of our world: a son crucified, a mother mourning. The ancient world? A mother goddess going to bed with her son.

Her mother, whom she has occasionally described as a whore, was, she believes, living a degraded form of an old, sacred calling. It was this sublime art of sexual self-cultivation the daughter wished to learn. You know her by now, know she will soon stop talking. You decide not to look at her. You walk with your head down, observe the way a wet leaf clings to your shoes. Yes, you think, that brash girl who set out for adventure from a taco stand on a California highway has continued to inform the woman.

She says she wants to live in the sanctuary of Ishtar. You recall that she was, as a young girl, fascinated by this place, which stood on a high cliff next to the sea. What you are to make of this wish she leaves to you. Or rather, to be somewhat more precise: she wants to live there for a time. And then travel. More or less on a pilgrimage, from one ancient shrine of the goddess to another. Someday, she is sure, she will reach Paphos, on the island of Cyprus. The mountains, their chalky darkness. Forests of fir and cedar. Spring rain in the barley fields. The place where Aphrodite first met Adonis.

You walk barefoot to the river, she says. The grass whips at your feet, stings you. Near the water a soft red clay, it oozes between your toes. At midday the river is still, withdrawn into itself so that you long to possess it. The place is considered sacred.

She opens her arms; walking backward, in front of you, she lifts her head, intends to look at you directly, avoids your eyes. It is a curious gesture, expresses you think an inability, an inadequacy to invoke the past. You want to hold her. This is the moment, you are familiar with it already, when you always lose her.

Part Three

ALMA RUNAU: A JOURNAL, A BROKEN SOLITUDE

SCENE: THE SOUTH OF FRANCE

TIME: TWO AND A HALF YEARS AFTER THE MEETING
     AT THE CAFÉ
     (ALMA HAS NOT RECEIVED CLAIRE'S
     LETTERS)

South of France, 1987

Autumn equinox.

On the eighteenth the first wave of swallows was gone. At a moment's notice the sky was empty as death. But since then small groups of swifts have been playing over the village and the rocks every day as if there were still no hurry on their passage south.

In the late afternoon I took a bag with my notebook and walked out into the meadows, past the cypresses of the cemetery. On the way I picked figs for my winter jam. The trees are filled with fruits, green, earth-yellow, and blue-violet figs, in miniature size as the trees are so old. I hid the bag, wandered on to the Pont du Hasard and climbed into the rocks I discovered last summer. I've been sitting here for a while watching the village on the rock flank and the plain below sink into silence.

The church bells just struck seven. A nightingale keeps recalling the first three notes of its mating song. In the south the young moon is standing. In some days it will be cut into a precise half, and I'll wonder again why or how this perfectly straight cut-line occurs since all the heavenly bodies are round. Living here, one day I might know.

I have grown weary of the city, but I know myself. The very moment I enter it, stepping out of the train at Gare du Nord or driving in along the Seine, it catches me. I grow greedy for culture, get drunk on it. I make do with my modest flat, modest life, with the extravagance of my daily café. I am content. It's only after having arrived in the country that I sense what I have missed.

Solveig's "stone desert" comes back to haunt me with

its truth. She left her mark on my beloved city. This way she would be sure to stay present even after I'd given up on her. I am lucky to have friends who keep sending me places "to heal my weariness." My Paris friends with their families and houses in the country, *comme il faut*.

I've been "healing" quite a while, battling with my translation jobs, my poems, my solitude, the unknown nature of scorpions, mice, animal sounds by night. I watch the days shorten, the sun's arc over the rocks, the shadows filling my little court. The summer goes. My soul slows down, curves in, settles into its solitude, prepares for something I don't know and yet know, for some descending that even without understanding makes sense.

Maybe one day I'll also get patient with the slowness of human change, this stagnation that alternately drives me mad or drowns me in resignation. What if equality between women and men takes as long as nature takes to level a mountain? I have to accept another paradox: to learn patience and still care.

Feminism is not one revolution, it's just rain. Provocative rains, thunderstorms beating down on that mountain. They wash away the wrong side, speed up, leap into vertiginous cascades, get lost in a crevasse, are gone, declared dead. All the while they rise from their way underground to wet the most unexpected terrains, grow, make themselves a bed, find their own voices, repeat and repeat their message to the rock, speak in the chorus of rivers, move on, open arms, hug islands, take in landscapes, forget the mountain, avoid mountains with the certitude of their direction, enter every new landscape's dream, grow heavy with their own richness, settle into a stately stream, beat the low pulse of balance, reach fulfillment losing themselves in the ocean that won't turn sweet.

I listen to myself and doubt that my patience will ever be free from resignation. My mood stoops with regrets. I felt it all day long, in spite of the treacherous heat:

The summer goes,
the swallows follow its path,
there are tears in the eyes of the fishes.

Still Solveig, I know, she won't leave me alone. On the way here I met my neighbor on his tractor. He shouted there was some package waiting for me at his house, something from abroad ... I immediately knew it was Solveig sending back my things—now that I've finally stopped reminding her. Why do these farmers have to ride around the meadows on their tractors anyway? Nothing grows there. Do they also have to control the hard-thorned shrubs and thistles? Do they need to move their tractor like a horse?

I had decided not to think about her. Always a restlessness comes with these thoughts. I want to be with the rocks, the plain, the village settling into the evening haze. How to keep my old slovenly enemy, nostalgia, from sneaking back in? I am weary of my own repetitions, how slowly my own changes occur while I demand immediate changes from the world. The stifling slow course of things is in myself. I want men to be different? Then women have to be different. I myself have to change.

A last swift just went by, noiselessly, followed by the first bat, and I am again stunned by the silence of such a rapid flight.

My passion for Solveig—because I couldn't have her— has fallen silent at last. I do not need to throw myself into the arms of strangers anymore in order to find her again in some other body. All those unsuitable, unattainable lovers I created in order to re-create her. Like a long fever. It's over.

What I want is to go beyond this kind of passion. Is there anything else? Nature, my unknown ally, my benefactress, has begun to appease me. Has she?

Last summer when I opened my eyes from my exhaustion this beauty was all around me. The young olive grove, its silver soothing the midday heat. The shadows cast in the moonlight, the shape of the huge cypress in the square, severe as in the sun.

I looked at myself then, my body screaming for this woman I didn't understand and had even come to dislike. It dawned on me that I might be in love with my own passion, my feverish longing for her, not with her. I said I loved her to despair, but then I wondered: loved? to despair? She was an alien whose mind I could never quite enter, enclosed in her visionary world. A mirage forever withdrawing at the pace of my approach. I must have loved my despair. I had more in common with almost every stranger I met. Even with the weird Claire Heller who never wrote and took her mystery home with her. A woman at least to talk and argue with. One who would listen and then come out with something I'd never thought of.

I remember myself at that time. The irony of my preaching equality while I was already hopelessly hooked by Solveig's difference. Solveig was a woman, an artist, a feminist, therefore I didn't want to admit the attraction her otherness held for me. Just as I didn't want to admit how Claire Heller in her feminine attire fascinated me. How I was shocked by my sudden longing to be a man and ravish this femininity that she offered and withheld. Her beauty bewildered me, the way she gave herself to my eyes, and then, reading my vulnerable desire, shook the spell with another laugh that said: Are you really inclined to believe my surrender to you would express your power?

Now, after Solveig's lesson, I know what happened to me at that moment in the café and at so many moments in my life: I desired like a woman, like one who doesn't know how to take.

Solveig's lesson—did I unknowingly choose her for that? How I would wait for her. Begging. The frailty of her body was misleading. She was tough like the shell of a hazelnut. Her bright blue eyes were sharp from suspicion. They softened when she withdrew into her dreams. I wanted her eyes, I wanted them to soften to me, to allow me in. She hated my begging, my burning for her almost touchable skin. She would lift her head from her painting and look at me, the one straight line of her frown cutting into her stubborn forehead: "Can't you stop your adoration? It's sticky. It won't let me move."

It was true. I wanted to hypnotize her, to pin her down like an admired butterfly. To inject my love into her like a needle so that she would be forever mine, filled with my love, with no choice left but to return this love to me. That's how I was, I suddenly see the irony: like the cruiser. In need, and impotent. I forced myself away from her every time. I was not wanted? Well, I would not want her either. I stayed out of her way, buried myself in work, spent hours at the café. Sometimes I even packed my travel bag.

Then it would happen. She would meet my detached eyes and try to hold my gaze. She would approach. Put her Gothic Madonna hand on my arm: "I'm sorry. Don't go."

Each time I hesitated, battling with my anger and my decision to be alone. She looked at me. Her hand went up my shoulder ever so lightly, but I could feel the tiny hairs on my neck rise. "Why would I stay?" I tried, keeping my voice cold, looking away. Her fingers forced my gaze back. And there it was, in her eyes. The sharp blue softened, covered itself with the finest veil of moisture. Her eyes opened to me, without begging, without shame, turning moist and letting it be, letting me in. There she was, her shell broken, revealing the soft, sweet nut inside, the woman. I grabbed her hair in a knot and pulled her head backward, still torn in my frustration. She caught her breath. Her eyes closed. Her blond lashes trembled as she waited for me. She knew I couldn't resist. Then I finally got what I wanted. Then, only then.

The plain is growing distant with the dark. I'll have to stop writing any minute. The moon-sickle is gaining silver, wandering south, toward the invisible sea.

If only I had known how to handle her! If I had already known what I know now . . . My thoughts about Solveig like to take this turn. My desire clings to the velvet of her eyes opening. I resist seeing anything else. I picture myself opening her now whenever I want.

Maybe it's childish, a stubborn way not to let go. Or it's a game, playing the old passion time and again. I see it reflected all around me: The sun is gone, mist is rising to swallow what is left of the fields, shapeless grayish blue lakes, but the houses won't let go of the light. It's more than a reflection from the sky. The sun beating down all day has been sucked into the stone and clutched. The village, the little stone cubes here and there in the plain stubbornly shine against the night.

Sept. 22, '87

Another hot day. The air is thick and holding its breath. I keep pushing my folding table and chair along with the shadow of the mulberry tree. The walls of my courtyard feel higher than the whole court is wide. Why didn't I try to borrow Mme. Petitpot's car this morning to take off to the sea—instead of chewing on words? This package sits in my thoughts. The neighbors won't understand why I've not yet come to fetch it. I bet there's some mean little note with it. And if there isn't any note, it's mean too.

It irritates me that Solveig can still bother me. I keep proudly declaring I'm far beyond her, and there she is again like a jack from the box! She exposed my foibles and opened up wounds I had wanted to forget with women. I can't forgive her that.

"You are like the men I've known!" I used to pout when she refused me or pulled out of my arms to rush back to her work. I didn't want to see that her selfishness and self-sufficiency were what attracted me. She having too much of them and I wanting some for myself. She used to laugh at my complaints or shake them off her shoulders: "I have to get some separation, you know, or else I can't make love." I didn't reply: "And I need some closeness, or else I can't make love!"

Had I really imagined that I'd solved my problems by choosing women, my equals, by loving without roles? *Hélas*, unless a problem is addressed and undressed, it'll always—

A *moment later*

. . . come back with a sneer. Like my mice!

This one I haven't solved either. The swishing up the wall near the kitchen window a moment ago could have been a lizard. I wanted it to be a lizard. I didn't particularly wish to hear the odd little noises in the kitchen. Every time I did stop to prick up my ears, *they* stopped. As though my state of alarm vibrated right into the kitchen! Finally there was the treacherous clicking from the metal cage—a sound I couldn't ignore.

I decided to sneak to the door and peek in. Sure enough, another little light-brown fellow with those huge Mickey Mouse ears! Eagerly struggling with an old piece of cheese that had dried out and stuck to the bars of the cage. Like an acrobat it had gripped a bar with one back foot for hold. Its body was stretched to almost double its length, reaching from the entranceway right across the trapdoor into the closed compartment with the bait!

It's their old trick. They obviously remember it from their first visit, some weeks ago. It took me longer to find that kind of nonlethal cage than it took them to "figure it out." It still puzzles me how. Had they been watching each other fall into prison when the trapdoor gave under their weight? Do they have guards, spies? Or did some prisoners manage to find their way back from a faraway meadow and teach the others lessons?

That's where I took them. I couldn't muster the kind of womanpower able to take (and give!) life. I still can't. I carry everything out: ants, spiders, butterflies, scorpions, and mice. I like to carry problems out. Mme. Petitpot gave me a curious look when I asked her where to buy a mousetrap that wouldn't kill. I insisted while she was rummaging in her kitchen for poison she fortunately couldn't find . . .

At first I took my prisoners a long way toward the rocks, my heart beating, I felt, as fast as theirs. I carried the cage under a scarf to hide the mouse from cats or dogs, and myself from ridicule. I also didn't want to see the little creature with its black-button eyes cowering panic-stricken in a corner of the cage. When I set the cage down in the dry grass and opened the gate, it often took a long time before the mouse found the exit. It would go on wildly sawing the bars with its teeth, stopping only, it seemed, to catch its breath. It never took any notice of the delicious bait that was now in its reach. It probably didn't even smell the fresh crumb of cheese I put outside the gate to give directions. I hoped nobody was watching me in this act of village sabotage or hearing me talk to a mouse! "*Allez vite,*" I used to say. "Get out of there, fast. Find yourself a new family. This way, little mouse!" Every time I was so pleased to see it run to the gate, stop, hesitate—and swagger into freedom.

But I couldn't do this forever. All those walks. And their number never shrinking. I suspected they came back. I began to feel defeated by their intelligence. But I didn't give up, not yet. I transformed myself into a hunter, eager to trap them with an even better trick. When I now heard them gamboling in the kitchen I stalked them. I slowly approached the cage and stood there waiting to surprise them in their circus act. Sooner or later the aroma of cheese would prove irresistible. In they'd go. And I, with a quick jump, would slam a wood plate against the entrance. Victory—and off with them to the cat neighborhood!

My patience didn't hold up to my feminist ideal. No

peaceful harmony between woman and nature, at least not between woman and mouse! My patience kept fading. I couldn't mark my prisoners to make sure they didn't fool me by coming back. I was fooled anyway. My hunter's satisfaction didn't make up for the time I spent motionless in the kitchen telling myself this was a Castaneda exercise, pretending to be a chair. Besides, I spent more and more time catching nothing although I put out more and more cheese. They must have learned to recognize me even in the form of a chair.

One day I caught sight of three of them running up the wall toward the roof. One of them was tiny, the next generation. They were crossing right over the threshold of my tolerance. This is it, I decided. My aggression was born. I ran over to Mme. Petitpot and got the poison. It made me sad. I kept picturing bodies in death cramps, dragging themselves across my kitchen floor. I was certain they would turn it into a demonstration.

Okay, I conceded, I'll give you a last chance. And that's what I told them, solemnly at the new moon's night, while burning incense under the mulberry tree. Go away, I said. Leave while there is time. Now.

I put a grain of wheat on each corner of the garden wall. Keep out, I urged, throwing some grains far into the neighbors' gardens. Death awaits you if you stay here. I promise you I shall cope with your dying. I had made a prisoner that evening and kept it as a warning. I carried the cage around the garden and into the meadows as far as I could walk in the dark.

No good. They are back. My patience isn't. The poison won't work with them either, I know it already. One or two casualties, and they'll know. I should have a cat. Trap a cat in my house to trap the mice that have trapped me?

Early evening

Just finished a big cleaning. The best thing to do with my restlessness—to stay in the cool of the house, naked, and wipe the exterior of pots and jars. Hadn't Mme. Petitpot warned me to leave nothing around for the mice? Not a breadcrumb, she had declared, laying her chin into impressive folds. No trace of oil, no smell to attract them! Now I've even hidden the smelly cage away. I was almost done with the kitchen when I heard the voice of the neighbor's wife outside. She knocked.

"I'm not dressed!" I shouted.

"It's a package for you, *Mademoiselle*."

"Could you just leave it there for me? Thank you . . . Where is it from?"

"Sweden? That's what the postman said, Sweden."

I knew it. I was feeling defeated from all sides. I didn't want to receive it. I refused to take it in. Solveig could wait in front of the door.

When the neighbor had left, I furiously finished the kitchen and distributed the pink grains of poison in all the corners, even outside. I heaped up two little piles at the foot of the wall from where they used to come in, running straight up to some crack in the roof.

I'm back under my tree now, with the fourth iced coffee of the day. There is still an hour before darkness. Solveig won't spoil my sunset.

It's ridiculous. I know perfectly well I'm only making myself wait. I've been holding off the moment since yesterday night.

What truth do I still fear?

The same night

An envelope inside a padded envelope. After two and a half years. A letter from Claire Heller!

Sent back and forth from Paris to Solveig to Paris, never getting to me. She must have wondered why I never answered. Just as I wondered why she never wrote. Claire Heller has kept her promise after all!

I took the "package" in before sunset. I quickly prepared myself a dinner and sat down to eat and read under my tree. My spinach turned cold. Half of my egg got eaten up by bees. This letter—I mean, this story is strange. I kept racing through it, always hoping to get to it, to find the key to it all. But it's exactly like the things she said—or rather didn't say—at the café. Riddles I'm supposed to solve—how?

This totally improbable girl. Knows all about men before knowing any. Knows exactly how a boy will react when he's tempted for the first time. Makes little bubbles with the bubble gum of Freud's penis envy before she spits it out. Ridiculous. A girl inventing everything, herself, her lovers, her supernatural powers. This secure, optimistic, liberated girl, haunted by nothing but sex! No culture, society, family to control her. No role demands, no gender terror, nothing to stop her from doing anything. Nobody running after her when she sets out—at age thirteen! No furious mothers and fathers, teachers and priests, chasing this young obscenity, this Lolita, out of her shack or mill. In Switzerland where morality is as clean as the sidewalks and order as loud as the cuckoo clocks. How annoying if this is supposed to be real. And if it's just a fantasy, why tell it to me?

The odd impression I had of her at our meeting—she was too much and not enough. Too damn sure of herself. Unable to tell things clearly, to make sense in a way that someone else could follow. She didn't want to be followed. Not by a woman. Not at least by me. So sexy—but don't you come too close. Still, radiating something I longed to get close to. What was it? Something I was afraid to know. This despair hidden in her eyes, this self-provocation in her pride, her female swagger. Somebody lonely, I felt. Alone in a dream world.

Now I regret that I didn't try to track any of her books in Paris. A heroine without fear. None of the despicable weaknesses and self-doubts of a "real" woman—like me. Is that why she chooses mythology? Ancient Greece? Mythical heroes, goddesses, gods? At moments in the café, a priestess speaking an oracle I would for sure misread. A sphinx, never answering questions. Making me talk and reveal myself. She stayed covered. Once or twice, I remember, I had to fight not to blush.

And then she became this Circe who transformed me into a man! I found her attractive, but her coy, secretive games irritated me as much as her pretense of mastery. She feared nothing from men. As if she couldn't be humiliated, raped, hurt. As if they were all in her power.

Her arrogance still provokes me. How superior she feels to a gender-impaired woman like me! A woman who was forced and forced herself into her role—instead of "choosing" it!

She doesn't convince me. What is this body-disposal-sex anyway? These anonymous gymnastics? Aerotics! Anyone can go out and expose herself to strangers. Even I.

After Solveig I managed to go to a bar and go home

with some woman. I learned it in my despair. Learned to
close my eyes and fantasize and be wild for a night. If
Claire Heller had told me her story at the café two and a
half years ago, I would have been impressed.

The loneliness when the fantasy cracks. When you
come down and the body's still hot but you suddenly feel
your heart cold. When you sneak out, with some nice,
embarrassed words, back to your splendid isolation. Then
the next fit of fantasy hits, and you start again from
scratch. Again at some/body's mercy. Always the same.
Will it work out? Will this body-makeup fit, can you use
it for what you need? Will it hold up long enough to
trigger your fantasy? Will it be short enough to sustain
the illusion and get you out of there in time? Don't tell
me about art, don't tell me there's any teaching or learning with strangers, Claire Heller. *Je vous en prie!*

Sept. 23

Early morning, not yet light.

I had to read the letter again, slowly. How has she found me? Has she followed me? The same night? She told me she had to leave Paris the next day. My concierge, the elevator, the boy next door ... As if she'd been spying. She may never have left Paris. She didn't drop the packet into the basket of my bicycle, that's for sure. The date is unreadable. There is no date. Who knows how long Solveig has been keeping it around before sending it back to Paris?

If only I knew when she wrote this. What if she wrote it right after our meeting and then didn't dare to send it? Not until one day she came back to Paris? Maybe she wanted to see me again. Maybe she hung out in the café waiting for me in vain. In any case, it must have been a strong memory for her. As for me. And I had thought she couldn't care less about me.

Now such an intimate communication. A confession, disguised as a fairy tale. She may have needed to disguise it. What if I didn't care? If I'd forgotten all about her? Or if I couldn't care less about a woman's story with men? So she is vulnerable too? Powerful with men but vulnerable with women?

Sept. 25

I keep reading her letter, paging through, looking for something—I don't know for what. Yesterday I even took it with me on my walk. I ended up on my rock, but then I didn't want to look at it again. I just sat and stared at the thick layer of heat over the plain. Not one swallow moving the air with its wings.

I wanted to argue and be angry with her, but the truth is, I've been sad since the letter arrived. Thinking about the vain effort of sex to silence one's loneliness. I've come to know it so well, not only with Solveig, and after her. Long before, with men. That's what I hear in Claire, a murmur beneath her story.

I envied men. Not their bodies, everything else. I saw their power—physical, social, cultural power—and believed in it. How could I not have believed in it, lacking it so badly myself? I never had solid ground under my feet. I hung in dreams—and fears—of love. I yearned for men's scaffold of thought, to hold on to in the ebb and flow of my moods. I longed for their structure of words, to spell my waves into a standstill. I wanted their bold stroke of opinion, to force the chaos of life into a perspective.

What were my tools to protect myself? I was a woman. No tools, just feelings. And no sex, Claire Heller! I had a caring mother. Her "good daughter" sacrificed her sexuality for love. Sex was for the others, the abandoned ones like you. Sex was for men. I had no access to my body, my "elemental powers." To belong to a man was my access. My way to observe, to learn, to steal.

I gave what I had. Tenderness, touch. My body. It was

a painful exchange. My defense—or should I say my revenge—was my silence. My caresses silently mourned my lover's body. His power had so little to give. Hard with fear. Not wanting to know. Afraid to wonder, to listen, to drift, to fall. I mourned something my own body knew without knowing, like a sleepwalker knows the way. Such longing—for what? This was the only body at hand. Whatever he wanted, whatever whenever—I never refused.

The perfect woman. In need. Begging for something I could not voice. Waiting. Available. Open. Opening to a void. Watching with awe my body, the unknown territory of myself, behave as it was supposed to. Wasn't this the ecstasy I had read about and greedily glimpsed at the movies? Watching my body arch, sigh, push, stretch, clutch the sheet. Re-creating the image, watching my performance with pride, judging it with a man's eyes. Sometimes this perfect woman I created, who could take and bend so lithely, turned me on.

But my efforts were for him, not for myself. How could I be disappointing? This creature in his naked effort, I pitied him. I didn't understand either his pleasure or his agony. I kept trying, patiently, tenderly trying to protect him from myself, my otherness. Wondering when the meaning of this strange battle would reveal itself. Offering him my throat, my neck curved in the enactment of passion, resigned to the bite of the stronger animal.

It still hurts. To think that my ignorance was supposed to protect my body, to keep it safely disowned. A man, brought up to be my opposite, was supposed to pierce the mystery. He, the first one, had to guide me through the unknown territory of myself, my silenced body. His body was supposed to have a voice. An imperative voice, capable of mastering my alien instrument and making music!

Not knowing oneself, one's own body, may be the

greatest impotence of all. The "mystery of woman" is that she is a mystery to herself. A being forever faltering along the thread of someone else's definition. What if I had started out like Claire? Vertigo . . . A woman knowing from the start what it took me years and years to know. I wonder if she knows her loneliness, too. She didn't search for love. Just for pleasure, adventure. Not needing love is an awesome power indeed. She doesn't seem to be aware of the cost.

Afternoon

Is there no other way to keep one's sexual drive? Does one have to stay out of love?

Or if one falls in love and grows close, does the initial fire have to die? Is this the cost of love?

Sex and passion, love and intimacy. Either or. Nobody seems to have solved this intricate intrigue . . .

Claire is right: men can't be the problem if the problem is the same for everyone. Against all feminist odds, there is some logic here. But if men are not the problem, why does she bother arguing about their power? She went for them, I fled them. In the end we find ourselves in a similar place. She, the wild one who can never get enough of it, lonely and in the end not satisfied. I could have told her. I'm not satisfied in my life with women—how could she be with men? She's tired of her power. So am I.

I wish I could talk to her. Or at least write her. No date, no address. She has to make a mystery of herself! What answer would I write anyway? There's no answer to a "story." Would I want to tell her my own story? "Dear Claire, I knew little about sex but now I do, as much as you . . ."?

Maybe I only want to ask questions. Dear Claire, why didn't you write for so long? Why did you write at all? Did you never love anybody? Did you really have this brother who died because you left? Was your mother a whore? Did she teach you about men? Is this really your story? Is it a dream? A woman untouched by the male domination of this world—is it your secret feminist dream? Tell me what it is, Claire. Tell me the truth!

Sept. 26

Up on my rock again. I feel lonely, like the Petit Prince on his planet the day he watched the sunset forty-three times.

Finally wind. Dust is rising at the edges of the fields where the earth lies bare. Small spirals of dust, bending southward. The wine harvest has started. The siren that now governs village life just howled the end of the workday. I can see the tiny tractors creep out of the fields. Loaded with grapes, they are headed for the coop cellars by the highway to be weighed. The open trucks, filled with people and followed by dust clouds, are climbing up toward the village to bring the workers back to their quarters. They have come from far, from Marseilles, even Spain, for the harvest. They earn more than what I get for a good translation: 34 francs an hour, I've heard. I can feel the excitement in the village. The little shop has shaken off its annual sleep. Everyone speculates about the new wine. The old men gathered every morning and evening at the square seem to be talking about nothing else.

"Ah, the drought!" They shake their heads in grief. "How small the grapes are! We'll have very little wine this year . . ."

"But the quality," they remind each other. "We won't have had such a wine for the past seven years!"

By night music and singing come drifting over from the workers' barracks to my quiet court.

"The mistral might bring rain," the shop lady with her sorrow-face remarked this morning when I got my baguette. "They better get on with the harvest! But even if not, the weather will soon change. It'll get rough with the next moon."

I went over to ask Mme. Petitpot if it was true.

"Oh yes," she said and my heart sank. "The first full moon after the equinox. That's the end of summer."

I won't like to stay in the little house with its one dark room when the weather gets bad and I can't spend my days in the garden. Yesterday night when I watered the flowers, I felt the first moist smell of autumn in the air. I wonder how long I'll be able to stay on.

I hung around Mme. Petitpot's kitchen, needing a chat. She made me taste her fig jam.

"You cook your figs for five minutes. Five minutes!" she ordered. (She called it *blancher*.) "Then, very gently, you add them to your thickened juice. See?"

Her little fat hands fondled the jars as though they were her babies. I didn't care for the oversweet taste but I liked the look of her jars with the immaculate figs hovering in the jelly.

At home I contemplated my own attempt. The thick, brown paste resembled smashed dry figs rather than jam. I had picked another bagful yesterday. I wasn't up for translating. I felt it might change my mood to outshine Mme. Petitpot's traditional fig jam with a new creation.

I threw out the brown paste and prepared the jelly with the juice of apples, nectarines, and lots of lemon. I added some skinned almonds. When it was done—the taste was exquisite—I set forth to *blancher* my figs, and carefully dropped them into the hot jelly. Afterward I caught myself fondling my own jars. The figs had not lost their color and shape. The little "gold buttons," the tiny blue and heavier green ones looked like air balloons floating in a jelly sunset with white almond clouds. What a feeling it will be to see my three jars on my kitchen shelf in Paris this winter!

Paris . . . Maybe I should go back sooner. I miss my

friends, my café, my cozy solitude amidst the crowds. I miss the rain, the fog, the gray.

I remember a dream. I remember fog. Amazing: there was Claire Heller in my dream last night!

First, I was on a submarine in blue-green depths. I was walking down a staircase on the outside belly of the ship. The water felt like my element and at the same time it worried me.

Then I was on a terrace in front of a house, looking at an autumn landscape. I was staring into the fog, the rust and purple shades under the layers of gray. A mandala. Next to me a man was also staring into the fog. "I see wild animals fighting," he said. I was deeply amazed, "I see something entirely different . . ." But I was torn out of my vision into a darker, anxious mood.

Then there was Claire. We were entering a house together. Women were sitting around a festive dinner table. We were both elegantly dressed, very feminine. I was wearing a long black silk dress, my body like a model's. I knew how beautiful we were. All the women looked at us. We hurried past them into the next room—to look for the hostess, we declared.

What a foggy dream of ambivalence! Claire was on my mind all day yesterday. I felt we were in a similar place of sexual frustration. In the dream we appear to *be* the same. Equally feminine. I am like her. I have her kind of body. How strange. We are in my world though, at a women's gathering. Or are we? There is a discomfort. We are using a pretext to hurry to another room.

An edge of discomfort is all over the dream, with the women, the man, the water. I don't know who the man could be. He sees wild animals fighting. It could be a sexual fight. I am totally unaware of the "wild things" he sees. Being reminded of them pulls me out of my peace, out of the fog.

Is that what Claire's letter does to me?

There is desire and angst in all this. Already in the beginning of the dream. Under water. I have no difficulty breathing, but I am anxious. The man's wild animals remind me of difference and danger. Then I am surprised about being a woman, one to match every man's dream. It makes me uncomfortable to be looked at. Am I suddenly too different? Too feminine for my feminist crowd? What is the next room, the next step?

I've always needed to hide and silence my femininity. I still can't bear to wear skirts or dresses. Anything overly "feminine" throws me off balance. Off my sense of androgynous balance. As if I were afraid I could still be drowned in femininity. This skinless state where everyone could move in and penetrate and take over. I had to cut it out. Make room for the wild things I needed. Intellect, a language, a will. Being less accessible for other people's needs. Setting limits, saying no, letting my anger out. Being self-sufficient, even selfish. Wanting, and daring to take . . .

And now? I know the masculine role as well as she knows the feminine. That's only one half. And the rest? Is that the reason for my fascination? For my anxiety? If dreams are wishes, I wish to be like her. A scary wish. Her way of being a woman seems to have little in common with what I've known. Her shameless acceptance of her body, her beauty. Her fierce and fearless way of giving herself . . . Could I ever be like that?

Sept. 27

Back to working. No rain. If it rains I'll have to squeeze my little folding table in front of the door in the kitchen to have some light, some contact with the green. I can't stand to be in the bedroom. Dark, stuffed like a furniture dump. Gusts of wind are sweeping through the court; the wind almost as hot as the air. I had to fasten my papers with clothespins. I got four pages done. I deserve a rest.

Two days ago I noticed that half of the mouse poison in the court was gone. I was pleased and terrified, trying to be prepared for the corpses. There were none. I kept hearing the mice gamboling in the roof, as always. I even saw some swishing behind the fridge when I suddenly entered the kitchen. I got suspicious and this morning I inspected one of the heaps. I had a shock when I saw it moving. The big pink grains were riding away, one by one, with ants! Poor things, busily filling their storerooms for winter. I might be creating some ecological catastrophe . . .

I decided to throw the poison away. The mice wouldn't be that dumb. Let them make their nests in the roof— what do I care?

It's a relief to be back to my routine. If I catch up now, I might finish the first draft before the weather changes. I've given so much time to Claire Heller and her letter. All this questioning and comparing myself! I am too easily caught by provocations of that kind. I'm different— why would I want to be like her?

It's so much easier to play the whole game without feelings. No need to boast. She probably doesn't even know the difference. Well, I haven't known for very long either. I came from the opposite side. All feelings. Loving, caring, tenderness, all carefully shared and distributed between equal-minded, equally willing women peers!

Then Solveig broke into my sweet sleep. (I'm glad it wasn't Claire Heller!) The Scandinavian boy in disguise challenged just enough of my feminist notions. She was self-involved like a man. She kept her distance. My desire threatened her. Desire was something she controlled. Something she evoked like a woman and cut off like a man. And yet her being a woman made me believe I knew more about her than she wanted to know herself. I would know how to crack her code.

I courted her secret. I played the companion, paid clever compliments to her work, and amused her with hazardous interpretations. I let her make the first gesture. That was my first mistake. The first gesture is a spell, spelling out the pattern of a relationship. I didn't dare to make it. I wanted her to reach out and want me.

I was in her territory. A cold Scandinavian autumn day, night almost falling into the afternoon. We were looking at a stack of drawings scattered over her huge table, warming our hands on cups with steaming herb tea and rum. There was a silence after something I said, something about the nervous roughness of her lines that seemed to cover up sensuous secrets . . . My heart fell into that silence. I turned away, pretending to look out of the window. But there was her hand on my neck—hot from the tea, her Madonna hand—ordering me back. I turned around. She let go of my neck. She was standing very straight, looking at me, and the veil filled her eyes. As if her eyes' surface was breaking. I slowly approached until my body touched hers. I still held my cup. In my faint swaying I could feel the tiny hair on the side of her face. She seemed perfectly still. I wondered if only I was holding my breath. But the moment I brushed my lips over her skin, very close to her mouth, I noticed the treacherous sign. The suppressed sigh, the hint of her head wanting to bend backward, inviting me in.

I felt I'd been pacing forever in front of her doors. I was amazed by my passion. It was made of fierce resentment and relief that it was my turn to take the power and possess and tame a woman . . . like a man.

My fantasy was to be a boy myself, the prince fighting his way through the thorns of Solveig's resistance to the princess hidden inside. That's what I wanted: to play the "aggressive" role, be wild, irresponsible, detached from any other feeling than this greed.

Sexual satisfaction wasn't important to me. Even when she made love to me, I would turn it around and make love to her. Sometimes, I remember, I loved myself when I was alone again, imagining that my body was hers. But the next time we met, I reembraced my ardent asceticism, resisting any temptation for release. I was drunk with my daring to meet an extreme. Appeasing my body would have meant to hand myself over. To lose the excitement, to touch ground. It could have been anyone other than Solveig. I was in love with desire. It was a new sexual coming of age.

Midnight

Can't sleep. The old cruiser haunts me again. Claire Heller's irony. Those glances of hers that seemed to strip me naked, revealing my impotence. Bringing back the memory of Solveig. The memory of my illusionary power. My typically female incapacity to handle a purely sexual adventure.

I got trapped, longing to be close; dependent, longing to be loved. Solveig's refusals subtly informed me that the power was hers to bestow or withhold. There had to be more to male power than being active in bed. What was this male power, this capacity to possess?

I lacked the right to my desire. The right to make a claim to a woman's body. I lacked the boldness to risk the refusal of my approach. To express desire, to go for it. To take the first step.

And more. To put my own desire first. To put myself first. To hold rather than surrender the self. To be in love with myself, my desiring self, rather than wanting to be desired. To dare believe in the irresistible power of my passion.

The hardest lessons for me to learn!

I was fortunate, having to go on reading tours with the authors I'd translated. I met a lot of women. I could pretend. I managed to slip into the role of the voyager who comes and goes and stays unattached. The adventurer who stays in control. Never surrenders. Masters the monster—the "elemental power of sex." Simply takes pleasure, then steps out, invigorated, and goes after the whole world, after every woman in the street ... This was my cherished fantasy, my self-imposed task. I practiced. Sometimes I found it hard to leave. But I preferred my loneliness. I still do. I don't quite trust myself. I might be tempted again to fall back into being a "woman," the woman in soft black silk, afraid of wild animals and aggression. I might again give up my self in love and follow another's desire.

How is it possible that this Claire Heller can't get enough of being a woman? I can't get it into my head. I can't even imagine. Unless she takes it like a man?

It sounds perverse. Another female impersonator. One who only pretends to give. She takes. She probably eats those men alive. She makes her lovers powerless, worse than Solveig. Solveig was unconscious, protecting herself. This one claims to be a teacher. I never understood the hostile image of a "vagina dentata," but now I do. It tells how it must feel to be with such a woman. This "goddess" with her always accessible sex is a user. An insatiable castrator!

I thought it was one of the foreign workers resting in the shade on my steps. A young boy, I thought. I put on an encouraging smile as I approached. He rose up in an odd movement, as if suspended and slowly pulled up on a string. Brown legs in shorts. His hands rested on his knees for a moment, his body slightly bent over as if preparing to jump out of there, as if caught. Slowly a T-shirt unrolled—a girl, a woman. I was confused. Something in her naked brown face, her dark eyes seemed to be expecting me. And then her eyebrows went up, the corners of her mouth pulled down into a regretful smile—it was Claire Heller, right there in front of my door!

I had the uncanny feeling that my thinking about her the past days must have materialized her. I didn't know whom to pinch first. I wanted to ask: are you real?

She opened her mouth and said something very fast. I only got half of it because as soon as the clown's smile disappeared I felt lost, I just didn't recognize her. She said she was only popping by and would disappear on the spot if she disturbed me. Which didn't sound exactly reassuring. It meant I would have to give her the signal to leave . . .

"Claire Heller!" I blurted out. "This is too much. And I just got your letter. Five days ago!"

"Five days ago?" She stepped back as if slapped in the face. I had never seen her embarrassed; it embarrassed me too. We stood on my steps staring at each other and I thought: Why don't I move and open my door for her? It was as though we were both nailed to the realization that there was something wrong with the timing. It was all wrong.

"Well, this is a surprise!" I decided to move on. "The biggest I've had . . . since your letter!"

The joke didn't cheer her up.

"Welcome to my humble shack," I proposed and wondered absurdly if that's how she had welcomed the boys. I quickly walked her through my darkened bedroom and the kitchen to the courtyard, aware of my usual chaos, eying the couch in the corner. There was a place to sleep in addition to my bed.

"Thirsty?" I asked and went to fetch a bottle of mineral water and glasses, thinking hard what to say next. "What brought you here?"

She set down her travel bag and gave me a questioning look. Maybe this was an oddly intimate question. I expected the spark of irony in her eyes but it did not appear.

She looked away, around the garden: "I'm just traveling . . ."

"Alone?"

"Sometimes." She turned back to face me. She looked weary. There was no provocation in her voice. Where was the mockery, the smile, the panache? This was a different person from the one I had known.

"How did you find me? Do you come from Paris? My concierge?"

"I've been at Avignon, the festival, you know. Yes, your concierge told me. Some time ago."

I could not concentrate. I rambled about the south, my friend's generosity, my work, wanting to make her feel more welcome. I could not listen to her comments because I was so busy staring at her, trying to find out what it was that had changed that much. It wasn't only the face, innocent of makeup, the shorter, ungroomed hair. She looked younger without her feminine attire and strangely familiar, but something was effaced. I couldn't grasp it. She, too, seemed to be searching me, or waiting—for what? I felt self-conscious and compelled to appear sure of myself.

I fixed a simple dinner, insisting that she stay in the chaise longue and relax from her trip. I wanted to have a moment to myself and make some order, in my room as well as my head. What has she come for? I wondered. I can't ask her, the question would sound like an attack. Does she want to force me into an answer to her letter? How dare she! Having kept me waiting that long . . .

I sautéed summer squash with garlic and tomatoes, added a few sprigs of basil from my window pot. Whatever happens, I won't let her assault me, I decided. I'll find ways. Of course, I will. I'll be true to myself. Just wait and see what she'll come up with . . . I opened a bottle of village wine and felt better.

"Dinner's ready!" I chirped. She jumped out of her chaise and, with a single leap, arrived at the table. As she had in the café. She grabbed the checkered napkin, wound it around her neck, and looked at me with obedient, expectant eyes. The model child.

I laughed, "Shall I cut your squash for you?"

She loved the food, she said. I thanked her for her letter.

"It's a great story," I said, sounding perfectly false. "I'd been so disappointed, you know, when I never heard from you." That rang less false. "Well, you kept your promise after all. When did you finally write?"

"I wrote . . . it may not matter anymore. I didn't send it for a while and you got it after you had long forgotten all about it, right?"

"Forgotten what?"

"Me?"

"*Me three?!* Never. I'm not used to meeting strangers

like you in my café . . ." There was the look I recognized. Watchful, checking me out. "Well," I veered off, "what have you been up to all this time? You've changed."

She looked hesitant. "Me? Not much. Some traveling . . . Affairs . . . And you?"

It was the first question she'd asked me. I heard myself say: "Oh, I had a mad passion for a woman and then killed myself to find her again in whatever other woman. In vain, of course."

There was a silence like after a shot. I was stunned by myself. Was this my answer to her letter—exposing myself in order to get even? At the same time the silence echoed inside me: And you have come in vain . . .

"I'm sorry," she said simply. I wondered what she was referring to.

When I went in to get bread and cheese I got the rescuing idea to talk about the mice. We loosened up. She even laughed, throwing her head back, when I mimicked how I carried the infamous cage through the village. Her features had begun to dissolve with the dark and I began to feel quite comfortable with her. I thought I saw something come alive in her eyes while she was listening. Not the spark I remembered. A warm, quiet glow. Who knows what she's been through—the lonely wanderer, I felt, suddenly protective.

"It's nice here," she said, stretching her arms to the stars. Then she leaned in as if to peer through the darkness. "I won't disturb you, I promise. Can I stay a few days?"

Her voice was dark and shy and for a second I ached to go over and hug her.

Oct. 2

She's respectful of my privacy. Every day she disappears for hours. Sometimes I catch myself waiting for her. When I go for my late afternoon walk I keep an eye out for the dark-headed wanderer on some little road. But I come home and there she is. I stopped asking where she'd been. I get nothing out of her except: "Oh, I've been looking around some . . ." accompanied by one of her graceful gestures fanning half the horizon. Claire, the clear one, Klara, the one with the most paradoxical name! I begin to realize it's no use questioning her. When we sit outside after dinner waiting for the night to cool the air before we go to sleep she will make a remark out of the blue. Something she noticed during her wanderings in the daytime. A sculpture at a roadside reminding her of a grave in a Sicilian cemetery. The pattern of tiles on the roofs or walls of a certain village compared to those on some island south of Greece. At the name of the village, St. Martin le Pauvre, I realized that she was getting around pretty far. She certainly couldn't have walked there in her flimsy little sandals. I glanced at her khaki shorts and T-shirt. I would hide my body better on southern country roads. "Still not scared of hitchhiking?" I asked.

She lifted her shoulders, smiling with a hint of triumph. Because she felt superior to me who's afraid of men? Or because I referred to her letter? It was one of the moments when she was her old self again.

I can still not bring these two personalities together, the one here and the one from the café. The one here is the even stranger stranger even though I can't stop wondering who she reminds me of. The nakedness of her face, without the shapes and shades of fashion, gets almost too close.

There is something carefully distant, however, in the way she holds back in order not to disturb me. It feels like a shyness that makes me shy, too. Her overfeminine café persona was at least aggressively alive. This one is like the shadow. A younger, gentle brother. Attentive to me but passive, avoiding an approach. Waiting for me to decide.

What seems at odds with this shadow persona is that physically she's not at all shy. In the morning she rises from her blankets (she prefers to sleep outside) and walks naked to the bathroom. Then, with only a small towel around her hips, she occupies herself in the kitchen, lays the table for breakfast. When I stagger out, wrapped in my body cloth, she doesn't seem to notice. She moves on as if being naked made no difference. Before we sit down, she takes her olive T-shirt from the washing line. She hasn't taken anything else out of her little travel bag. She never seems to be cold after sundown or even at night. Always in her T-shirt or naked, a towel wrapped around.

I must say, I like watching her—as much as I dare. I am fascinated by her body. It's a feminine body and at the same time it's not. Compared to her waist her shoulders are broad, no gently falling curves. Her breasts, however, curve. They are surprisingly full. Her buttocks, arms, and legs are muscular, but there is nothing too thin. Her back is longer in proportion than her legs, just the opposite of mine. That's probably why I remembered her taller. The storyteller, dream-castle-maker looks closer to the ground than I, the skeptical realist. An interesting paradox. Maybe our bodies express something we need to be.

I noticed that she hides her belly with the towel, not

her ass. But hide is the wrong word. She doesn't appear to have any shame. Is this the early, innocent acceptance of womanhood she dressed up in her story as "creating her own body"? She's a mystery for me. A mystery wrapped in this little white towel she probably wears so as not to offend me. It's like a mere decorative emphasis of her brown nakedness.

I've always been riddled by the aura of innocence in certain women who are the very opposite of innocent. Certain stars, Bergman, her daughter, too. Kinski, Anita Ekberg, Monroe, of course. They are sensuous, sexual, experienced, but somehow not conscious of it, at least not self-conscious. I think that's what makes them goddesses to other mortals like me. We stare at their faces and bodies, worshiping the paradise vision of sexuality embodied in a never-lost childhood innocence.

Claire is one of them. It's not so much in her face. It's in her body, in the way her body seems centered, grounded, at peace. All her movements flow out of that. Her movements, too, have nothing to hide. But the most touching expression of this "innocence" (as it appears to me) is in her neck, in the way her head is connected to her body. Her head is posed on an almost sturdy neck in the precise axis of the spine. Something one rarely sees on women, except on statues from ancient Greece or other cultures where women's strength was permitted to show. It's what has always fascinated me, what I used to envy in boys. No frailty, no swan's neck delicately twisted, curved, or stretched into "feminine" grace. Not even a dancer's proud, tense carriage. A neck solid and relaxed. Unseductive and unconscious of its stance, its message: this is where I am and who I am—this is myself. What a charm then, by contrast, in the inclinations of the head! Every movement out of this poise has natural, animal grace.

Her makeup and longer hair in Paris must have dis-

tracted me from noticing this. Now I see—and I would
love to just watch her move around like that, in her
shameless sensuous way, and not have to talk with her!
It's the talking that creates the strain. It's all repetition.
As if back in Paris we had already said too much and were
now locked in our extreme positions, our opposition. The
woman-who-can't-get-enough-of-them and the prudish
feminist! I fear the minute I open my mouth to comment
on her letter it'll be the same old pigtail. I'll be locked
again in this person full of rhetoric and sexual apprehen-
sions. I can't stand being this person anymore, especially
not in front of her.

Oct. 4

Yesterday evening I told Mme. Petitpot that I had a visitor. "An old friend from Paris," I said. She looked at me over her TV glasses. "I won't need the car tomorrow. Why don't you show your friend around?" She gave me a benevolent smile. I know she wonders about my sitting at a table for hours, filling papers. She finds it unhealthy, to say the least.

I accepted the offer. I wasn't sure I'd feel comfortable spending a whole day with Claire. But I needed to take a break, get out of my beloved prison. Claire liked my suggestion to drive into the mountains, "just following our noses."

"Better take a sweater or something," I said. "It's cooler up there."

"I'm never cold. Should we take some fruit and water? By the way—" She turned around from the fridge and faced me for a moment. "We don't have to talk about my letter."

I was shocked with relief. I put two sweaters in the trunk.

On the way I picked up a Michelin map. I wanted us to be able to follow the smallest roads, wide enough for a single car. Cool air blew in through the windows. The sky was cloudless. We passed through the shade of old almond and olive groves, the sound of crickets deafening. Suddenly blatant sun. Silence. A naked plateau. Down into a *chaos*, dried-out riverbeds, nothing but rocks. Stubborn patches of wild rosemary and thyme appeared between them. The rock grew into blocks, then disappeared into a forest of oaks. Low walls of small, heaped-up boulders accompanied the bends and bumps of the road.

"Old roads of Europe . . ." Claire said.

"Faithful old roads," I agreed.

She fell back into her reverie, one knee drawn to her chest, her arm out the window. I restrained myself from looking to the side where my glance would brush over her. Every time I did she seemed unaware, nestled into herself. Once she had her eyes closed, her head tipped back. I quickly tried to take in her face. She looked more familiar when her eyes didn't keep watch. Still there was something strangely undressed about her face. I couldn't get used to her mouth. Without the lipstick there was no aggressive pout but an expression of frailty and longing. What was she dreaming of?

I stopped looking, afraid her eyes might open and catch me. Afraid it might bring back the embarrassment. I told myself to stick to her generous offer not to bother about the letter. It was the past. Now she was here. But why was she here if she didn't want me to know any of her secrets? Something must have happened since she wrote that letter. I thought of the loneliness between her lines. Maybe I should bother. And be generous in return.

She had raised her head again to look at the mountains. I pointed out that the earth-warm white and yellow stone was the same as in my village, in the walls of my court. We saw some villages in the distance, built in this stone, each sitting on the fortified throne of a hilltop. They looked so luminous against the scenery of scarce mountains and shady valleys. Inside, the romantic defiance of the walls and rugged rooflines crumpled into a desolate atmosphere of abandon.

"How can one live in such a place." I shuddered. "Cut off from the world. And so small! Not even a bistro . . ."

"I often don't mind being far from the world."

"But here the world is the others. Everyone eying each other all day long, for sure."

She didn't reply. I pondered about her being far from the world. Did it mean even far from men? Was this why she seemed so different? I tried to picture her as some kind of a hermit, wanting to get away from it all . . .

We came to a medieval town nestled on two sides of a ravine, a lively place where we found a restaurant with tables outside. After three hours of driving it was a relief to eat and drink and see people, even one or two tourists, walk by. We strolled through the crooked streets with well-restored houses, ended up at the foot of a huge town wall. Cypresses were towering above. Claire gave me a sign with her head and started walking. I followed her upward. How had she known there had to be a path?

I remembered her remark about her suitors: "They either look away or they follow." How easy it is between women and men! Any attraction is immediately clear. Between women it can go on forever. Following, looking away—none is necessarily a clear sign. The question stays open. Is it the old cliché? Women are interested in so much more than sex? In sentiment, friendship, intelligent exchange, closeness, companionship . . . ? How to know? A man just wouldn't meet a stranger, write her his sexual life story, look her up, and spend days with her . . . without a sexual interest. Well, would a woman? A woman like Claire?

We reached the top, a sort of terrace bordering on another wall, and arrived at an open gate. Two majestic stone posts, old and bent. We entered a wilderness that must have been a park a hundred years ago. A knee-high wall enclosed it, moss-covered and rounded by wind and rain. We followed its bend toward old stables. A house with a slate roof, a *manoir*. We looked at each other. Nobody around.

Carefully we walked alongside the house to the front. Two large, high terrace doors were closed with shutters, nailed and overgrown with vines. Thick stone snails framed the single window above, in the gable. Beds of lavender cut into geometrical shapes gave the house a tender, ironic touch of a castle.

"A miniature French garden!"

She gave me a quick look. "I love French gardens!"

"Me too . . ." Did she remember our conversation from two and a half years ago? Then, I had preferred to disagree. In fact, I'd always loved French gardens. I even find it a pity that she herself isn't a French garden anymore.

I went to inspect a hedge on the left. The vegetable garden must have been behind it. Thick, dry grass and a few apple trees were all that was left. A flat stone in a corner under the hedge was inscribed in a child's hand: "*Ici repose un moineau mort été 73.*"

"A sparrow's grave," Claire said, coming up behind me. She bent down and touched the stone, tenderly brushed off the dirt. "Maybe nobody's been here since 'seventy-three . . . It reminds me . . ."

"Reminds you?"

She laid her hands flat on the stone for a moment, got up, and scanned the house and garden.

"A haunting place . . ."

I sat down on the grass carpet under one of the apple trees. From the side, the high, pointed roof of the house looked like a witch's hat. Another terrace door had not been opened for so long a young tree in front of it had almost reached the roof. Claire sat down next to me. Small triangular dormer windows without glass were looking at us from the roof. Eyes, curious, inviting.

"They're sad. Abandoned . . ." Claire said. She lay down on the grass, her arm covering her eyes.

I searched the rest of her face, her mouth, wondering if
that was how she felt herself. Again there was something
unsettling about her. A stillness. A childlike yielding to
whatever it was she was feeling. I had a *déjà vu* as if I
were all of a sudden seeing her little brother. I couldn't
explain it. I had the strange certitude that I had known
him. That this part of her story was true.

"Tired?" I asked after a while. "Tired of life?"

She moved her arm an inch to look at me.

" . . . ?"

"You look so different. I mean, your letter sounded
tired, too."

"Different? After two and a half years? Wouldn't you
worry if you were still the same?"

"I'm certainly tired."

"Of confusing every woman with the one you couldn't
get?"

"And you? Tired of teaching untalented boys?"

Her arm went back over her eyes. I felt she didn't want
me to read the smile she was fighting. Then there was her
old ironic glance.

"Women are still better, right?"

"Well, who has been teaching whom?"

"I wouldn't prove anything . . . to you."

"What do you mean?"

"Nothing."

She picked a stalk of grass and chewed on it with
squinted eyes. Then she sat up on one elbow and put an
appeasing hand on my arm.

"Alma, couldn't you forget about that letter?"

"How? Why?"

"It's old. *Dépassé.*"

"Outdated by what?"

She fell back on the grass. "How would you translate
the wind?"

I tried to hide my irritation. "Tell me."

She gave me a grave, questioning look. "Alma . . . Do you believe in time?"

"Oh, another story?" I could have bit my tongue. "Sure, I believe. Try me."

"You are too literal, aren't you, to believe in any story?"

"Not when I can tell a story from the truth."

"I've got stories. Nothing else."

I could see she had already withdrawn.

"You've got nothing but secrets that you manage to keep!"

"Isn't sexuality always kept secret? Above all from the ones engaged in it?"

Oct. 6

I wanted to stay in to work as usual. But I had no milk left for my afternoon *café au lait*. My addiction hit. In these lonely workdays the cup of coffee is my sole (soul) companion. The only shop in the village is closed by noon and doesn't carry fresh milk anyway, only that disgusting sweet and oily nonrefrigerated stuff. It was almost four, time for the shops in the neighboring villages to reopen. I hurried over to Mme. Petitpot and asked if I could borrow her car for the errand. How are the mice? she asked. Gone, I lied. The poison's all gone, too. She smiled, pleased that she'd been right. She handed me the keys. Take your time, she said.

I don't know what got into me. I didn't drive to Tierrac, the closest little town, as I usually do. I found myself driving to St. Martin le Pauvre. I wondered what it was that Claire had seen there. Something special, something "Greek" about the walls. Did her eyes see more than mine? I didn't quite believe it. Anyway, why should I care? But I wanted to check it out. I wanted to know something about Claire.

I had driven through the place many times without paying particular attention. To me it looks like any of the other little towns around. A narrow round stone bridge (traffic stuck on each side) leading over a meager river into a cluster of houses. Dark streets, the houses forbidding, their shutters always closed against the heat. The beautiful old sandstone hidden under the after-war coat of gray-brown mortar. I find most of these towns depressing. Their inhabitants seems to find them depressing, too.

They tend to have a gray-brown ugliness about them and a hostile curiosity toward anyone who is not also trapped there.

Winding up the main street to the little supermarket at the other end of town, I watched and stared in disbelief. How could she find anything appealing about this place? I strained my eyes to capture whatever might be unusual. Suddenly, there it was. In the center of the town the street opened into a square. With two bistros on opposite corners, a bakery and a newspaper shop, it was the only life spot in the whole place. The tables outside were all occupied, mostly by men. But one table at the bigger bistro was visibly the center of everyone's attention. All heads were turned to it. And there sat Claire Heller.

I was going slow because of the traffic on the square: in a second I grasped the whole scene. She was surrounded by four men, beer-drinking villagers, all of them roaring with laughter. Claire was throwing her head back in unison, her mouth glaring red.

What if she'd seen me? I was certain she would have read her victory in my face. I was ashamed of that face. What's wrong with me? I thought. Can't she amuse herself as she pleases? I don't want her to hang out all day in my stuffy court, do I? This is obviously what pleases her. I'd better get my nose out of her life. *Laissez vivre*, remember?

I parked the car in front of the supermarket and went in to cool off. It didn't work. I blindly gazed at the potatoes, postcards, plastic sandals. I tried to think. I couldn't stand the idea of having to drive back across the square. Of seeing her again with those men. Maybe this time one of them would have his arm around her. Or worse. I wouldn't want to see it. But I wouldn't be able not to look. How can she do this? She puts on lipstick and plays the woman-of-the-world for them. Shows off as the foreign attraction of the marketplace. And what does she play for me? I felt betrayed.

What did I expect? Had I not read her letter? But how can I be that boring to her? How on earth can the company of gross, beer-drinking provincials amuse her? Calm down, I told myself, and get your milk. They amuse her, believe it. Didn't you want to know something about Claire? Isn't that why you came here in the first place? So, just take it in. This is learning. I went and put the milk in my basket. If this is the truth about Claire, I decided, I'd better know it. This is my chance to figure her out.

I placed the milk back on the shelf and left the supermarket. I returned to the square by foot. I was going to spy on her. Stalking her like a mouse, to catch her in her circus act. I reached the bistro from the side street, stopped at the corner, and pretended to study the menu. From there I could only see her back, but she would for sure not see me.

By now there were two more men at her table. Most of them leaning forward to be as close to her as possible, their hairy elbows on their knees. One was pushing up his beret, scratching his skull in some visible effort—trying to stay in his seat, I suppose. A well-dressed young man, already puffed up with village responsibilities and red with sweat, was twisting his blond mustache, hiding his complacent smile. An old good-for-nothing with a broad yellow tie and a student's straw hat was leaning on his cane, his big lower lip pushed forward in his concentration, peeping through finger-thick glasses. The *garçon*, looking like a schoolboy, stood glued to the next table— where they were all twisting their necks—his tray with empty glasses suspended in the air, his free hand holding on to the table as if otherwise he'd lose balance. Seeing him I suddenly understood that they were all listening to her. Claire Heller was talking. In French. There her graceful hand went up and all the heads on the bistro terrace went up to follow its arc through the air. She stopped, shrugged, and they all laughed again. Clapped each other's shoulders, moved in their chairs, drank, lighted cigarettes, all talking at the same time, relieved from the spell for a moment . . . until she went on.

If that's not a circus act, I thought. But she's the director. She's got the control. God knows how she's doing it, but they seem to behave. No paws on her. No obscene gestures. Just as her story claims! They don't laugh about her, at her expense. They are laughing with her. They are fascinated by what she's telling. What on earth can it be? And what on earth can she get out of it? Is it that they're all wanting her, courting her, competing to get her? Each showing her great respect as long as he hopes to be chosen?

If I were one of them. To sit in this circle and listen to her. To have her talk and talk and smile at me. To be forgotten. Forget to listen and just stare, get lost and stare at her mouth moving, her lashes covering and uncovering her eyes, her hands tracing arcs in the air. To be one of them and not worry what she might read in my face.

Maybe that's what she gets out of it. Their faces are open, they have nothing to hide. She can read her power in their faces. She sees every reflection of her attention, follows the effect of every favor she accords or withdraws. What a power—being desired and having no fear of it! She draws them up like moths, watches them dance around her flame, checks them out and chooses the ones to burn and the one "to teach" . . .

I in her place would have had no doubt about the choice. Indeed, that one worried me: the handsome boy with his half-open mouth and the childish ecstasy painted on his face. The table wouldn't hold him for long, I could see it already. He would drop his tray and everything else at her feet. She would find it charming. What if she didn't come home tonight? And even if she came. I hated the idea of any of them driving her. I suddenly hated to picture her in a car with her Warren or any other guy. And then being delivered back to me!

I had to do something. I couldn't stand there letting this happen. I wished I were outrageous enough to just walk to the table, pull up a chair, and join the staring. Shifting a cigarette from one ear to the other, licking my lips. Or at least to sneak to a table right behind so that I could listen in and spy for good. How could I get in touch with her and yet keep a safe distance from them? Have the bartender carry a note: "Someone's waiting for you at the bar?" She would turn around, spot me, and wave me over to the table. *Quelle horreur!* Tell her I'm waiting at the car? And then wait in vain? No, I'd have to make it difficult for her to refuse. I'd have to make myself visible. Put myself out there in some way or other in order to get her.

I had an idea. I returned to the supermarket, grabbed the milk and a bottle of champagne. Jumped into my car, nervous that she might leave or that my courage would leave me. Checked my hair in the rearview mirror, took a deep breath, and got going. I drove up to the bistro speeding up, then worked the brakes to a roisterous stop precisely in line with her table. Everyone's head flew around. Now I was the center of the town's attention. I casually leaned out of the window. I met her eyes and put on a grin.

"Want a ride? And a surprise?" I shouted, opening my hand in a sweeping invitation that said: if not, *tant pis,* too bad for you . . . I gave her exactly three seconds to choose me.

I caught the flash of delighted disbelief in her face.

ALMA RUNAU

With the same flash I understood why an admirer got chosen. The corners of her mouth went down into her Mona Lisa smile. She took her time while all the heads turned back for her reaction. She contemplated the proposition. I held my breath. Her hand went into her shorts pocket and she dropped some coins on the table, still smiling to herself. Only then she rose up and turned to her table companions: "Well, *messieurs*, that's it for today. *Bonne soirée*."

A pity, the *garçon* didn't drop his tray! She lightly walked up through the tables. Reading my triumph in the flabbergasted faces around her, it suddenly struck me that my scenario ended here. I had not thought out how to go on from the moment my plan had succeeded. What if she'd seen the panic in my face? I managed to pull myself together and gave the villagers a good last grin before taking off with my loot.

"Well, Me Three!" I said once we were out of sight. "Looks like you spent an awfully lonely afternoon . . ."

"And you? Spent your day driving around picking up women?"

"How did you know? Does it show?"

I couldn't tell if her laughter was mocking me.

"Luckily I came to your rescue, didn't I?" I kept my voice innocent. "Seems to be my destiny . . . "

"Fascinating."

"Sure. Like in Paris, remember?"

"Oh, Paris. Where you rescued the table you'd wanted? I see. What are you rescuing this time?"

"You."

She burst out laughing again. I wasn't sure I knew where I was going.

"From those guys, I suppose?"

"From your loneliness."

I heard my voice cut into her laughter. I had not in-

152

tended to sound serious. Her sudden silence made me nervous. I didn't dare look at her. Had I hit the target?

"Never mind," I tried to sound cheerful. "Once again *saved*!"

I gave her a quick glance and perceived the contempt in her eyes.

"And safe, I suppose?"

I suddenly hated her. Why wasn't I better at this game? I didn't manage to be either serious or funny. She wouldn't let me. I had made the allusion to Paris because I secretly wanted us back there. I longed to finally recognize her. And she promptly tried to trap me in her typical Paris way!

"You are addicted to them, aren't you? Why do you put on lipstick for them?"

"I am addicted to life," she replied haughtily. "That is, to pleasure."

"Oh yes, those village dopes must be pleasure *par excellence*, I can see that."

"Enough to make you jealous. I can see that."

I stopped the car at a sand road branching off the Nationale.

"I suppose you'd prefer to go back to them!"

"Why do you think I've come?"

"Claire Heller." I turned in my seat to face her. "I wish I knew why you have come. I have no idea. No idea why you even wrote to me. I can't recognize you really. Who are you? What are you saying in this letter? Why don't you tell the truth?"

It was finally out. She didn't look at me. I sat back and stared at the road.

"The truth. I see. That's all you're looking for in my letter. The truth? *Your* truth. You can't see me or recognize me because you won't accept my truth. I'd have to be a manhater, like you, to be recognized."

"So you think what you need to seduce a woman is to

show up at her place without your lipstick—et cetera—war paint?"

We fell silent. I felt I had gone too far but refused to feel guilty. Finally, both wounded. I went on staring at the road winding through the hills, the dust-green thicket of shrubs. The rush of cars past us kept breaking the wild chirping of crickets.

"Why don't you drive on?" she asked. "Let's not talk here. It's too hot."

I gave her a quick look. She didn't seem destroyed. Her face was thoughtful, neither haughty nor offended. Not even closed off. I was relieved, then realized this was the second time she'd taken the initiative.

I got back on the highway.

"By the way," she pursued after a while, "what's the surprise you promised?"

What does it take to knock her off her balance?

"The fact that we're talking!" I decided I would tell stories, too. From the corner of my eyes I saw her amused smile. "I got a bottle of champagne." (One smile was enough to draw me back to my truth?) "It's the full moon tonight."

"Let's talk at dinner then. I need some time."

We drove the rest of the way in silence. I dropped her off at the house, fetched my notebook and her letter, a bottle of water, gave the car back, and climbed up to my rock. Now I'm here. I need some time too.

She's right. I want her to be like me. It has to be *my* truth. And hers—I've been totally blind. Her wandering, unattachedness, the men following her. Even her insecurity in front of me. She can't read me, her effect on a woman like me. We're not in a café surrounded by men. She's my uninvited guest. The intimacy makes her timid. Like the little brother, trying hard to understand, to be *à la hauteur*. Seen from now it does ring true. Never mind the flourishes, exaggerations, the bragging. There's even something moving about it.

Isn't it part of my own dream? A woman, uncrippled by patriarchy? Uncastrated?

Well, let's not exaggerate. She still serves men. She still resembles the stereotype. Vamp, whore, nymphomaniac, *femme fatale* . . . But there is no other image. No name for what she is or tries to be. Do we have goddesses, priestesses, sexual angels?

That's part of the pain I feel looking at her, reading her story. That's why I said she was unreal. She pains me because she simply, naturally has what I don't have. What I've longed for my whole life and have to struggle to work and sweat for inch by inch: this feminine version of sexual boldness, self-assurance, pride. This power.

If I still had any doubt about it, this afternoon threw it into my face. How she reigned over them at the bistro, made them behave, got from them whatever she wanted. They were all under her spell. A mystery like art. Ask Michelangelo or Gertrude Stein how they did it! I'm in envy and awe. *Voilà* my truth.

In fact, there have always been women like that. Rarely recognized by feminists because they were only too well recognized and claimed by men. Great courtesans. Liane de Pougy. *La Dame aux Camélias.* The first "modern" woman of our century, Lou Andreas Salomé. But Sappho must have been one of them, and Natalie Barney, too. Everybody worships them, just like the *femmes fatales* in the movies. Only most women aren't conscious of their worship.

I've been raised as a powerless woman. Feminism taught me to suspect any power that would drive others to their knees. It taught me to keep my own knees straight. No more submission! Beware domination! Not kosher, this power. Has sexuality ever been?

I was right to say it's a torture, a perversity to give

oneself when one has no self! The mere idea of falling to one's knees is an unbearable vertigo. Losing the last hold, the very rest of one's vague, unanchored self.

My truth? Giving myself in love is fake. Ninety-nine percent of women—who aren't "goddesses" but humans like me—fake giving themselves. We come with backs bent like slaves' or with our proud straight knees, and it stays at that. We don't touch ground. We don't know our ground.

I had a sudden realization strolling home. Found a shady bench here. I can't write in my notebook when she is around.

Her letter was simply not what I'd expected. I wanted some kind of sexual theory. As if theory were more real than a life story. Even one's own life story, "rewritten and corrected by the author." I get caught in this bias over and over. Theory, the "masculine" form, is superior. I myself look up to it. I look down at my own diary writing, my "diarrhea." The telling of life experiences is suspect. Can't compare to that crystalline thought, the abstraction. Too muddled up with contradictions and paradox.

Claire could have conceptualized her stories in a few sentences. *Men are less powerful sexually than they want to seem. Women the opposite. If women are victims, they are victims of an illusion about men.* In order to make sense out of such a theory one has to go back to life. What experience is it abstracted from? How come a woman in partriarchy sees that the emperor is naked? As the French feminists keep asking: *"D'où tu parles?"* Tell your own story!

Her theory disguised as story. It goes step by step. Each story a stage in the development of a woman. A development that even contains feminist insights . . . Am I now giving credit she doesn't deserve? Making up theory in order to redeem her outlandish tale?

Story 1: A girl sees through the swagger of the male hero. The neighbor, the man on the bus, the supermarket guy . . . A girl believes her own eyes. (Where did she get her special glasses?)

Story 2: She decides not to be a "hero," but to become a woman instead. She senses a mysterious superior power in women. (She doesn't see that women's power is the pedestal. Men put women up there in order to mystify their use.)

Story 3: She creates her own outrageous rite of passage. She takes the first step instead of passively waiting for initiation. (But she has to become aggressive. The loud-mouth girl sacrifices her tender, poetic dream world for the crude reality of sex.) She sees sex as the art of cultivating body pleasure. It has to be learned and practiced like any other art.

Story 4: Delusion, disillusion. Sex can't be learned as an art in a culture of body hostility. Especially not from men. She sees that men are profoundly insecure in their bodies. They can't match up to the inflated phallic image of the father. They can't match up to the awesome orgasmic power of the mother. (But she still tries to teach them.) She picks boys as the easier target. The ones not yet entirely possessed by the male clan. Even with them, however, it's too late. (She can't raise them all!)

Story 5: She hints at a quest for sexual knowledge that takes her beyond this culture's limitations. (Still with men?) It seems to be a quest back in time to some ancient culture where women can be worshiped for their sexual power. (She phases out of patriarchy. Open end of the science fiction . . .)

How could I have missed it?

Her stories are too exotic at first glance. Her strange metaphors, her mythology, Adonis and Aphrodite's temples, choosing one's body, sex as art, whore as artist . . . This outspokenness, brash sex talk, then wrapping it all into mysterious, mystical smoke. This woman-in-a-bubble: she sees the irreality of sexuality and doesn't live in reality herself. Dreaming herself out of patriarchy . . . That's what I also wanted and tried, with women. It's the most paradoxical twist of all. She reaches the same conclusion that I as a feminist have reached. I could almost say we agree. We have the same longing for body wholeness. But she won't give up on men. When will she understand that she'll never succeed?

I almost ran back. I was dead hungry and suddenly scared she might have vanished again. What if she took offense at my long absence or thought I was offended and wouldn't want to talk with her after all?

It was a relief to see light in the little house. It wasn't dark yet. The sun had scarcely set, the moon scarcely risen behind the rocks. She'd put a light on in the kitchen to prepare dinner. Outside, the table was laid under the mulberry tree. She had cut a geranium and placed it in a wineglass on the table. Olives were put out in a little bowl. I was expected for an intimate feast.

"Sit down," she shouted from the bathroom. "I'll be there in a minute."

I took the champagne out of the fridge and chose the two least clumsy glasses. Funny, I thought, what are we celebrating? A second arrival? That's what I had decided to propose to her when I left my rock. I intended to tell her that I knew her story was true. I wanted to welcome her after all.

I was preparing the bottle—and almost dropped it when she appeared. She stood in the doorway dressed in a tight red summer dress, barefoot, one hand on her hip, her nails red, shoulders naked, eyes blackened, her poppy mouth without a smile. Her face was calm, her body motionless. She stood as if painted into the door frame.

My heart jumped into my throat. I was speechless. I didn't know whether I felt like a rabbit staring at a snake or like Adonis at the apparition of Aphrodite. Should I fall to my knees or doubt that this was real? It was an intense discomfort, a rush of delight and embarrassment. I couldn't let my eyes wander over her freely, making her an object. I wanted to. Was she trying to turn me into one of her admirers? Or to comfort my jealousy? I suddenly felt shabby, out of place in my everyday shirt and shorts. Unworthy of whatever this was, gift, challenge, invitation —to what?

"Is this what is needed to seduce a woman?" she asked. There was only the slightest edge of irony in her voice. It was enough. My heart fell back into its place. I recognized her.

"Let's see . . . " I proposed. I suddenly saw the magician's box. I remembered: in order to avoid her traps I only had to take a step ahead. "Turn around!" I ordered.

She obeyed. Her movement had a puzzling ease. She got up on her naked toes, turned and looked over her shoulder to give me her face in profile, taking her time. I wondered if what I was seeing was again the innocence that doesn't need to either shade its erotic nature or add any extra effect. Or was it simply what I was feeling myself—relief at my proposition? I couldn't tell.

"Nothing else could be needed! But as I am the only woman here"—I pretended to search behind me— "would you kindly give me a moment to dress up to the occasion?"

I held a chair for her like a cavalier, forcing her to approach. Now the doorway was free for an elegant escape.

Looking through my clothes I debated if a quick shower would reveal any intentions. I wanted a shower —intentions or not! Feeling the cool water wash over me, I knew with a sudden excitement that I didn't need to worry at all. This was my game. We were playing in my territory. She wouldn't dare to take the first step, having no experience with women. And I, I would know how to take it . . . in case I wanted to. What did I risk? I could simply relax and play.

I slipped into a pair of white pants and a white smoking shirt. I tried my moccasins from the Italian flea market, but decided for my high-topped tiger tennis shoes. Slicking my wet hair straight back, I could see that I was moving into my power. No curly wisps to soften my face. The more severe lines of my cheeks and jawbone stood out. I saw excitement, arrogance, sensitivity. I smiled at myself in the mirror. This was what I wanted—and she, too, was finally where I wanted her. In Paris again.

When I sat down at the table, we exchanged the pleased look of accomplices. She had served artichokes for an *hors d'oeuvre*. I poured the champagne.

"Thank you for the dinner," I said and lifted my glass for a toast. "I've seen you before. To recognition!"

"To mystery." She answered, looking at me over the rim of her glass while she drank.

"Do you remember our toast in Paris with our last drop of cognac?" I lifted my glass as I had done that day: "To sameness!"

"To difference!" she echoed, her voice holding the same old challenge.

"Have we advanced a single step in our dance?"

"Why not speak for yourself?"

"Do you recognize *me?*"

"The hermaphrodite?" She smiled, teasing me with the desire I had confessed to her that day, to be both, masculine as well as feminine. I was again struck by her memory—and her unaltered refusal to use the word *androgynous*. "You seem the same to me," she went on. "The same boy who ran from Marathon when the seven Persian ships were cut down."

"Achilles dressed as a girl?"

"The same and different. I can see that you have lived."

162

"To recognition once again! I admit, you are a mystery to me. But I want you to know I believe your story."

"You believed me the first time, in Paris, didn't you?" There was the old spark of mockery in her eyes. "What mystery seduces you now?"

"You're a feminist in disguise! What a disguise. I read your letter again. Claire, you are a *féministe manquée!*"

"No kidding. A mystery I've missed?"

"Your theory is great. But men have more to them than their false image. They've got a whole culture to protect them from knowing about their inadequacy. They've found excellent ways to make women bear it for them."

"I? Bear it for them? That must be an analysis of *your* relationship to men."

"Oh yes. You are the only exception from the rule. You sound like you're not living in this world."

"I live in the world as I define it."

"Have you defined this costume you're wearing? The *femme fatale*, the whore?"

"As always you miss my irony. Isn't it ironic that in this costume you seem to recognize me?"

I stared at her. It was true. Here we were sitting at the table, peeling our artichokes, one dressed up as the "boy who ran from Marathon," the other as the archetypal seductress. And I was trying to discuss feminism! Tomorrow, I decided, tomorrow I'll tell her that theoretically we have more in common than she knows.

I tried to relax and enjoy the dinner. She had prepared ratatouille *à l'américaine*: eggplants, green peppers, squash, and tomatoes, all cooked together in the same pan. It was delicious anyway, delicately spiced with herbs and *piment*. Sensuous cooking, I noted. No meat added although she doesn't mind it as much as I do. The last course was goat cheese, *crottins* she had discovered at some road stand, and grapes I had picked in an old neglected vineyard: the smallest, sweetest, untreated grapes.

I got her to talk a bit about her travels and she got me to talk about my life. She wanted to know about this woman who had occupied my past years. It was when I told her about Solveig that I noticed the strange ease I was talking with. As if the woman in red whom I had finally recognized had turned too familiar already. It puzzled me that I was not more thrilled by the telling. The classic situation: two women secretly attracted to each other, each unpacking the backpack of her life experiences in growing excitement, showing the other her treasures. This time my excitement didn't grow.

Maybe I was still keeping my guard. She, of course, stayed as evasive as always. I didn't get any further with my questions about her letter. Why is it, I started to wonder, that I am not seduced? This is the perfect setup for a romance. We've quarreled, reunited over a sensuous dinner, the night is warm with an occasional breeze. The moon is coming up over the garden wall, a fat, promising peach. Why then does my desire not come up?

Isn't this the most attractive woman I've seen in all those years at my café—now sitting at my table, the light of a candle licking her naked shoulders so that I can't get my eyes off her? A woman I've so often thought of, sometimes fantasized about, and who has pronounced the word *seduction*?

Maybe that was the problem. It had been pronounced. The seduction felt planned even if it wasn't clear by whom. It blocked my imagination. Eros was certainly hovering in the air—but with no arrows in his quiver. It's too predictable, my mind, observing us, kept telling me. It may also be too risky. How can you tell a *femme fatale* from a goddess? I recognize only too well the form she's chosen for being recognized. Her role is defined and so is, by simple deduction, mine. There we are again, in opposition. It's too late. If she'd come sooner—a year ago I would have jumped on any occasion to train myself in the male role. She would have been my goddess then, more perfect perhaps, more challenging even than Solveig had been.

It's a different challenge I'm looking for now. I want a meeting, a confrontation of peers where the excitement is *not* to know who will take which role. Who will surrender to whom.

Yes, I remember. At the café, I had envisioned us in an arena performing precisely this dance. I saw myself on an armored horse galloping against a masked stranger who claimed to know all about sex because she knew all about men. It was a chivalrous combat, each advancing and striking and turning, playful and serious at the same time. I was unsure if I really wanted to win and convince her —or if I'd rather be defeated and learn what this skillful stranger knew . . .

Could she turn a prince into a frog? Could she make me feel like her men must feel: insufficient by compari-

son to a fairy tale? Or do they? It will be I, however. I
will have to turn her into something new—a woman-
lover. Evocative silence or at best stories from a distance
—that's her way to touch a woman. We aren't peers in the
arena, meeting in the mystery of true challenge. No, I told
myself, you're only half a mystery, Claire.

Then I knew why I was talking to her in this false
familiar tone. Not just to get even with her story, her sex
revelations, but in a deliberate attempt to teach her something. She's so arrogant in her sexual power, I wanted to
put her in her place. That's why I kept spilling out little
intimate secrets, exaggerating my conquests, bragging
even about my wild hunt for compensation after Solveig
was gone.

"How did you find all those women?"

"How do you find all those men?"

"As you have seen with your own eyes . . . "

"There's not much difference," I conceded. "Going to
a man's bistro or to a woman's bar. I guess I did it like
you. Traveling."

"A female Casanova."

"Two of them at a table, right?"

"Did you never get tired? Getting women must be
pretty hard work if you aren't a man."

"My 'Casanova-ing' may have been less tiring than
yours. At least my role has been clear. With men it's more
complicated. You always have to mislead them and pretend. To make them feel that *they* have the initiative or
power or whatever. Pretty hard work, no?"

"Are you sure your woman lovers have not been misleading you, as well? How would you know? And you—
have you got tired of misleading them?"

"*Pardon?*"

"You just said it yourself about men: playing the male
role is a fake."

I caught my breath. "*Touché.* It's all a fake. The female role as much as the male. While I was thinking of Solveig, the others were thinking of whoever, each acting out her predictable fantasy. I got frustrated with it."

We were silent. She had kicked me off my horse. Were we in the arena after all? At last I found myself on the ground.

"I know you're dissatisfied, too," I said. "Your story tells. You can't teach, educate, develop a stranger. If you do, you get attached. Then your passion falls asleep, and you end up longing for another stranger. You never get further. You're always after the mirage of the perfect adventure with the perfect stranger. All stories—not only yours—are made from the same fantasy. Because it can't be."

"Even if you once find it . . ." she said after another silence. "One way or another—"

"—the stranger vanishes." We looked at each other and I felt the first recognition between us that wasn't some kind of game.

"Have you ever met him? I mean, her?"

I didn't answer.

"Strangers in the night . . ." She lifted her arms as she had done the first day. The moonlight, stronger by then than the candle, fell on her lifted chin, her throat, her splendidly sturdy neck. I had a sensation of *déjà vu*.

"Maybe I have . . ." I hesitated. "That last time before I gave up trying."

"Tell, tell," she pleaded with sudden excitement. "Tell me a story!"

"I'm not quite as good at it as you, you know."

"Yes, yes, you are. I loved your Soleway story—don't tell me you didn't invent her!"

I smiled. Her pronunciation of the name sounded like a road to the soul.

"Let's have some more champagne." She flew inside to get the bottle back from the fridge. How right she is, I pondered, struck by her sense of metaphor. I did invent Solveig—again one of those surprising things she knows. What if she knows much more in fact than I expect? Hadn't I already had this sense of her in Paris? I watched her move, bring the bottle, fill the glasses, place the geranium and the candle at my side of the table as if for a ritual. She's got nothing superfluous in her movements, I marveled, even when being watched. Purest simplicity ... if one forgets her vampish attire. But one forgets it indeed, she transcends it. That's why I love to see her in it. She always transcends it with her animal grace.

She sat down again and opened her hands in an invitation that seemed to include the whole night and the chubby moon. Then she leaned in: "Where was it? At the North Pole? In Africa?"

"It was in Amsterdam. Or let's say in Hamburg ... "

I could read in her face that I was on the right track. I was all dressed up as Scheherazade.

"It was New Year's Eve. A big house near the harbor," I began. "A terrace surrounded by old plane trees, overlooking the water. You could see the big ships sailing in. The basement of the villa was built like a nightclub. A bar, little tables, a dance floor, a disco ball. Even lovers' corners. The house belonged to a man who was famous for his parties. They always had a theme, something like a color, a historical epoch ... "

"*Rouge et Noir*, King Arthur's Court—"

"Do you know the man?"

"It seems to be a European tradition. I've heard about such parties while I was traveling."

"Apparently the whole villa would be decorated for each event and people would come in costumes. Mostly gay people, that is. Like my friend Jan with whom I was visiting at the time.

"Jan had a sister, Mieke, to whom I'd been attracted for a while. Or so I thought. The two were like two sides of the same coin. Both tall and blond. But Jan, who had a big, muscular body, looked and acted the feminine part. He was an actor. Mieke had a more delicate body, but her appearance was edgy, controlled. She was a lawyer and clearly the male of the siblings. She used to loosen up though and get a little wild as soon as her brother was around. I loved to watch them. I was in fact mostly attracted to their quasi-incestuous relationship.

"Jan got us all invited. Mieke's latest lover, Angela, too. The party was supposed to be a *bal masqué*. A costume wasn't obligatory, just the mask. The theme was the Silent Night. After the New Year had been welcomed the moment would be gonged in, and the party was to continue without a spoken word until a gong would sound again. We were all excited. It promised to be a great piece of theater to be performed in silence during that space of time.

"I had my own theme. It wasn't only the year's end for me. I felt I had come to the end of a cycle. I had decided to end my traveling, my fruitless one-sided affairs, my tiresome conquistador role. I wanted some rite of passage, you know. I wanted to embody the boy one last time, for good.

"The *bal masqué* was the perfect occasion. My friends were my accomplices. They helped me create my outfit. A black tuxedo, black-and-white Al Capone shoes two sizes too big, a long white silk scarf. Every detail was accompanied by Jan's little shrieks and Mieke's calm, competent comments. Jan trained my smoking and drinking gestures. We tried all kinds of makeup and beards. In the end I decided on a dark little mustache and a black catlike mask with a nose. My hair was parted in the middle. Gel, some spray effects of black and silver. I even colored the tiny hairs on my hands.

"Because of my costume we came late to the party. It was a foggy, rainy night. We hurried down the cobbled streets, freezing. We crossed a bridge and there was the house. It looked like a hearth with all the bottle-glass windows glowing. We four were a pretty group. Jan wore a short white cape with a low-cut black lace top hidden under it, black tights, and a girlish Pierrot mask painted directly onto his face, the tear included. Mieke looked almost a boy too, with her white tuxedo, diamond bow tie, and neuter pantomime mask. Mieke's lover, Angela, had chosen a phosphorescent miniskirt, punk boots, and a black face with a phosphorescent mouth. Three boys and a girl. Among them I looked outstandingly normal. But as soon as we entered the house I was relieved to feel I could disappear among the multiple tuxedo outfits in the crowd.

"It was almost midnight. We strolled through the rooms admiring the decoration. Everything, the furniture, staircase, entire walls were wrapped into dusty white cloth. As if Christo, the artist, had come by to make an *emballage*. It was an atmosphere of silence. A statue in the hall had her eyes banded with this cloth of silence ..."

I stopped, unsure if Claire was listening. She was staring into the night sky, pursuing a vision of her own.

"Claire? Where are you?"

She shook herself. "The silence. It's extraordinary. I'm seeing it all."

I was reassured. I shouldn't have been. I went on.

"The noise of the crowd was shocking by contrast. The voices shrill with excitement. Soon there would be the gong. They would have to stop. One could feel it in the air. Then the church bells chimed and everybody rushed out to the terrace for the fireworks. It was the New Year. One could hardly see the knotty plane trees in the fog. But one could hear the big ships. A chorus of ships, fog-horns, and bells. Rockets shot up from the terrace, hissing, and dissolved into sugar in the drizzling rain. It was a delight. The fine wetness on one's face, the wet champagne, the kisses we all shared.

"New Year was a pretext for kisses. I insisted on watching the siblings kissing away. Ah, once again! I encouraged Mieke after she'd bent over in a fast, timid movement to my mouth. She obeyed, in comical confusion. It was all a kid's game. We laughed, rushed back into the warmth.

"Then the lights went low. A huge Asian gong was rolled into the hall by two naked men. Their bodies glistened under a projector beam. Everyone gathered. One of the men positioned himself in front of the golden disk. I saw paillettes flashing like stars on his back. There was already total silence when he swung his arm with the drumstick. The deep gong vibrated and wouldn't stop. The house was flooded with a slow spherical music. Projector lights came up bringing the crowd back to life.

"But it wasn't the same crowd. Compelled by the silence, the music, the light, people started to slowly move. Some walked, some stood, some lifted an arm. A notion of gravity seemed to enter the bodies, a notion of movement informed with meaning. It was not them, not us anymore. The costumes came to life.

"As if a cloth were ripped from my eyes, I saw them, singled out. Red ostrich feather sweeping down on naked shoulders from a black robber's hat. Yellow-green cockscomb, wrists chained to an iron collar. Pink tuxedo being hugged into a huge ermine coat, a crown rolling to the ground. Leotard opened into two circles of flesh and a rose. Two dainty luggage carriers of stewardesses advancing in step with two pairs of hairy legs in pumps. Dark sleeve, hand in a white glove, a lorgnette approached to the feathered sex of an angel. Arid *décolleté* of a Scarlett O'Hara dress. Beard draped into a light blue boa over a bathing suit. Boxer shorts with a rabbit tail. Gray Nosferatu fingers creeping over the morning gown of a six-foot-tall geisha with breasts. Ass pushing against tiniest leather miniskirt, zipper from belt to seam . . .

"I was watching the etiquette of a lunatic's court. People promenaded, solemnly greeted each other, raised hats, bowed in deep reverence, curved languishing heads over shoulders, pointed, waved in slow motion, circled hips, held back screams with fingertips.

"After a while, when the music took on a beat, I went to the basement and found my little group on the dance floor. It was a different atmosphere down there. A night café scene from *Unter den Linden*. Distinguished tuxedo outfits ringed around the wilder fauna dancing in the center. Laughter, occasional words, busily hushed.

"Eyes greedy to stare while staying half hidden behind their mask. Eyes hungry to be watched, ready to use anyone's look as a mirror. Narcissists rolling their pelvis in front of mirrors in fake exclusivity. I caught the ones who looked gone, in a sensuous trance, dart glances at the spectators. Only Jan, still in his white cape, seemed innocent. Swallowed by his mirror image, he executed huge pantomime moves like a desperate crane. I got a shock when I fell into my own reflection—an elegant dark feline staring back at me.

"Eyes kept wandering over me, and sometimes I didn't know whether the person was a man or a woman. When a feminine costume, long white lace, a white umbrella, turned out to be indeed a woman, I was disappointed. It was like a balloon going limp. The lack of contrast wiped out any erotic tension for me. I watched Angela swing her phosphorescent hips like a jungle creeper. She didn't turn me on. I joined Mieke for a leisurely-gentlemen pas de deux. A tango followed. She took off her mask. I took the lead. Of all the women I had crossed that night I liked her best. It may have been the same for her. I suddenly read it in her glance. At the same instant I saw Angela's eyes fall into an abyss. I withdrew.

"Mieke sat down at one of the little tables. I danced on alone, eyes closed, playing with the fantasy that her eyes were still on me. But when I looked at her, her eyes were somewhere else. She was absorbed, in serious concentration, by a couple of young men, kissing.

"I felt a pang of jealousy and quickly took care of it. I stopped dancing and placed myself at a strategic point from which I, too, could watch. I quickly forgot about Mieke and the rest of the party.

"They were standing at the piano in a niche of the room. Two equally tall, beautiful boys, both dressed in Great Gatsby suits. Long jackets, pleated pants, body-tight vests, all in sand color, only the shirts snow-white. The simplicity and elegance of the outfit, doubled in this perfect twin look, made it a costume. They were wearing the same narrow leopard mask.

"The boy leaning against the piano had darker skin. His hair had the thick silky quality of Asian hair. It was razor-cut over the ears and neck, stood up on top of his head like a thick calligraphy brush. A shock of it fell longer onto his forehead, off-white. There was a padded softness to his face, an almost girlish delicacy around his mouth, chin, and nose.

"The brown hair of the other was tightened back into a short braid. He had pale skin and a strongly marked face. The skin was tight over his bones, the cheeks hollow, his mouth finely drawn, driven. His face had the heightened nobility of someone who hasn't slept for days because of passion. He appeared to be the older of the two, the guide. He was gently assailing the other, pressing and nestling against him. He whispered into the soft one's ear, wandered down his neck with tender little kisses. He took him by the chin, smiling, then, with the same tenderness, kissed his lips, took a bit of his tongue. As if to catch his breath, he leaned his face against the other's face and, in devotion, rested there. He moved back to look at him, spoke insistent lover's words, shamelessly breaking the rule of the night. The soft boy answered, his eyes glittering. They talked, their faces close, until the wanton lover fell silent, again approaching the other's skin. The Eurasian boy never made the slightest movement toward him. He gave in with a note of hesitation, surrendered, again and again seduced.

"I've no idea how long I watched them, seduced myself and envious. Peers, I thought. Beauty that is neither masculine nor feminine. Two boys loving each other with the knowledge and emotional fervor I believed only women could have. Only we. I marveled at the refinement and tenderness of their touch, at their persistent fire. Was there anything they could envy women?

"Fascination is always mixed with envy. With the fruitless longing for identification. The longing to take part. Such boys carry a dream for me. The dream of an elegance that has cast aside the adored beauty of woman and replaced it with itself. Their self-assurance and ease is carried by a whole male culture and is secretly worshiped. They do not only embody themselves. They strive for a godly image old as the world and eternally in fashion: the hermaphrodite. The female embodied in the male.

"Where is my own godly image, I wondered. The archetypal cultural image I could embody in one of its endless glorious variations? A female image of human completeness and self-sufficiency? A painful void. I dream about those beautiful, decadent boys who have each other and the world at their feet. I train myself to play their role, I try to copy them. I put on their costume. I fantasize being one of them.

"I looked at myself again in a mirror, and smiled at the striking similarity. Three felines of apparently the same kind. I looked back at them—and fell into someone else's gaze. Someone was studying, and perhaps comparing, me!

"The pageboy had been there the whole time, leaning against the other side of the piano. I hadn't paid attention. Now I looked into an adolescent's masked eyes. A round face, a straight-cut fringe of henna-red hair trimmed to a very short page cut. A short purple velvet vest. The arm in a white, romantic sleeve posed on the piano, holding the contemplative head. Legs in white stockings and lacquer shoes, leisurely crossed. Short baggy pants of the same purple velvet. A simple black mask that gave the face a grave, grown-up note. His limbs, his whole body had the relaxed deliberateness of a child. One who is too young to participate in passion but knows its promise. Who had brought him there?"

Claire had not touched her champagne. She seemed to be sitting on the edge of her chair. Her face, hit by the candle, looked pale. Her red mouth stood out eagerly. She was leaning forward, as though she wanted to push into my story.

"Are you all right?" I served myself another glass. "Shall I go on?"

She didn't move from her tense position. Her voice, almost in anguish: "If only you wouldn't interrupt!"

"*Pardon*. Where was I? Yes, the boy . . . Having noticed that I had noticed him, he slowly lifted his head out of his hand, two fingers still on his cheek. It was a movement of startling grace. I was struck by the directness of this acknowledgment. My interest wasn't perceived as an intrusion, on the contrary. Was this the next generation of boys—growing up with androgynous men, allowed to assert themselves with grace instead of aggression? I moved my glance back to the two lovers, then gave it another try. Was I mistaken about his age? Could a precocious child possibly play that way with an adult?

"His eyes had followed mine to the couple. They rested there for a moment, his head inclined, returned to me with a coy pride. He must belong to them. A young brother? He bore no resemblance. In fact his dissimilarity was striking. I noticed his hand, now resting in the air, the palm upward, the two last fingers curled in, the others slightly stretched out. I flashed my glance down to his feet—tiny, unlikely feet. Then upward again, searching his body. With an uncanny promptitude he changed position. He placed his hand on the piano and rose up as if to show me what I was trying to see.

"The picture formed. I saw the breasts under the folds of the ample shirt and bolero. A woman.

"I had mistaken her for an adolescent boy because of her delicacy, her costume with the short pants, her frankness. Now she didn't look that young anymore. A woman dressed like a pageboy but not trying to hide her sex. A woman interested in men? Ambiguous men like those two? Like myself? Was she taking me for a man or had she seen through my disguise?

"What if she had watched me dancing? She would have seen me with another woman, not with a man. I had a flash of a thought: if I were a heterosexual woman myself, my greatest desire would be to get one of those refined, decadent boys. I would watch them, stalk them, try to pick out and capture the one, the special one interested in a woman as well. At least in a woman resembling an innocent boy.

"My heart started beating. Her interest was so free of probing, veiling, securing, I concluded it was set on preestablished rails. She was taking me for a man.

"She kept looking at me with the same grave curiosity. I put my hand on my heart and bowed. The hint of a smile crossed her face. She lifted her chin, a prince waiting for further worship. I went a few steps closer and bowed again. This time she imitated my gesture, placing her hand on her heart. I repeated it with every step. She didn't move out of her position. She was simply standing there, calm and relaxed, her left hand on the piano, her right hand on her heart.

"With my last reverence I arrived in front of her. I tried to read her age, to look behind her mask. She waited. I lifted my hand, I reached—"

Claire's body went straight back in her chair. It was a movement as sudden as the return of the bowstring after the arrow is shot. "Why are you telling me this?"

"What—what do you mean?"

"Are you sure this is your story?"

"My story?"

She came forward again, frowning, her gaze trying to pierce the darkness. Trying to pierce my skin.

"What's the matter, Claire? Can't it be my story?"

"You must be kidding." Her sidelong gaze continued to measure me out. "A *bal masqué*. What else? Strangers, masked identity, no risk involved. The easiest fantasy. How predictable! You want me to tell you how your story ends?"

"I can't wait." I'd never seen her in such a cutting mood.

"Do you really think you change anything in that banality, that age-old conquest fantasy, by changing the sex of one person? Nothing changes, I tell you. I know the story by heart. Everybody does."

She flung one arm over the back of her chair, advancing

her shoulder in the proud, provocative way I recognized from our first meeting.

"So. The woman guides him out of the bar. He follows her up the stairs. He'd follow her anywhere. She knows the house. They arrive at a room. She takes a hidden key. Opens the door, locks it behind them. The room is a boudoir. Of course, a fire is burning. There's no other light. She leans against the wall. Lets him touch her, standing. Then takes him to the chaise longue. Lets him take her but not undress her. Not take off her mask. Then she sends him away. End of the story . . . 'your' story."

"Pretty good . . . " I was surprised by my husky voice.

"Pretty banal, isn't it?"

"*Your* story," I nodded, hurt by her scorn. "You are missing the details."

"Such as?"

"When we arrived at the room, having passed the statue in the hall, I blindfolded her with my silk scarf . . ."

"Oh yes, the scarf! How could I forget . . . Mystery added to mystery. No romantic story without blindness, right?" She paused. I was alarmed by her anger. "And what has happened to the scarf?" she asked, leaning in with a false smile. "Have you ever wondered about this detail?"

I stared at her. Was she intruding into my story? Was she part of it? I rushed to shut her out: "The woman has kept it forever after that night. Nobody had ever made love to her like that." I saw her raise her head to hold back what seemed to be bitter contempt. "She kept it as a symbol of her blindness," I insisted. "Because she let the stranger go, unknown. The lover of her life—she never knew it was a woman."

"The lover of her life. What else? A woman! And how would your story claim a difference? Didn't your woman try to act precisely like a man?"

"My woman?" I smiled. "My story tells that a woman is different with a woman—even if she thinks the other is a man."

"Of course, Alma Runau. That's what it's all about. Your old story: A woman is better than a man. You would love to prove that to me, wouldn't you? But you have no proof."

"That's right. There's no proof. There are only details. There are secrets . . ." I reminded myself to get on a step ahead of her. "A woman will not reveal her intimate secrets to a stranger, a man taking power over her. Her body will take the pleasure it can take from the situation and keep its secrets. Only a woman, one of the same kind, can read her body. Touch, find the gate, the spot under the left arm where the blouse has a triangular hole cut in it to ease the movement . . . Once a gate is found, the body can't resist telling."

Claire rose up as if to shrug off what I had said. She went two steps toward the mulberry tree and followed the scars of its bark with her fingers. Then she leaned her back against the tree. I couldn't see her face in the moon shade. But I saw the defiant movement of her head as she addressed me: "The lover of her life, right? And she didn't keep this miracle-maker. Instead, she kept the scarf!"

"I was blind, too. Another detail you would have missed. I had never met a woman who gave her body so freely. When I left her, the second gong resounded through the house. I went down the staircase, through the hall where everybody was screaming, applauding, taking off their masks. I wandered about, looking for Jan and Mieke. I felt sad. Something momentous had happened. More than a banal conquest. The perfection I thought I had reached in my role, had been hers in a way. She had told me her secrets, I had told her nothing about myself. I couldn't give up my mask, give myself. I envied the woman who had found a lover like me. I had never found such a lover. Not even among women.

"Was this the rite of passage I had wanted? This knowledge? I had thought I knew all about my role. But now I saw. It is the woman who creates the male role. Her surrender creates his conquest. She, giving herself, creates his ability to take her. No woman had ever brought me to the realization: it was I who was created and I who received."

I paused. In the silence I heard the breeze. Claire in the shade of the tree had not moved.

"I had a great longing to see this woman again, show her myself, know her . . . learn from her. I ran back up the stairs to the room. I looked all over the house. I searched for the two beautiful boys as well . . ."

Claire stepped out of the shade. She leaned onto the back of her chair. Her face came toward me, full of clownish pity: "The lady vanishes . . ."

She disappeared into the house, tossing back over her shoulder: "But you don't ever know why, do you?"

Part Four

CLAIRE HELLER:
A LETTER, AN INVITATION

TIME: SHORTLY AFTER LEAVING THE SOUTH OF FRANCE

CLAIRE'S SIXTH LETTER

I could apologize, Alma.

The sudden arrival, my equally sudden departure. Unannounced, was I welcome? I do not imagine you have grieved over my absence. Your cherished solitude, swallows, the mulberry tree, passionflowers growing over the stone walls, cornflowers in a wineglass on your work table. I have not tried to forget you.

Perhaps you already know. What I have not managed to say, what I tried to tell, could not tell you, had never tried before.

In the small garden, near the village. It might have been said. What you have meant over the years. Why you? The question cuts, exposes. Shall I admit loneliness?

There are people like that, they long for late nights, will talk until morning, arrive exhausted at the same locked door. Then leave you, driven away by desire for truth, it's improbabilities. It is not possible to say good-bye, kiss you on both cheeks, plan another meeting. You, who would listen. How shall I tell this story to you?

I drift. Build deception. Try hard to give you the code. Retreat again into hieroglyphic.

Early morning, the village is dark. Shall I write my name in lipstick on the town wall?

On the plane home, I ask for paper. We will arrive in

New York at the end of a page. This letter, like so many others, may not make its way to the mail.

Are you reading? I imagine you reading.

You have made sweet syrup. From elderberry, growing wild along the road. You lean back in your chair, sip from the tall glass. Now that I have dared, there is much to say. Impressions, hoarded over a lifetime. Saved for the one whom I must have known would appear some day. *Par hasard.* On a park bench, waiting for the bus, at a café table.

It happens like that, perhaps always. On the deck of a ship, in darkness, the last night before embarkation. The face of the stranger scarcely visible, the far light of the lounge. A word or two, slipped past the sentries, smuggled out. There are such people. They dread above all to be known. Invent one tale or another. Anything will do. Put your ear to the wall. You hear them knocking against their cell. Desperately tapping out their story.

It happens like that. Without a word, in a house near the harbor. The stranger whom you might recognize and fail to recognize. The one to whom one day you will tell your story. Have I told it already? That place, beneath my left arm, where I have hidden my longing to hand myself over.

When did you recognize me? I would say, not yet in my red dress. Still not as you told your story. Perhaps the moment I vanished. Because I had been recognized? Because I had not been?

The woman who disappears from the masked ball. Perhaps I wish to live out her part in your story. Force you to find me in the one who had gone by the time you returned. Did you return? I doubt it.

Either way, the question remains. Why did she leave? Because she had recognized you? Because she hadn't? This part of the story you cannot know. Her uncertainty. This tale you cannot tell. Groping in darkness, will it be male or female, does not matter.

This rather: ballroom snuffed out, mask askew, eyes unfocused. Woman lying in her own piss. Cat licking up vomit. The taste of that dawn, its deadly certainty, the next and the next will be no different. No, I do not believe you turned back. I do not believe you were able to do it. I do not believe it was your story.

You, too, cannot be certain. Am I writing myself into your tale? Taking it over? Spinning a thread of connection between us? The boys, for instance, what shall be said about them? The leopard brothers, your androgynous apparitions of beauty. Who were they?

I would say . . .

Warren, you remember him? had known them too, had gone out with another boy one night to beat up those queers in the alley.

I would say . . .

Those boys, they ran into me later. One of them, his name was Geoffrey, told me he'd gone to my brother's funeral.

It had been raining, he said. A terrible day. Saw the announcement in the papers, went by himself. Threw earth on Dennie's coffin, he said.

Even now I would say: he was the first who lived the life of the body. The others, warriors, throwers of beer cans, in armed shirts sitting on the stoop late summer evenings, I knew their story by heart. Take them to bed, they hide behind muscle, from first touch cower behind flexed biceps, not to be reached, in flight from sensation. A man sure of his body does not swagger, a man capable of sex does not swagger.

It made sense, finally; I understood the offense, the outrage to which the warriors were subjected, catching sight of men who set out, as I did, to live the body. He knows, the muscular one knows: if it is possible for them, it must be possible for him. They pass him beneath the streetlight, fear of contagion, temptation to soften, reinhabit his senses. He lifts his arm, gets to his feet, shield ready, calling out insults, warding off danger.

I touched him, husband, brother, fellow-traveler, arching beneath me. A boy like that. Sits up in bed, bends over to place his cheek on my thigh. Remembers the girl in the sailor suit. The shack in the garden. The rose vine growing over the incinerator. The little kid sitting there, waiting.

Secrets, I'd imagined, a lost world. He builds it between his hands. I move to the edge of the bed. Hours pass, he is still there, breathing memory.

The other sits on the balcony, smoking hash. It can't last, he knows it. Sentimental interlude, he is drinking a glass of brandy, cracks pumpkin seeds between his teeth. Geoffrey goes to him, out there it's morning. Kneels at his feet. I hear them, my go-out-and-do-anything boys, laughing.

Geoffrey wakes from a bad dream, rose burning on the nightstand next to his bed. His skin has erupted, he cannot be touched, cries out, starving for sensation. I watch, from across the room.

Is this why men seek women, call it lust? Deeper, there is dread, to wake at midnight, crying in darkness. Those who swagger want to crawl, those who thrust long to creep into. The urge is sadness. What they call instinct, that is the knowledge: he is alone, could die of hunger if she does not touch him.

His breathing is shallow, he is afraid to waste away without me? That is the fear he calls by the name of sex? The itch that drives him, to find a woman, take her? Even if she cannot touch. Even when tomorrow, he spits out time, gets rid of yesterdays.

The bully, stripping pants from a small boy, pushing him out from the schoolyard, legs too suddenly naked. He grows up, he says he wants to be laid. Believe him. Lay this child to your breast. Another. He leers at the girl in her striped pinafore on the parched highway. He pulls over, leans from the window, cries out he is longing to eat her. Believe him.

You, far away, in your garden, moving your table inside because of the storm. You imagined, I suppose, a different marriage? You stand at the door, watch the sky darken. Water settles itself in the mulberry tree, pours over the stump next to the window, gathers between the sharp stones, scatters the redtails.

If only you knew them as I do. Their loneliness, disguised as desire. Timidity, hidden by the thrust. Archaic sorrow they want you to weep, their small hand groping. That man whose power you imagine, why is it you cannot strip him? Decipher his need, uncertainty?

My husband, his lover: they come to me arm in arm. Geoffrey has tied flowers in his hair. Eyes blue, skin the color of quail's egg. Dark hair, braided? it falls to his shoulders. The other lies down on the bed at my side. I undress him. He takes my hand, leads me to him. Waits for instruction.

He fears motion, does not look at me, his lips are dry, he is afraid he will choke on my tongue. Says I want to possess him, says he does not want me to possess him, pleads with me to possess him. Enters, hides his head in my arms.

I touch, remember a lullabye, say nothing, lift his body, lower it against me. Geoffrey is holding my head in his hands. I teach the other to move. He lifts his head, searches the distance, looks for my eyes, is helpless, desperate, throws the night around his shoulders, wants to go on, wants to go on.

Look at me, the other had begged. Does it please you? Touch me, Geoffrey had said. Is it softer than yours? His skin had been softer.

Skin, its inhabiting, infinitely patient courtship of flesh. And we had, the three of us, done it, we had buckled. Uncombed desire. Entangled ourselves with desire.

The way nipples rise, ask to be sucked. The brief pride of the male sex, its downfall, shrinking to childhood. Sorrow that comes after. Lonely ambitions of flesh stripped naked.

Geoffrey walks to the door. The world, he says, throwing back the shutters. The other accepts, stands up on the bed to spread his arms. He runs to my boy, throws his arms around him, carries him out onto the balcony, rocks him above the streetlights, perilously.

The loud-mouth girl. Ask her, she'll tell you she

crossed the world with them. The trip took thirty-eight days. Three months, eight weeks. Or years, does it matter? Didn't sleep, she'll insist, that whole time. Ate nothing but fish eggs and oysters. Got a bad tan on the deck of a small boat. Tracked them down the harbor where they traded in powders. Left nothing, not to imagination.

You remember her? Setting out from a taco stand on a California highway, seeking knowledge? Her hunger for the body. To throw herself over its rapids. She wants you to know, she left no land virgin, unexplored. Went higher, without foothold. Knew fear, finally, the one essential: what if this stranger, or some other, becomes necessary? That place, beneath her left arm, where she has hidden her longing to hand herself over. What if this stranger, in a house near the harbor, learns her so well she cannot do without him?

Ask her, she'll tell you: Sex is only possible after that fear. Until then, the body withholds itself, guards its delights, keeps them secret. Lies to itself about the scale of its pleasures, knows nothing until it meets up with that fear. And survives it.

She has come from far away, has been inflected with the exotic, carries the odor of distant places. What is sex, she asks? You recognize the irony. Looked at objectively, she says: a mere question of touch, brief or prolonged sensations. Touch the body yourself, hand it over to another. Put parts of his body into yours, take him. Roll, writhe, tumble, grasp, push, stroke, rub. Cry out for the return of that pleasure.

Much of this familiar, nesting, fondling; some catches

your breath, makes the pulse hammer beneath your breast. Touch places not usually touched, open where opening did not seem possible. Close down, be opened again, find the way to him, cross, climb up, be tossed down again. Beads of sweat along the upper lip, flesh cringing away, afraid of the lightness delivered, pleas muttered, breath beneath breath, why this? why this terror?

Inexplicable. Unless, unless this risk, exposing these chasms of preference, known only to you, in that rhythm and sequence, where to go hard, where to tread softly, what must be said, what at all costs must never be spoken, demands certainty. The infallible promise of being there, to do it again. But you know, sliding his hand to that place and no other, how fragile, impermanent, this bond of sensation. Tomorrow, he will look the wrong way down the street, will dance into some other crowd, disappear from a masked ball, keep walking, never turn back. It happens.

I remember the night. Cobbled street, gabled roofs, a town near the sea. I remember, a house near the harbor, windows of bottle glass, a terrace, plane trees on the water. We had walked late, from abbey to mill, Geoffrey whistled, kicked a stone. The other, pushing a strand of white hair out of his eyes, kicked stones, unquiet as leaves.

I caught sight of the question, crossing the bridge, trailing after, looking out from shuttered window, limping behind us. Was it worth it? My life, unrolled at my feet, tearing downhill, hitting the stone wall, trapped there, unable to escape it. Was it worth it?

Let's dance, says Geoffrey.

Let's go to Egypt, smoke hash, traffic in fake antiquities.

Is that all, I say?

Hey baby, come with us.

Yeah, says the other.

Bone weary, weary in flesh. A night like others, unlike any other.

Was it weariness, fear? Whether I left them, they went on without me, does not matter. Grief draws grief to itself. A room in a house near the harbor. At dawn under the plane trees, on a terrace. Somewhere I stopped, couldn't go forward. Had done it all, everything. Left nothing, not to imagination. To mourn one is to mourn the other. Now and before indistinguishable. All loss is the same loss; chosen or endured, the body weeps sweat, tears, urine, blood, does it matter? And weariness, that old tune so full of sadness. Can you tell it from fear?

I know, it's hard to accept. The front seat of a car on Hollywood Boulevard. The slick bad boy behind the blackjack table. A window that opens on the river. Boys at school. A boy who remembers. The masked ball, the stranger. The women's quarters, behind the sanctuary. The place where Aphrodite first met Adonis.

Pomegranates grow in the walled gardens. That is how I tell it, am unable to tell it another way. Want you to understand: there is no choice. To survive is to get there. From that weariness, or call it fear, one asks only that it be far, long ago, impossible.

CLAIRE'S SEVENTH LETTER

Over distance, in your small house in the country, you have been made into the listener.

The one whose gaze remains steady, who leaves the telephone ringing, does not need to sneeze, does not rummage in her pocket for a crumpled bit of paper. In this form you can be trusted, briefly.

What might have been said.

That day at the old house. A tree growing up over the front door. Did we speak of it? A sparrow buried in the garden, the grave marked by two stones. We walk back from the old house, stop at a restaurant. It rains. *Madame* (who has warned us, nonetheless has seated us outside) brings out a striped umbrella.

We are silent; there is difficulty; the rain, all that we are not speaking. The girl in her blue dress runs out to save the doll who has been lording it over us from her cement throne beneath the tree. The child screams, runs back into the kitchen where we have seen her, shelling peas. The large yellow dog comes back across the courtyard, a dead kitten between its teeth.

Madame has come out to stand in the doorway. She stamps her foot. *"Ce chien sale,"* she mutters, *"il est toujours comme ça."*

We do not manage to smile at her tolerant disgust. I stare at my plate. It is you who tell me. *Madame* has wrapped the kitten in newspaper, carried it out through the kitchen. You do not think it will be buried in a marked grave, in the garden of a house no longer visited.

A death in the family, I ask? Is that why they did not come back? Or did they know it was the last summer? The husband perhaps knew, but did not tell his wife? Or the mother, her children? Afraid. The farewells, the impossible ceremonies of absence.

You fold your napkin next to the wineglass on the table. Watch the rain. It is making small oceans, ruined fountains in the stone court.

Silence. We look at the stones in the old town wall, see moss growing, gather a handful of rain. I think I will anoint you with it. Let it slip through my fingers.

Small white cups, basket weave at the rim, coffee arrives finally. We busy ourselves, stir darkness, neither of us takes milk today.

Late afternoon; we have emptied the basket of bread into our pockets. You feed sparrows on the way back out of town. Probably it has not occurred to you I have tried to tell you about myself. In the next minute, perhaps. Rounding the corner, standing before the gate. If the hinge squeaks something may be said, something started that cannot easily be stopped. There are such people; once they begin you have them on your hands for a lifetime. As if you've saved them from drowning. As if they owe you so much you can't get rid of them.

And if I dared to tell you I do not believe in time? Have crumpled it, tossed it away into the corner. Stepped out of it, kicked it from me. Shed it. Raw, without skin, stood free then. Naked.

Is it so hard to believe? Life wears thin, like anything

else. One day you cannot go on. Catch sight of yourself. After the ball. Besotted shadow, slithering homeward. Some people never get out. I managed.

Yes, I managed.

If you had done it, you would have asked, how is it possible? I never asked. I wondered only, why this place rather than another? Perhaps the mountains, their chalky darkness when I arrived the first time. The old man, he was my guide, went on about the forests of fir and cedar. Later, I saw carob trees, spring rain in the barley fields. There were vineyards, climbing slopes from which it was already possible to glimpse the sea. And the gardens, the women's quarters behind the sanctuary. Walled gardens, I'd imagined them that way.

We traveled by mule: over hills and ridges, ate tangerines, bitter almonds, rode through orchards. At nightfall a simple meal, hard bread, olives, dried octopus. Looking back I wouldn't say it was an easy journey. The rivers were old, they had made deep beds for themselves, we crossed them at daybreak.

In time it became apparent I knew the way as well as the old man. Would pull myself up to cry out the name of a village, the whitewashed steps, the fields of anemones.

My brother, Dennie, he asked me once:

How do I know?

Know what, you eggplant?

How do I know I'm not a boy in some other boy's dream?

You can't know, I told him. Maybe the boy back there has dreamed you up, to keep me company, does it matter?

A Letter, an Invitation

At road's end, where the ball ends, you do not ask
about the road that finds you. If it leads to a small village, river nearby, grove of walnut trees, you accept it.
Farther off, the river foaming from a cavern at the base
of towering cliffs. I recognized the place, rank vegeta-
tion, fissures and crannies of the rocks, knew from the
first moment the green veil spread over the stream in the
chasm below me. It was the place, they said, Aphrodite
first met Adonis.

The temple: hewn stone, columns of granite, I have no
theory. For the first time I believed my brother was
dead. Walked beneath walnut trees, looked up through
falling water to the top of the cliffs. And the white goat
grazing at the edge of the cliffs, all familiar.

You could say, grief cannot tolerate time, chafes at it,
wears it away. You could say I went back there because I
owed it to him. A queen between the sheets, I'd promised myself. One day, much later, I figured it out. That
kid died because I left him. Couldn't go on without me,
turned to ice.

Why this place rather than another? There were of
course the mountains, their chalky darkness. Villages
hidden among groves of fig trees. Hawks nesting. And
the teachers, the old women. They said it had all been as
nothing. My life, nothing. Sensation without meaning,
flesh profaned, body torn from the sacred. They knew all
about it. Been deceived, choked to dust on sensation.
Came back from afar. To the walled gardens, a mile from
the sea, behind the sanctuary, to teach the ones who
might be chosen the following spring.

Will it be possible? To lift you, as I lifted my brother,
to transport you? Will you be moved? Is it probable you

can be seized, carried away? Will you come? To begin
with I was lonely. Or perhaps: for the first time acknowledged sadness. Alone, among the others. Women of all
ages.

The first time we went out to the grove. Wandered,
our eyes closed, fingers groping. How tell the god's tree
from the others? But I knew: it would be better to ask no
questions.

Pines, the darkness of pines; palms, tangerines, the
flowering orange, almonds, and cypress. Telling you
now, I fear you will take it as dream, a vision. Oaks,
sycamores, black poplars. Do not take it like that. It happened. Dawn of the second day and we had gathered. It
was, I thought, a tree like others. One of the women,
(had she taken pity?) pointed upward. Yes, I saw: wild
roses growing up through the tall pine.

Shall I explain? Shall I leave you to bear the confusion, as I did? Surely by now you know. Why I could not
easily tell you? Why I have not been able to tell this
story before?

We were joined by the men. The tree, dug out: we
bore it between us. In silence, single file, barefoot. The
tree carried on our shoulders. In silence, planted it in
the garden, behind the sanctuary. The old women, they
dug the earth in a circle, surrounded the tree. Planted
barley. It had been done before.

That first time, I did what I could. I recall: the drums
beating. The uneasiness; my arms, moved by a will of
their own, by memory? Arms linked, from dusk to dusk,
we moved in a circle, the old men and the young boys,
singing.

The second day: the blowing of trumpets.

The loud-mouth girl. Ask her, she'll tell you. They danced all night. Fell exhausted, cymbals screeching, drums crying, trumpets wailing, flutes droning. Ask her, she'll say it had been for this she left the brother.

You remember the girl; the long march through the sexual desert. Trading herself for a handful of water. Sun-blackened, washed up finally on a far shore. From the wooden shack near the alley. To the walled garden behind the sanctuary. A straight line? The next station?

I ask again: can you be seized, transported? To ask, a confession.

The third day. The body, prepared. Procession to the river, white robes, robes of saffron, water splashed from tortoise shell, the girls chasing the girls chasing the boys, the matrons laughing, rubbing the body with cyclamen, with oil of violet; bathed, we spread ourselves out on the banks, were rubbed by the old men with Tyrian oil and the doves flew over, hovered above us, fanning the air, in love with the smell.

If you could catch a boy, you caught him, sprinkled him with rose water. If you could be caught, you were sprinkled with sage from the mountains. From a terrible distance, I watched the others.

The third night, a ring of fires. Silent. The old women had grown beards. The priests dressed in women's garments. They had told us, from among the women, from among the men: two would be chosen.

That first year, it could not have been I who was chosen. I, in my weariness, afflicted by flesh, still wearing its burden. Could not imagine my legs spread, calling the goddess. That seduction. My eyes, darkened with kohl. Wary, suspicious. Could not conceive my arms enclosing the frail, the timid body of the god.

That night, we gathered to watch.

The woman, she was still fertile, took the boy, lay him on a bed of leaves, raised him, straddled. Why this one rather than another? But I knew: ask no questions. Breasts heavy, thighs majestic, the fleshy gravity, an earthy slowness. Yes, the goddess. She must have looked at her boy like this.

That look. If I am unable to make you see. Its sadness, triumph of possession, a certainty: what will be done that night must be accomplished. And tenderness, like no other: it swallows his fear, his virginity. How can I tell you what I know about sex if you cannot see?

She takes her breast in her hand. Should I be watching this? The fullness of her. As if she fears she will burst, drown him. Is it I who want to cry out?

The heat of her. Her heaviness: ripening toward him. Will he be smothered alive? Crushed by the weight of her? She lifts his head, moves him toward her. As if she knows: he wishes to run, fears to be crushed, is afraid to be buried alive by her. He closes his eyes. I see: she has opened his mouth.

The boy feeds. On her eyes. Cups his hands. He nuzzles her breast, worships. Goes to his knees, he plants her. She has spread herself out, he roams through her. She has raised herself up, he climbs. She is midnight, pours down over him. He is small, curls up at her side. She dawns. He is shaken to life, arises. I, too, would not have been able to imagine: virility's grace, its sensuous ease, endurance.

By dawn of the next day, the god has been slain. That is their story. Cut down in the fields. One drop of his blood a crimson dew on every blade of sprouting barley.

The boy rests in her arms. He knows, she can pound his bones, mix him with wine, swallow him whole. To strengthen her, endow the earth, with which now, toward morning, she is covered. And she will rise, whole. He will be cast off on the river.

The boy rests between her thighs. Ceremonial actor, he imagines the terror he might feel. The willing surrender. The accomplice-sacrifice. The old women, they are at work. Shaping a man of earth, dressing their sacrificial doll in pine needles, laying the little god in a bed of bark.

The god has been slain. They lift a knife, stab him. The man of earth bleeds violets. He has been cut down. They raise a scythe, slaughter him. The earth man bleeds corn.

The boy watches. The woman holds his hand between her legs, soothes him. His terror has become real. She wants him to rise. Strokes his sex, woos it. With breath, with spells and lips and fingers. But he has fallen, given it all, been drained of his sap. And so they mourn him.

Dawn. High noon. Twilight. Darkness.

When it is all over, after the mourning, the fasting, the shaved heads, the procession to the river, the casting off of the man of earth in his boat of tree bark, the boy who had made love to the goddess was given to me.

Someone, behind me, pushed me forward. The boy, standing in the river. Someone, next to me, lifted my arm, cupped my hands. I sprinkled him with water.

Claire Heller

Why, I wondered?

That night there was joy. Why me, rather than
another? And wildness. Trumpets blaring, flutes beating,
drums wailing. We came back from the river. Drawing
the goddess. The woman who had carried her all night
was carried by us. To pipes and tambourines, the path,
strewn with flowers. And we were told. Yes, we were
promised. The boy would arise again the following
spring.

I should have told you. About time, the slowness; they
all seemed to feel it. The ones who went back to their
villages. The ones who remained, in the walled gardens,
behind the sanctuaries. Except the woman who had
been chosen. They used to send for her. When someone
was ill, birth impending, in the days of her blood. Then,
she was sent out to cross the fields, walked there, her
head uncovered.

Sometimes I followed. The boy watched us, his bare
legs dangling over a wall of the men's quarters. He kept
an eye on us. No word was spoken. But somehow, in
time, things were imparted.

I noticed. The traffic between our house and the men's
quarters. Sometimes, there would be a new woman
among us. Dressed like us, tending the crops as we did,
sitting with us after the night meal to hear the old
women tell their stories. Was she a stranger, straggling
about outside of time, as I was? In time I discovered.
Beneath her garments, she was a man.

Occasionally, one of the older women, or a young girl,
would be missing. I would catch sight of her in the pine
groves, selecting wild herbs, the dark berries, the cut-

tings of a particular bark. Bearded, she was learning their lore, I supposed. Whatever it was from which I was still excluded.

The day's tasks; what they were I scarcely remember: the usual things, I suppose. Weaving, carding flax, crushing the grain, squeezing berries.

A warm, still evening; the boy came for me. He carried a basket. The heavy bread brought over mornings and evenings from the village. Wineskin, purple figs ripened on the flat stones of the wall. Goat cheese.

The mountains, closer than usual, goats visible, grazing at its peaks. I did not ask where we were going. Did it matter? His manner grave, uncertain; he gave the impression he had been sent to do this.

Long legs, I had noticed before. Dark skin, baked into him. Dark gold, or brushed up, like the hide of the donkey. He rode behind me, hands crossed in front of me, holding the reins.

I'd seen him riding before, lonely in the twilight. His back straight, legs stretched forward. There were places, known perhaps only to him. He pointed to flowers and trees, named them. Carob, the long, dark fruit; the olive trees that grew with us, up into the mountain.

In those days, still the beginning, I repeated everything to myself. I am here, there is the river, dropping down from above us, eagles soaring.

He surprised me with small villages, thrusting up out of the stone face, hidden from view, from below. The sea caught his attention. He stretched out his hand. Now the sea, too, picking its way, plodding upward, with us.

Alma, if I insist, do not take it as dream, as vision,

what do I mean? If I say, it happened: what kind of sense will you make from it? I admit, it is strange.

Holm oak, he tied the donkey beneath it. Uncovered his basket, spread a cloth. Leaned at the tree. He had pomegranates, split them open against a stone. The red juice. On his hands, on the white rock. Do I mean it took place in the realm of the senses? Yes, I remember. He fed me. Drop by drop, squeezing the thick blotched skin of the fruit between his palms.

I had the impression: this boy is trying to teach me. I thought: he has made me naked, has been told to touch me. I said to myself: I am here, between his legs, leaning against him, my head tipped back. He has a small, hard strawberry between his teeth, it is not yet ripe, he has pushed it between my lips, I am receiving.

A cypress; it must have been a cultivated garden. Near us: flat, circular stones, ash-gray in the long twilight, a silver sage growing between them. A stand of lavender, late bees hovering between purple stalks. I tell myself: he gives himself. He is something to eat. I am enfolded.

Far off, a donkey calls to ours, its cry rusted. He has trickled a river of wine across my breast, licks me dry again. I yawn, he breathes into my mouth. White moth rocks at tip of lavender sheath, flits, rocks, sucks, possesses. The boy bends over me.

I had thought him slender; he closes my eyes with his lips. He has grown large, his hands enclose, he turns my head; there is wind, it remembers salt, there are fields of white moths that are, he says, flowers. I am sinking, falling away, there are limbs, they wrap him; there are fingers, they walk all over him. There are breasts: they are his? mine? another's?

Heavy, he has straddled, has come toward the place where there is a question of entry, crossing. Wetness, an invitation. The pulse of difference, outcry against separation. Offers himself, his sex overfull, nippled, asking to be delivered.

My legs, they open; there, where hunger has not before declared itself as hunger, I suck: he ripens, carries over into, has brought to fill, to feed me, his milky whiteness.

Has been sent to teach this, the man-mother? Rocks, croons, his milk runs down between my thighs. Been taught (by whom? how? to what end?) so to present his ripening pod. As she, who bears, offers breast for first feeding? A thrust, inward, beyond tenderness: the knowledge, flesh entering flesh, life depends on this.

I want him back, have I never before been put to the male sex? I grope for him; have I been filled before? He says: the milk has been drained; I must wait, teach him to fill again. He lays himself out at my side, loses his heaviness, grows lean, timid, remorseless: has gone back to being a boy.

Homeward: darkness, the moon riding steadily downward. If he has been given to me, for this. What is my purpose?

CLAIRE'S EIGHTH LETTER

I imagine you recognize: the practice of magic. To make crops grow, earth fertile, keep the world sap flowing. It is hard, I know, to know it as worship. We, who do not inhabit the flesh, take possession over the body, regard it as property: my hand, your skin, his lips, her belly, their sex, cannot easily understand. To worship, with the body; find sacred, not only flesh, but its behavior; to know this longing to be inhabited, seized, possessed by the goddess. To call that desire. And surrender, that awe-filled giving over to the world's necessity. Do you understand it? Perhaps you, more easily than I?

The old women, nighttime, in the walled garden. They told us: All who worship, who serve, perform the sacred sexual act, carry between hands, lips, thighs, the earth's fertility. We were all, they said, Aphrodite, and the boy. The eagle sowing its nest. The barley sprouting. The south wind gathering pollen. The snake endowing itself. The egg flowering.

There are things, impossible to tell if the other does not already understand. That is the fear. To give the best-kept secrets. What if, lying beside you on the grass, next to a garden overgrown upon itself, near a house with eyes, one reached out to trust another, and found the distance between you so large the one lying beside seemed to grow steadily beyond reach of your fingers?

What would happen, I ask, if we, too, understood sex

as world necessity? Fundamental, magical act? Without
which, and the hands that have made their way to your
breast, the lips that open you, fingers that search out
your pleasure, there would be weariness, withering,
parching, dying back among things? The rose parched
on its trellis, the geranium dying in the garden, swallow
unmoving below the eaves.

If we, too, falling to bed, believed that from this sweat
that flowers between us, the cornfield prospered? From
the juice that spurts, the mouth that receives, the womb
that quickens, far from us, in swamps, in deserts, what
must live and be born is brought to conception?

I want to tell you. More than anything else. About this
boy. His melancholy, the distance between him and
others. He came to live with us, in the women's quarters,
behind the sanctuary. Or perhaps, had been there
already? Long before?

Mornings, I would see him, before the others had
wakened, near the stone wall. Trying to turn himself to
stone. Or to flower. I saw him, at midday, watching the
snakes cross the compound. Trying to shed himself,
learn to slither? Others spoke, called out to him,
repeated his name: he was far, they might have crossed a
world to reach him. Stretched out their hand, found him.
Still, beyond their fingers.

I go to him; at the first touch he is aroused, wakened.
Has come to life, is rooted, pinned back to us. Have I
been given for this, to keep him here, preserve him?
The old women, they say: Touch is the sacred.

Yes, I know: it can't be easy. We, who use sex in the
vain hope to get back to the body, long for the terror, the

torment of desire, imagine passion as alien intrusion. What can we make of this people? These, whose sacred forms embrace the flesh?

The story we tell; our tedious tale of forbidden desires places itself against culture. The woman who falls because of desire. Marries the carpenter, runs off with the gypsy. The man haunted by a fallen woman. The child born out of wedlock, nameless. The nobleman who murders another man's child, driven to destroy his wife's transgression. Women of the streets, the sad men who buy them.

Modern statement of the old theme. The husband's folly takes a mistress. The woman runs off to Paris. Another, tracked down by her husband. Man dies on the beach for love of a boy.

Our secrecy. The locked doors, dismal hotel rooms, ornate palaces of black-sheet pleasure. Eyes closed, lowered, shame of the flesh. The terrible streets of our transgressions. Belligerent assertions of freedom, sexual cruelty, desolate liberations.

He is young. How young? Unbearded. Since then I have imagined: this boy longed to follow the god. Be cut down in the cornfields. Escape the senses. The body not yet fully developed. Dennie, as he might have been if he'd grown older. Was it for that? To keep him alive, to make up for my brother? He throws himself down. Disappears in the grass. For now, he is slender. The hair on his arms, the sun turning it high-red, golden.

A question of touch. How to reach him. It is a matter of urgency. Perhaps, among them, none would have felt it but I? As if I, who had set out to live the life of the body, was growing finally into a body. As a child might. Drop by drop, that time, the blood-juice of pomegranate on my lips. And now, in return, owed the favor to him?

If that was sex (the slow ride into the mountains; the silence, the shadows that climbed the path before us, the heavy air beneath the tree), what was the other? In the parked car, in the streets, in the closed rooms, with the others?

What we call sex: the itch that cannot be stilled, the melancholy violence, that shame that comes after, the haunting loneliness that drops the lovers, beaches them, in their solitary plot of rock and dryness. Later, I understood what they had been trying to teach me. In the walled gardens, behind the sanctuary, the year, ripening upward, toward spring.

That first winter, learning to grow back into my senses. I was placed at the wall, sat there unmoving. Dawn, dusk, I heard the stones growing. I touched him; the boy, the man-mother of the mountains. He grew small, curled into me, made a nest of my limbs. Mornings, we wet the stones of the compound. Dripped oil, the water of almonds. The boy, close at my side, kept an eye on me. I heard the stones breathing.

The woman, she took my hand as we crossed the fields. In time, I, too, was invited. To offer my blood. I witnessed: the first shoot, the sprouting barley, the golden flax. She pointed, named them. I saw: they were I.

Since then, I have wondered. The obsessions that drive us, our lust: is it for this? To fall back into our hands, grow back out of the grass, be turned to earth and planted? Violent, we call that desire. Because we cannot make fruit grow from our passion? My breasts, they turned green. Oozed, split open. He sucked, his lips groping their way back to me, tasting of fig.

So what, you say?

I sense it. The way you stand up from the bench in the garden. Throw down the pages you are reading. Grow furious, take a few steps toward the gate, as if you imagine it would still be possible to go after me, call me back, sit me down opposite you in a café somewhere, make me listen.

When a man goes to bed with a woman, you say: does he allow her to lay him . . . in a bed of leaves? Suppose even: our culture built on the loss, the denial, the hidden quest for this mystery. Does that bring her to life? Restore her? He has jumped out from behind the wall. Has spread her beneath him. His hands on her throat. Does it matter, you ask, if he looks for the body's magical potency, its sacredness?

Shall we argue again? Shall I, in turn, grow wild, impatient? Get to my feet, crumple the paper, toss it aside?

The uses and abuses of theory. Isn't that what we wished to explore, examine? An exchange of letters, we said: laying back skin to reach the essential, the hidden.

And why is it I cannot tell what I know? The meaning, for instance, of this traffic. Between the men's quarters and the women's? Haven't you wondered?

In time, the timelessness ebbing, my senses clearing, I saw: the old question of gender. This careful division we make, at all costs preserve. They had undone it; bearded the women, given breasts to the men. The boy, living among us, must have been taught. To take the role of mother, assume its activity, assertion. To make use of his sex: to feed, to nurture.

Each time, entering me, the mountains our cradle, night folded on us: it was he who was woman. I, the child. So that in time I learned. That is what men seek in the sexual act. It is the role of mother they wish to assume, to master.

We look closer: the active and passive. The rules of gender. We place them in nature, insist the roles are there in our genes. Could it be: the two genders, they are always only mother and child?

The man: he who initiates. He determines the act. What does that mean? He takes her. In his arms. Sweeps her, off her feet. Carries her, to the bed.

Does, what mothers are always doing?

The question of gender: do I mean, it is hiding the old story of mother and child?

The old questions. We lift them, hold them before our eyes, turn them a new way, see them differently. A missing plane, neglected facet. The way gender hides truth; how sexual role disguises the real meaning of sexual desire; the way we have made instinct of lost memory, have attributed to the urgency of the flesh our unwept sorrows. The man, driven. To take woman. Longs, secretly, to play mother, to feed her?

You protest. Take up a pencil, mark the page.

Among us, you say: the woman, she who gives herself. She hands herself over to his need, takes care, lets him take pleasure, make use of her body. Surely, you say: that is what it means to be mother?

So, we dispute. As we have done, from first meeting. Will do, I am certain, the next time we meet.

You, are you unable to imagine the mother's assertion? You, too, must have known it. Fed when you were not hungry, filled when your mouth had not yet opened, broken into by that transgression, her uninvited crossing of boundary. Made one with her, when you wished to be one with yourself. Held captive. Delivered up to her rhythm. Overpowered by her need to fondle, to touch, to hold, to join. The fear of her thrust; that horror you cannot recall. The dread, primal: the breast penetrating, forcing entry, colonizing, possessing.

Have you imagined phallic, what was once, originally, the breast's power of intrusion? Have you imagined it all as fear, of him? Fear of man, the active gender, he who thrusts, you say: breaks into, enters?

The mother you imagine: helpless, subdued, subordinate being. The father you create: the phallic bully. Have you given to him her transgressive power?

And therefore you cannot imagine the man's longing to feed you, in the sexual act. And therefore, cannot conceive: the man-mother, who feeds.

The time came, it was inevitable; I was sent to live with the men. Was dressed in their clothes: the short robes, heavy sandals. Was taught to wrestle, to hunt, dance, run wild: up into the mountains, after the wild goats, leaping from the rocks, tumbling down through grass meadows.

The old men, at night they sat by our bed. They told

how the world had been made. Delivered up out of the one who had made herself. From rain and from dust. And she was alone, lonely; from her thighs, she made mountains; from her wetness, desiring herself, made seas. Trees grew from her tresses. When she sang, when she danced, when she walked, lonely in her nakedness: she spit on the earth. There were birds; the serpent biting its tail, the egg conceiving itself.

They told: their dread of that one who had made others. Her magnificence. The size of her, larger even than the world she made. Can you imagine?

I, in time, began to remember. Memory, they said, was the meaning of flesh. In time, I began to recall. They called that the body.

CLAIRE'S NINTH LETTER

It began with the senses. The itch of palms, longing to touch her. The ache of lips to enclose her. The way flesh crawls. The dread: to be crushed, annihilated by her. To drown, in the outpouring of her. Burst with her fullness, discharged into me. To be torn, broken. By her entry.

The old man, he who had once played the god, held me against him. He, who had known and endured her, knew how to become her. To soften his splendor, temper the power of his overpowering, fill, feed, enfold, fondle.

In the walled gardens, behind the sanctuary. Was that their mystery?

I, who have never been able to sleep. Wake, climb from the bed. Read, write letters. Tell myself stories. It was so, in the shack near the alley. On the long road, parched with desire. The old man: wets my lips. Closes my eyes.

His touch. Can I describe it? Fingers breathing. The way skin weeps, tells its story. The infant terror, waking in darkness. He is there, his hand, on my head. I remember Geoffrey, the skin erupted. Dennie, the shack in the garden. Stories, how they never managed to fill, feed, enfold, fondle. He is there, his touch carries fragrance. Wind enters, through the tall grass, moves through the window.

Do I mean: remembering the mother . . . he had no need to inflict her?

A *Letter, an Invitation*

I admit: I had not seen it before.

Man: driven to inflict on woman what he has endured from the mother? His fear of her size, her overpowering, her breaking into. What he calls sex, the urge that drives him to take a woman: impelled by this need? To make her suffer what he has suffered, and cannot allow himself to recall?

I admit: I had not seen it before.

And therefore, he cannot: soothe, gentle, caress. Soften the distance between them. Cannot remember this oldest way to restore union, gently placing part of his body in hers. Is that what they had to teach, in the walled gardens, a mile from the sea?

I, too, I have wondered; then, since then, still now, writing to you.

Then, I did what I was instructed to do. There came a time, difficult to locate in time, when I met the boy again on the mountains. This time, children together, growing older. We were sent out to herd goats, slept in the mountain pastures, covered ourselves with skins. Fed ourselves with souring milk left to curdle in an earthenware bowl, beneath juniper bushes.

As if, the two of us, we had to do it all over again. Go back to that time, we call it innocence: before loss of the body, its easy knowledge of pleasure.

The nights, cold; mornings we woke covered in dew. I had the impression: he, who had been chosen, had played the god, had known the mother, had missed a step, couldn't go forward. Had been intended to take the place of the man. The old one who touched, told stories, sat by the bed, guided the others.

With me, he was learning, all over again. To play.

Race after the goats, dragging me with him. We bathed
in the rivers, charging up through falling water. As if the
sacred rites, they depended on this. Each of us, learning
to play the roles of the sexual act, to be mother or child,
woman or man, must begin again with the senses.

What was wrong with the boy?

I had the impression: he yearned to live apart from his
body. More extreme than others, had drifted farther
away. Could not tell with his body the god's story of
willing surrender, in service to nature. Was unable to
enter the life of the mountains.

Night, he slips through my fingers; adrift in darkness,
he is digging stars. Looks down at me, from frozen
absence. I tie the goatskin around us. Afraid he will die
of cold. Be washed down rivers. Never return in his boat
of bark.

It is again, the shack near the alley? Two children,
skin weeping, unable to tell, unable to sleep. It is again
the boy I married?

There came a time, inevitable, when I was sent back
to the women. Then, for a time, lost track of the boy.
Perhaps, with other boys, he kept to his games in the
mountains. Learning to dig himself back into kinship.
With goats and rain, the ripening of cheese, the ferment-
ing of berries. Had I failed to learn what they expected?
Must now be given to somebody else to be taught?

An old woman, impossible to guess at her age.
Stooped, withered, stiff, toothless. She had her tasks:
watering sage, the dense, green unflowering basil, picking flowers. Mornings, she sweeps the courtyard, gathers
branches, burns them along paths outside the compound. I work with her.

A *Letter, an Invitation*

What the boy had taught: to name the carob, the holm oak, suck the pomegranate, useless here. The old woman, her method was different.

In time, I had the impression: she was special to them. One among many. Understood, from her stillness, watching the fires, she had a story. Must have been young once; taken a boy between thighs, the drums beating, flutes wailing. There was something about her. Slowly imparted. Perhaps, in her youth, this role, this enactment of goddess, of mother, had been repeated? One year following another? The boy, always another. The woman, always the same?

With her, I was boy-child. Ran out to fetch and carry: the almond water, the oil. Tended the doves, bathed, fed them. Late evenings: the beating of wings over the compound. She looks up, fixes them with her gaze, raises a finger. The others fly off, into the mountains. The white birds return.

She smells of old stone; tastes of flint. Her breast bone-hard, it is barren ground. This oldest fear: the mother runs dry, is exhausted. Can I endure her? She lies down at my side. Will she survive?

Have I spoken of cold? How she is not there in her flesh. Has gone underground, is covered in ice. How my body retreats from itself, cannot touch, grope, feel, reach her. How it abandons itself, grows vacant.

She touches my forehead. I know for the first time, fully. The way skin builds a shell for itself, scabs over. To keep her out. The body's retreat behind sinew. To deny her. The bulging of muscular will. To fight off the wish of her.

She wants me to touch her. The longing of cold to be

melted. I touch. Far off, the arousal of waters. She is young again; black hair oiled, curled over her shoulders. My lips at her. The small green drives upward, under my breath. I feel the weight of her hands on my back. My youth enters, makes its way through her, drives sap.

She branches, bends over. I sense: we have reached the secret, the mystery's core. The woman's burden, never spoken: he, who casts seed, will never know birth. Can I describe it, her pity? What else can it be called? This sorrow that melts her. He cannot breed; he, who makes fertile, cannot carry it through. He plants, he cannot conceive. She gathers him up, puts him against her. To console. This grief, unfairness of nature. For her, that is the sexual act. To lavish, to give. To chart his way back to her. So that he, who cannot be woman, becomes one with her. Becomes her.

How time lives in her hands. Is extended into my arms: opens out. From egg, creating itself; from seed, planting itself; from wind, carrying; from pollen, transporting. She weeps; rubs her tears into my skin. The rains have come; from the mountains, the boys and the girls dressed like boys return with the goats. Carrying the smallest. In the villages, the old women and the girls and the boys dressed like them set out the barrels. Rain falls from the eaves, the nights are long, day passes quickly, the years turn in on themselves, bite their tail. The cycle roves through, begins again, is repeated.

One day she speaks: the year, turning; the rain, the sprouting of sun, its lengthening shadow, ebb and flow of the moon: these, she says, woman. And man, her child, serves.

A Letter, an Invitation

The boy. Returning from his mother's village, fingers
purple, he has been gathering berries. I see the awe in
his gaze, he has caught sight of me, striding the path
toward him. My long white robe spreads through the
dust. The braid tightens across my breast. I am barefoot;
mine is the earth, to tread with deliberate footstep.

I touch him; he endures it. Falls back into his body,
grows out through his skin. He wants me to touch him
again. What is sacred is called down out of the distance,
lodges itself between my hand, his fingers, entangled
with us.

For the first time, he knows: this is the fate of that boy,
the god. He, who wished to roam a perpetual childhood.
At play in his mountains with the boys. He must return;
lay aside spear, bloodlust, give up the flight from knowledge. Must endure awe, envy, the dread of her power,
she is life, cannot be held, hunted, can never be killed.
And he will die; cannot evade it. Not even by making
the wish for death his. Must live, owes her his seed.
That is his meaning.

I touch, we turn to dust. Age in one another's arms. I
bury him. I have saved him from death; his seed will go
on. He hides in my lap. Worshiping, he will grow old.
Yes, take his place with the others. Grow into the old
man, tell the story. The promise of this, uncertain,
moves into his eyes.

Kneeling, his touch carries this knowledge. So light, it
can scarcely be felt: it intends to give pleasure. Mother
and child are laid to rest, divested. The old skin has
been shed. We return over the great sea, to breed in the
marshes. Snow runs down into flowering shrub. We are

sunlight, playing over the stones of the courtyard, dissolving into them.

Yes, I know, I see: what, before writing to you, I had not seen. Among us, the sexual act cannot reach this power of magical play. Because women pretend. Hide their sexual power. Hand themselves over to him. To make him believe. In his power: over the body, against nature, over woman, against the mother. Because they pity him, the barren one, the hunter. And do not allow themselves to know their pity.

That was the time. The beginning again, of time. I saw, as for the first time: linden trees, the long march of them down into the village. The flowering fields, the dense sea of them. Swallows. Skimming, pitched upward, soaring in sharp flight to fall, to flit again over green fields.

We gathered, were gathered: the linden blossom, for tea. He takes to flight. Stings me away from white flower, protective leaf. Our arms full, we creep back into the village. The ox returns, turns dust to gold, the treading begins, my feet stamp juice from him.

Lizards hide in the stone walls. Children, carrying baskets; they kick pears in the orchard. I have the impression: I will not see this for long.

He says: I am goddess of the cornfield. He wants to gather me in. He says: my hair is yellow, it grows over my fields.

Trumpeting of cranes. I am bowed, the plum drags me with ripeness. In his armpit, cicadas beating. Grain yellow on the threshing floor. We are harvested. The corn is laid up to be shelled. He thrusts thyme between my lips,

218

prolongs me. The heat, great. He must be laid to rest near the fountain. Babble, pass by overhead, rise out of the corn to cry at nightfall.

It is too hot for the larks.

The old women, they told us: all who worship, who serve, perform the sacred sexual act, carry between hands, lips, thighs, the earth's fertility. And we were all, they said, Aphrodite, and the boy.

We heard them, from the walled gardens, behind the sanctuary. While we played. Procession to the river. White robes, robes of saffron, water splashed from tortoise shell. We knew, from among the women, from among the men: two would be chosen.

CLAIRE'S TENTH LETTER

Was it madness? A flight to the past? To escape the past?
I would say, rather: It was a return. For one, who had
lost the meaning in things. It was meaning.

Fundamental, a bedrock. From which, somehow, in
time, I was returned to time.

What is memory? A few stones, picked out of the river.
Reassembled in a garden. You can make a wall of it, a
skeleton, a bench, stone table.

What is sex? All of it, maybe.

What eyes say, before speech. The world of the body,
its memories. First sensation: the way it fell. Into her
arms. That is the way it will fall: in love, from a steep
place, down a river, over a waterfall.

What is sex?

In childhood, the body learning, to grow into itself.
Later, the child older, the need to keep the body. Hold
it back from the exile. To which the others wish to subject it.

It is, younger brother curled up in a shack, listening.
Impossible stories. Girl, making it, rite of passage, in
parked car off Hollywood Boulevard. A way to learn. All
that the body has forgotten. Learning it back, insisting.
Marking the stages of progress, the stations. Leaving
home, the taco stand on the highway. The train moves
off, crosses the world. The appetite: to know, take it in,
all that it offers, what it is, the risk, the unknown, the

taste of its fruit. And what is forbidden: the body's ghettos, the wrong side of the track, its impoverishments. To enter, restore them.

A blackjack table. Stolen car. Stealing back what has been stolen. Setting out again. Crossing the seas. Unlearning the laws, the prohibitions. Terrible streets of transgression: the cult of sensation. Haunted by this: something is lost, missing, cannot be reached, connected.

Man, the other. The longing for him. Surely he knows, has preserved what we have cast out? The disillusion. Nobody knows. None of us. The boy fishing, the sun on the river, footsteps on the marble stairs. Can he be taught what others have forgotten?

The rage of forgetting. The frustration: we kiss, hard; we embrace, violently; we leap out, we attack, we tear open, we force entrance. And still cannot touch, reach, contact. Always, it eludes us. The body, swallowing its secrets; pleasures hidden, memories at bay.

And then there is one: more vulnerable than others, seems freer, will do anything, does not swagger. Remembers childhood, might be brother. His skin has erupted, he must be touched. To him then: open the doors, the hidden desires. Go further, admit fear with a stranger. At a masked ball, risk loss. Unleash sensation.

What is sex?

Disillusionment with the body? That too? Desert of sensual pleasures, night of the flesh, its aridity. The way you cannot go on, have reached, it seems, the end station. The train stops: the last risk, it seems, taken.

Meaning dries up; the body withers, scorns touch,

grows barren. Someone is in mourning, they say. Perhaps the goddess of grain. Her daughter has been stolen, gone underground. It is an old story. Or maybe the boy she loved has been killed by a boar.

What is sex?

Above all, it seems, a question of touch. The way touch remembers, has preserved childhood. The way the body knows, has never forgotten. The fear of falling. The dread of being small. And her magnificence. The stories flesh tells: rocked back out of urgency in earth mother's arms. Touch: a question of memory. The ultimate risk, the train's return to the first station.

If you go back, there; the walled gardens. Stay a while and then come back again: the secret treasure you smuggle through. But of course you know by now: that is the body.

Vulnerable as dew, infinitely fragile, scarcely yours. It must be offered, at first tentatively. If you are lucky, she is one who remembers tenderness, calls it the old way. Perhaps she straps you to her body. Naked, a single skin encloses you. The beginning again. She wears you on her hip, slung on her back, goes about her tasks. When you are hungry you suck. She does not let you cry. Part of her, she senses your body before you do. Your legs kick. This means: soon you will wet, discharge, relieve tension. She takes you down from her back. Your fingers tighten. You are back in her arms. You watch, from your perch: the way she digs yams, plaits a basket, plucks berries, frees an iron gate from its rust. Then slowly. Detaching the small from the large, stumble out, they are your legs that totter. Her arms, there when you fall, you fall back into her. This body that will become your body. Apart from her, never too far. One day she places you near the door of the hut. When you are ready you walk. Away from her. Turn back. She is there. You reach out. You touch her.

It is your first sexual act.

Have you noticed? It is almost three years. Since we met. More than four months since I left you. Did not write my name on a stone wall. It takes time to remember.

Tomorrow, I shall drop these letters in the mail. Imagine them arriving, somewhere. In Paris, are you there? Sent on perhaps by the concierge. Following you across Europe. Meeting up with you, finally.

As for me: I shall go home. I mean: the city where the wooden shack stood. Next to the alley. The first time since I left. Returning, briefly. Then north. The road she took. Setting out into the world in search of the body. Ironic, or perhaps even: sentimental journey? Does it matter?

A city, near the sea. A house in the hills, it looks down over water. I bought it, when? On a whim, suddenly. Driving up into the hills to visit a friend. Before we parted, Geoffrey and I; before the masked ball, the walled gardens. Before I met you again in your little court. You see: I am trying. To give an order, coherence, sequence. Perhaps you already know?

What is sex? Our original question. The reason, to begin with, these letters were written. Now, they will have been sent, all of them. Finally.

Do I mean: whatever has to do with the body? Its

need for the other, earliest knowledge. It will dry up, wither, without her. Sex: this groping, from one stone solitude to another. Do I mean: this confession? Taken up, tasted afresh, in the arms of one who can be trusted? Enough, anyway.

An act, the most hazardous, let us say, of recollection? Mutual memory of childhood?

And therefore: a step forward. Less than a promise. But worth the risk. A possibility.

And above all, in case you have not understood: An invitation.

Part Five

ALMA RUNAU:
A LETTER, A CONDITION

SCENE: A CAFÉ
TIME: NOT QUITE THREE YEARS AFTER THE FIRST
     MEETING

Claire,

I've been so mad at you I swore I'd never have anything to do with you again! All those stories of power, and then to walk out on me like that! I saw it as impotence. Cowardice. How you got rid of me and my story, lying to me. You were "too tired to say another word before the morning." You must have been lying in wait until I'd finally stopped writing, and then sneaked out. Your bed rolled up, you left almost no trace. Had you ever been there? That's what I concluded: you had not wanted to be there at all.

I couldn't stand the idea, to have driven you away. To imagine you leaving the house, wandering through the dark, through the dead village, alone. Walking along the empty road. Hoping for some car to pick you up. Were you awake enough to watch where he was going? Going where? Did you even care?

If you'd at least written your name on the town wall! What if I'd woken up in time? Another lie? I wanted to leave, too. Get out of there. I stayed, in case you might change your mind. The lady reappears—and I never know why either, do I? She might send a note after all. An address. The mail is slow in the south. I drove around to check out the bistros, the village squares. The rains started. I hated you for doing this to me.

The lady likes to reappear when one has given up on her. No hopes, no expectations, no commitment. How big a distance does she need in time and space in order to approach? And even issue an invitation?

Four months are long enough to make one cynical. This time, at least, your letter got to me without delay. An omen?

Yes, I do understand. Neither of us could take the risk. We each had good reasons to cherish our doubts. Even now you keep a back door open. Don't worry, so do I. I've been cursing your need to hide behind any disguise. Costumes, stories, vague allusions, silence. But then I, too, had been disguised in that New Year's story. And had needed to blind your eyes.

When reality is not enough—or maybe too good to be true—one needs a story. I recognize it. Writing oneself into the other's story, writing the other into one's own. Isn't that what is called falling in love? Making up a story together. The vagueness is there, as much as the flourishes, to cover the uglier truths. I've done it too often. It's always a strain. Pointless. Was it me, was it you? We are almost strangers, we've never been anything else. You've sent me a new letter, another story. This time I shall try to answer you.

You'll like this. I won't miss your point by asking if the story is true. I got the message. I finally learned to believe what I read between the lines.

Do you know where I'm writing? You guessed it. At my café. "Our" café. It's far from being the first spring day. Paris at its grayest. Gusts of wind. The draft is coming in through the windows. I bravely hold on, thanks to my leather jacket. The same old table. Everything else is different. Today they would let me spread out over several tables at the window if I wanted to. A subdued silence, even around the few people chatting. A single person here and there. New surly waiters. The *patronne* sits on her throne behind the cash box, grim and pinched. People come in for a quick coffee, hurry out again. Every time the door opens, the gusts push in. I'm tempted to have a cognac with my next *crème* . . .

I don't know when I'll have the courage to return to the country. I dread having to put up again with the mice and scorpions and spiders, even though I managed so well. (And in the end Mme. Petitpot's nephew did come to close the mouse entrance in the roof, as you'd suggested!) It's easier to be in Paris right now. Nothing unknown to be confronted here. I just wish I'd made more jam to take home. I see my friends more than I used to. Maybe I had enough solitude last year.

Solitude seems to be our mutual theme. I never know whether I should worry about you or not. I did worry. Is she happy? Amusing the men in some bistro, somewhere in the world, with her stories painted in the air? Is she in despair? Each possibility used to feel equally probable. Each still does.

So, that's where you went after the *bal masqué?* Cyprus. Aphrodite's temple. A place that protected you, hit you with enlightenment, took away the burden of yourself . . . for a while. Was that what you tried to tell me when you came? Was that what you came for?

It would never have worked, Claire. You say it yourself, there are things not to be spoken. Not to be heard. The public spectacle of sex. Hard enough to be read. Reading one can at least keep things out. The dry old woman's tears. Jump over words or carefully walk around them, shroud images with one's own imagination. I understand why you had to jump up, interrupt, walk out.

Do I have to be seized, transported? You're not that hard to follow anymore. I've been close enough in my own sexual search to what you are writing about. In the sanctuary of an ordinary meadow, right here in the city, in a room next door—simply being in love. Yes, I can see that you would transport yourself to strangers with a culture and language you don't know. As far away as possible from yourself in order to remember . . . But what you remember sounds as lonely to me as what you'd told me before. Even your realm of the senses, embedded in nature, "making the world sap flow." I hear the lonely heart.

What is sexuality?

What you describe, certainly. Being stripped naked. Thrown back into memory, back to childhood. Yes, earliest terror and bliss. Embodied. How beautifully you describe it. All of one's primordial experiences of the body suddenly present again, in the presence of the other. Coming to the lover with the naked hidden truth of oneself. To be recognized.

But how can you be recognized when you are wearing a costume? I've seen you dressed as a profane goddess for men. Now you wear the costume of the Sacred Marriage. Goddess-impersonator with symbolic god. Another disguise. Another metaphor. Always strangers. Always evasion. Even with the spiritual dimension, the training to understand the mother-child enactment, I would say, there is evasion. It's impersonal sex. Symbolic. Not quite real. No real people struggling to bear through their nakedness in order to get to each other finally. (Do you know? Making love in the German Bible is translated, *And they recognized each other?*) It's never simply Claire, simply in love.

You never use the word *love*. You never mention the experience of loving. The only love I sensed in your stories was your tender, presexual love for your little brother. Has it all died with him? Is all your sex a mourning? The ultimate confirmation of your mourning for your mother? Torn from your heart and buried? Sex—the desperate attempt to disappear into the body, forget the rest of yourself. "Cosmic sex," so it seems to me, rides on the same despair.

There is also evasion in the roles. The goddess and her hero. A patriarchal myth of difference reconciled. But there is no girl here, no daughter in her love for the mother. No celebration of sameness. No mourning for the difference and separation inherent in it.

I mourn the loss of the daughter-lover to the mother. The loss of desire, loss of difference within sameness. All desirable difference is extirpated from the female, projected onto the male. He's defined, confined by his violent otherness. She's got nothing of it left. Poor him. Poor her. He can't remember being like the mother even though he is of her flesh. She can't remember being like him even though she made him. Two opposed genders celebrate and mourn their reunion once a year!

If in your temple you were all taught to change roles, why not also celebrate a Sacred Marriage between two women or two men? Between a human being and a tree?

Certainly we are part of nature—which a culture hostile to the body and in love with reason tends to forget. But we are also separate. Remember Georges Bataille, the French philosopher who defined culture as the radical human *no* to nature? I mentioned him at our first meeting, my favorite sexist informant. Lately I discover a certain weakness for this *no* of his. I like to be able to step out of nature when I choose. Deciding about my own body, giving birth or not, my own living or dying. Deciding how to make the world sap flow by choosing to desire whomever I love.

I am convinced our human destiny is to be in *and* out of nature. Not split into two gender-halves, men "out," women "in." It's gender impairment on a global scale!

The balance I long for is the constant dynamic between "in" and "out." On the one hand we are unconscious, just "being," like plants or animals. Caught in the flow of life. On the other hand we are conscious, "knowing." Knowing, for ex., that we have just "been." The play of "in and out" is so fast both seem simultaneous. Isn't this precisely what sex makes us recognize? We are "in" and "out" of nature at the same time.

Am I getting metaphysical? Back to the physical. I'm cold and hungry. I'll return to my elevated thoughts at home, eating dinner. I hate either-ors, as you know.

Later, at home

Mushroom soup and dandelion salad. A glass of wine. A hot-water bottle on my knees. I'm warming up. Back to your temple.

Your travel into the Goddess-Hero-Mysteries has reminded me. The beginning of the gender drama, when the boy discovers he's not the same as She. The M/other. He can't be one with her creative, orgasmic, nurturing powers, the cosmical cycle of life and death in her blood. He's separate. Frail. His body exposed. He is her child. She made him. She pities him. She tries to bind him to her mysteries by letting him live and bleed, love and die. Her sacred rite: she makes him once again part of herself.

Don't you see the implications?

I know this pity, the immense pity I had for men as soon as I "knew" them. Even though in my eyes they had all the power I pitied them. Split-off beings, desperately struggling into context, into meaning. So ill-equipped.

How to heal the gender-wound if not by giving up our power? Making ourselves smaller, looking up to him. Giving what we need ourselves, giving in to the need of the beloved. Always wanting to restore his sense of oneness, his *yes* to nature.

In my women relationships it's been the same. The fear of overpowering the other, of being more, having more. The guilty need to take ourselves back. In groups, too, in the early women's movement I noticed our ambiguous drive to be strong, but never stronger than . . . No comparison, hierarchy, competition among us! Not even with men.

Being powerful beyond the equality line was a sacred scarecrow for most of us. How could we be sure that our power wouldn't be "power over"? How could we be sure we ourselves hadn't brought patriarchy about: with our power over our sons, with our need to make up to men for their disadvantage according to nature? Had we created men's need for revenge?

I understand what your temple training aimed at. Teaching men and women to face their primordial condition. Helping them reach awareness after millennia of trying to forget. In sculptures from the Bronze Age the boy-child sits on the goddess's lap, replacing the Stone Age daughter. Then he sits next to her on the throne— her husband, same size. In early Egypt, she has her arm around him, protecting, guiding him. She has initiated him into her mysteries. She lets him share her power, then lets him use his power over her. He grows and grows. In the end she is no goddess anymore, she's only the mother of God.

Isn't it still everybody's story? Is it women's own choice? A sacrifice? Crippling our own body and mind so he can expand? Sacrificing our health for his well-being? Excising the pleasure from our own body so his pleasure can be without a rival?

I suddenly remember our first conversation, our first disagreement about equality. I had paraded my favorite argument: Women have to develop their masculine, men their feminine side.

You said, "Great. Everyone alike. Where's the attraction supposed to come from?"

"Can't you think of sameness as attractive? Don't you like yourself?"

"Opposites attract each other, folks say."

"Same and same befriend each other. Folks seem to disagree."

"They aren't talking about the same thing. It's a matter of choice. One's taste for extremes, drama, passion—or comfort. Equalizing is certainly nice. Peacefully going to sleep at mother's breast."

"How do you know? Have you tried it?"

"Tried what?"

"Each individual is already so different from every other, it's hard enough to get close. But if you add the gender gap it's hopeless. Men and women are bred like two different species!"

"That's why they need each other so passionately."

"They need their own missing half. No other person can make up for what is absent in oneself. It's an unappeasable, desperate need."

"Hmmmm!"

You sounded as though you were tasting a gourmet dish.

Remember?

I decided to slaughter my last pomegranate. It had been lying around since Xmas. Hard like a walnut. I used a screwdriver to get the seeds out. Do you like this *hommage à toi?*

I remember our conversation, something you said struck me as true: "Falling asleep at mother's breast." I didn't want to admit it but that's precisely what happened, sexually speaking, in each of my relationships with women. There was an exhilarating sense of oneness, belonging, sacred marriage, yes. But at the same time, with our ideal of sameness, we kept each other from our otherness. We grew into each other, slipped under each other's skin. We knew each other by heart, sensed our moods already outside the door. We made the other into ourselves.

But it's the dilemma, isn't it, of every relationship? (Is this why you never enter a relationship?) If there's no "other" anymore, desire dies. Wanting to encounter the stranger—wanting to keep everything familiar. The contradictory needs between which passion falters! We try to get around the conflict by keeping both needs apart: sleepy domestic security, fatal attraction to the stranger.

Your stranger. The one who has to be changed with every desire, every season. Who is chosen once a year. I would like to find the "familiar stranger," the one I can learn to love and fall in love with again and again.

If lovers would allow each other to change, find their own direction, their unique path . . . Wouldn't the en-

counter with difference keep reproducing the stranger
one longs to encounter? Then, maybe one would realize
that the desired stranger is also a desired part of oneself.
An unknown possibility one longs to become. A possibility one longs to learn from the other.

In my experience, the risk was avoided. The risk of
change, estrangement, loss. My relationships became a
cradle. A place where we could heal our wounds from
being women. A place where we protected ourselves and
each other from our difference. We were outsiders, sepa-
rated from the rest of the world by our love for women.
Difference, roles, anything that could separate us from
each other, had to stay out. We protected each other like
mothers protect their children from the world. From too
much adventure, challenge, unequalness, competition.
In short, from life. And thus from our truth.

Sex, I suppose, in such a cradle, can come to be felt as
part of the danger of life. How can one be totally naked
and open if there's a need for protection from some truth?
From the memory of men in our bodies. . . . From the
compulsion of gender. Shielding ourselves from the con-
ventional notions of sex (domination, passive surrender,
giving up self), we came close to eliminating sex altogether.

These sexual fears, you say, are not about men? They
are about the mother lurking behind them? Behind all of
us? No matter the gender—what sex enacts is always the
drama between mother and child? It does ring a bell. I
can't deny it's a tempting thought that my rage against
men has been a coverup for a much earlier, hidden rage.

It's true. Being the helpless doll of an all-powerful
mother must mean being fed on the best as well as worst
of life. The mother is every/body's wonder and terror.
Every/body's initiation into the frightening ambivalence
of being. (Isn't it ironic that you, the "bad girl" with the

"bad mother," can allow yourself to know this? You obviously don't have to protect her, or your memory of her.)

Nevertheless, there's something you don't seem to know. Women are in a particular situation, loving other women. Womanloving brings the mother-memory as close as can be, "for better or for worse." (Reason enough to stick to men?) There are memories of a sweetness without any equal in the world. The beauty, lushness, the sensuous softness of a woman's body is without any equal in the world. But the memory of having been over- and underfed, possessed and abandoned, overwhelmed and rejected by this same body, source of life, of love—indeed also invokes an unequaled fear.

No wonder you avoided it. No wonder I did, too. The dogma of tenderness meant calling up the safe, nurturing m/other. All-encompassing, presexual sensuality rather than sex.

Most of the time my lover and I felt so closely bonded, already quasi inside each other, it was quicksand to enter and be even closer, more intimate. We had already given too much. How could we give even more of a self we didn't possess?

(Have you ever been close enough to anybody to feel this mother-*angst*? To be swallowed alive? S/mothered?)

Like any "married" couple, we would make love from time to time. With the body ease of our familiarity, we were likely to be satisfied. Or should I say, pacified? But in the sweet nest of our bodies the longing to recognize the stranger, be the stranger, to conquer, seduce, surrender, had gone to sleep.

It bothered me as a feminist to still find myself and my lovers in the same old shoe, "Sex is male, love and intimacy are female." I wanted sex. I began to wonder if I, if women, even feminists, had something to learn from men?

It bothers me, Claire, that you are still wearing that shoe. You leave out love and intimacy, you worship impersonal sex. I hit upon the right question three years ago when I asked if you were a female impersonator. You are.

I told you about Solveig and my sexual quest. I don't think I mentioned my frustrations with my "male" training. Isn't it funny that we each went into sexual training? You went for the sacred, I for the most profane. One thing in common: sex with strangers, right? Coming each from the opposite end—how are we ever going to meet in the middle?

Not at "our" café. At the Coupole this time. It's such a strong wind I couldn't have made it farther on my bike. Here the *crème* is *minable,* as you might know. They never use fresh milk. But I'm sheltered from the draft in the soft banquettes with their high plush backs. Farther down, Truffaut actor Jean-Pierre Léaud cowers in another banquette in his eternal trench coat. The usual old ladies in furs, pearls, and heavy makeup are hanging out, chatting and flirting with the waiters, preparing to go up to the 5 o'clock *thé dansant* with their young gigolos. It's a place where nobody cares how long you hang out. My traditional bad-weather café.

I want to finish my letter. I read yours again. I want to come back once more to our favorite topic, the stranger. The mysterious lover, the irresistible *étrangère*. The one met at a bus stop, on a boat before sunrise, in a house near the harbor at a *bal masqué*. Passion incarnate.

I must have been practicing for that New Year's night. Cultivating my detachedness: my control.

What is passion?

Distance. To yearn, dream, pine. The delicious torture of putting off a rendezvous for the sake of waiting, resistance, pleasure postponed. The rising expectation: feverish anticipation, desire whipped up to an unbearable peak. And finally *Erlösung*, finally release, in a rage of body thirst. Violent greed for fulfillment, another sweet torture, so short, alas, always already possessed by the need to tear myself away in order to let desire slowly rise again . . .

Sounds familiar? No kidding. What a great *mise en scène*. Two beings forever apart, with the momentary illusion of being together. A longing not for satisfaction in fact but for longing. Provoked sensation. Why?

For the past three years this kind of passion has been my drug. An ecstasy of cultivated pain, a sickness in love with itself. It has nothing to do with love. It's not even concerned with the "beloved." The lover has to fit my game, fit into the costume I hold out for her.

It works as long as the other stays remote, unreal, always a step out of reach. An apparition, a sexual mirage. A fantasy-body that lies between me and my lover's naked flesh. As soon as there is closeness, intimate knowledge, a real face with its ugliness, a real person with her otherness, the game is over. Once I look behind the mask, remove the blindfold, once I am recognized beneath my costume, I fear the consequences. The gap opens between my love illusion and the truth, between my act and who I really am. The stranger's irresponsible daring is lost. A shyness sneaks in, a fear to show too much of myself, to give it away, to give in, to be taken.

A terror falls. To lose control over my need, to depend on the giver of pleasure. To become a slave to pleasure. The terror of wanting a fulfillment that goes on forever, never stops, leaves me incapable of tearing myself away. Leaves me addicted to a bliss that is not of my making.

(The reason I left the room at the *bal*? The reason you didn't hold me back? The reason you left before I got back? Did I dare to come back?)

I keep running. Everyone does. To the safe distance, the costume, the ritual, the sacred symbolism, the unfamiliar stranger in the night.

(Do you want to know the true meaning of the New Year's story? The two women were so hidden by roles they couldn't possibly recognize each other.)

241

When I started watching myself acting, acting out passion, I found that I intensified all my other feelings in the same "passionate" way. Do you remember how I loved the swifts? Their screams were my screams for my lover, their vertiginous plunges were the vertigo of my desire for her. Their beauty wasn't enough by itself, it had to be heightened. My feeling of love wasn't ever enough by itself. Without the ache, the intensifying drug of pain— what was I able to feel?

"Without pain, no pleasure," as folks say.

Why not?

"Patisseries, croissants, chocolats . . ."

The lady with the red uniform and weary face is pushing her cake wagon through the rows of tables. No request. She doesn't expect any. I secretly bite into the croissant I bought at the bakery across the street. I'm an expert at hiding food in my lap. In "our" café, I know how to choose the tables that can't be surveilled by the *patronne. "Une petite tarte, Mademoiselle? Un p'tit cognac?"* She has trained the waiters not to be content with a simple order of coffee. It's *pousse au crime,* a shove into the lap of crime.

Outside, wherever one looks, advertising pushes one into the lap of sex. Ready-made s/excitements, to be easily consumed. A bus drives by, showing Mr. Muscle holding a newborn baby against his naked torso. The photo cuts below the belt; the zipper doesn't quite close. One hand supports the baby's head, amazingly tender. The other, gripping the baby's ass, seems to suggest that even the tiniest body calls for rape. Across the street a movie poster exposes the full, naked breast of a man in bed; the woman next to him has her breasts fully covered. In the neighbor poster a man yields to a woman who comes up behind him and peels the jumpsuit from his upper body.

Her face beams with loving authority. His is in agony, taking pleasure.

Are they ahead of our time, as your letter would suggest? Or is it that feminism has repudiated women's attributes—babies, breasts, surrender—and already men are taking them over, making them theirs? Turning them into men's sexual attractions? Coming attractions?

I wonder if it's not the same arrested state of affairs. Now a woman possessing. A domina. The roles exchanged, the same old roles. Always the illusion that some kind of authority, violence has to come in, has to be embraced in order to overcome one's resistances. To be forced, to force oneself into the pleasure one can't take.

The illusion of passion has the same function: creating the aloof, unattainable other. Distance, resistance then have to be torn away in a storm that leaves you no thought of failure, no feeling of frailty—just sweeps you off your feet into, finally, ease.

Always illusion of ease. In the advertisements, the fantasies, the temple vision, the childish wish for the dream-lover, the prince(ss) charming with X-ray eyes who recognizes you without a word. Guesses all your secret desires, has the perfect authority to plunge your abandoned self into the seventh heaven. (The lover I, in the New Year's story, pretended to be?)

It doesn't work. Not for me. Not anymore. To me it all looks like a mad search, doomed, even if you call sex art or the sacred. Paradise lost. An obsession. A greed that doesn't care about the taste of food, the pleasure of eating. Mere need to fill a void. A desperate drive to forget for a moment how separate one is from it all. From oneself, the other, the universe.

It sounds absurd to me to ask the body for "art," or even the "sacred," for high and subtle sensation, if heart and mind have nothing to do with it. Who are those others, your lovers, those boys? Long legs, pimples, erupted skin is what I learned about them. Nothing about their hearts and minds. The emotional poverty, the anonymity of what you call sex!

Yes, you're right, I am dead-scared of the elemental power of sex. Everyone is. Women and men force their difference upon each other to avoid the dangers of elemental love. The nearness of goddess and child. You do, too. With another woman, however, the dangers might be unavoidable. That's what you might be able to learn with a woman. Not in the role of a boy-child. As a woman yourself.

Will I ever finish this epistle?

I read my last pages again. I suddenly heard my raving. The feminist galloping on her white horse, brandishing her flaming speech! I don't know why I still get these attacks of rage at you. Because you aren't "further"? I'm sorry. You would say I'm still avoiding what you're saying. I'm mostly interested in speaking myself, in peeling my own onions. *Une fâcheuse tendance, je le reconnais.*

I don't tell you how your letter provoked and inspired me. And taught me. I'd still rather shake you. Don't you realize, I want to shout, that this spiritual quest of a sacred eros is part of feminist thought? That it's been happening right here in front of your doorstep, for years? Women creating their own rituals, shrines, rites of passage. (Re)creating their new and ancient myths. The goddess, indeed, in every woman, the goddess and her heroine, mother/daughter, sisters, clans, dreaming their sacred eros into being.

How detached you are, disconnected. How far you have to run. How everlonely you are!

I probably want to shake myself. Shout at myself: Stop making speeches! Stop making ideology! My sacred eros: How? My taxi to the temple: Where?

At least you don't pretend (anymore) that it's easy. If you see sex as "art" in the sense of work—the stubborn, passionate tenderness of work—I could agree. I told you, I want the elemental power of sexuality to speak in a personal tongue. I want the familiar stranger. I want to learn the erotic passion of love. Teach the lover who I am. Learn how to read the other's body which after all even between women is not my own. To risk handing over to the other my wishes, my unknown self, my fears.

I've always imagined how it would be between lovers who told each other the truth of the moment. "Not there, like this, try here, I am lost, I don't know how to bear this, help me, I'm scared to go on . . ." Not whipping one's body into the loss (even cosmic loss) of consciousness, but listening, consciously, to its wants. The body's voice may be so slow, shy, hesitant, deeply withdrawn under its immediate cover of skin. How to reach it, read it? How to touch, how to speak in its tongue? How to fine-tune one's listening as well as one's telling the truth?

Imagine the relief it would bring, the release of muscle, the real ease of mind. The sweetness your heart would feel for this lover taking your truth, taking it in. Bearing it. Bearing through it with you. Wouldn't you love yourself for the courage, wouldn't you want to embrace the other for this recognition, passionately? Truth, I imagine, is the most powerful aphrodisiac of all.

But it can't happen if only one person desires it. It needs a certain equality. Not the one I've known, not the equality that counts strokes and pleasures and anxiously compares powers. I imagine the equal willingness to take the risk of truth. And a similar capacity, I should add, to recognize it.

In this e/quality the either/or of roles, of giving and taking dissolves. Letting go, coming along, going toward, advancing, coming open, going beyond oneself . . . The attunement of all my senses to my lover and to myself creates a simultaneity, an exchange of signals continuously transforming each other: now the taking gives and the giving takes. My hand touching receives an answer from her skin, which makes my hand explore the gesture with a pleasure that seems to be her pleasure in being touched by me . . .

How to make such moments last? The dance of eros. Free-floating games of polarities, beyond opposition, beyond fixed roles. How make it last? Playful inventing, sensuous finding of sense. From the little I know about it I love the pleasure of making sense within my whole being, body and soul. Knowing the other who knows me is knowledge beyond me, is knowing all.

But how to talk about the sacred? I can hardly talk about the profane. And anyway, are you listening? I give the question back to you. Even though I have to admit that I don't really know who I am talking to. Who is inviting me and into which world? I feel we are mostly talking like visitors out of alien worlds. Why do we talk at all, not knowing each other's language? Why would I want to follow your invitation if you don't even know the basic facts of my feminist time and space? Do you expect me to teach you my ABC? I'm no initiator. Like you, I sometimes indulge in a fantasy about a school of love, but I'm no temple-teacher. I think I'll send you a list of books. The basic columns of my house of thought. It's up to you. It's an invitation, too. And, in case you haven't noticed, a condition.

Alma

Part Six

CLAIRE HELLER:
A DIALOGUE, A MEETING

SCENE: THE BERKELEY HILLS
TIME: THREE YEARS AFTER THE MEETING
    AT THE CAFÉ

1

Early morning, not yet dawn. The car pulls up in the parking area. Two women get out and begin to walk fast. One of them hesitates, turns back.

"I better do something about your suitcase. It's not exactly Paris, but you never know about a place like this."

"Is it far? How long will it take to get there?"

"If we walk fast, not more than fifteen, twenty minutes."

Claire Heller opens the back of the car, covers the suitcase with a blanket. "Are you cold? Shall I take an extra jacket?"

"I'm okay. I don't want to miss it."

They walk fast again, single file. At the entrance to the path there is a gate, fastened with a heavy chain. Claire reaches it first.

"Why is it locked?" Alma Runau asks.

Claire climbs up, straddles the gate, offers Alma her hand. From there, they look down over grass meadows, early dusk. A faint light has just begun to outline the low brown hills. Claire points out the lakes, visible now and again in the shredding mist.

Claire says: "We'd better hurry. You'll never forgive yourself if you miss the sunrise."

Alma has stopped to read the printed sign on the far side of the gate. "You have the permit, I suppose?"

"Pay no attention to it. I've been here hundreds of times."

"Are there really mountain lions?"

"I've never caught sight of anything but cows. A deer once. And of course birds. There's a breeding pond down there. Last year, when I came back from Europe, I drove here straight from the airport. It was evening, there were more birds than we'd see now. Hundreds of them. I wish you could have seen them. Every few minutes a new bird would fly in, settle on a reed at the edge of the pond, make a wild, cooing sound, fly to the far side of the field, alight on a bush, cry out, fly back to the mating pond. Or suddenly a flock of them would fly up out of the reeds. I mean dozens of them, in a single rush. Winging out, crossing the field, circling back."

She has stretched out her arms, swoops them back and forth above her head.

Alma says: "Are you nervous?"

"Excited. What about you?"

"I hardly recognize you. Do you change every year? Or maybe this is what you look like in America."

They are walking fast along the dirt path above the valley.

Claire says: "You must be exhausted. Did you sleep at all?"

"I had three seats to myself. The plane was half empty."

"You don't look like a person who's just crossed the Atlantic for the first time."

"How would that look?"

"A little less sure of yourself? Although I can't say I've actually known anyone in that condition before. Do I seem to be chattering?"

"Talking nonstop."

"It's a big responsibility. What if you don't like it here?"

"I like it already."

"You do? Really?"

"You sound surprised."

"I never imagined you'd come. I thought you'd say to yourself, 'What do I have in common with that Claire Heller?' I was sure you put in your ridiculous condition because you hoped I'd never agree to it."

A young black bull catches sight of them as they pass below him on the path. He lifts his head, regards them intently for a moment and begins to run very fast downhill. A few feet behind them, at the gnarled tree growing from the path, he pulls himself up short and gazes at them with an unexpected, forlorn friendliness.

Alma Runau says: "He must have lost track of the herd. He looks lonely."

"Nature, lonely? Nonsense." Claire walks ahead, then turns back. "I thought you'd want to know all about my homework. Plato, even in Greek, would be a light task compared to this feminist reading list of yours."

"I made up my mind not to ask."

"Shall I speak frankly?"

"You, frankly?"

"This obsession with power!" Claire has raised her voice. "I've read your epistle a dozen times. I've made my way through your tedious list. But did you or your

worthy sisters just once bring in an actual body in bed
with another body because it is fun to be there?"

"Have you rehearsed this speech?"

Claire bows her a compliment. "It used to be the holy
sacrament of marriage that served as a screen for simple
body pleasure. Now you've cooked up love-and-
intimacy. But you yourself have never known how to
live it. Why not just drop the whole thing?"

"Is this another invitation?"

"If you want intimacy, go to the laundromat and gossip
with your neighbor. Sex is theater, a sacred game. It is
ritual drama, it requires roles."

"For most women sex is still a social drama." Alma's
voice is sharp. "The pleasure they achieve is men's."

"Why are you so worked up about other women?"

"I'm part of the crowd."

"What does that mean? You feel guilty otherwise? You
have to share every pleasure you have with your sisters?"

Alma smiles vindictively. "Why not at least with
one?"

"I have always assumed I was responsible for my own
pleasure."

"Isn't this what happens every time we meet? For one
moment we feel at ease. The next moment, back at
square one, in our old opposition. If the problem doesn't
exist, what have we been arguing about for three
years?"

"I can never bring myself to believe you actually hold
these ideas. Surely, you only bring them out for sport?
Everything divided into us and them. They who make

use of us and get pleasure from that! We who do not, cannot possibly, have never had pleasure!

"Of course you'd laugh."

"You can hardly manage not to laugh yourself."

"But what are we laughing at?"

"How seriously we take ourselves?"

"How seriously we take one another?"

"Alma Runau, I love it when you smile like that. But you shouldn't. Such unabashed childish pleasure! It doesn't go with your pessimistic world view, sister."

"Me? The pessimist? I who can imagine human nature fundamentally changed."

"Don't any of you ever wonder whether human nature is not just fine the way it is? It is you who are unable to come to terms with reality."

Alma imitates Claire's bow. "People like you always retreat into reality when you've run out of arguments."

2

The sun is rising. There are cows grazing, mist burning
off above the lakes. The brown hills have turned a pale
gold, the luminous dirt path through the fields is also
golden. The power lines are flashing with silver light,
humming in the early breeze.

Claire takes off her heavy sweater as they walk.

Their silence is awkward.

The sun moves higher.

Alma puts the sweater over her shoulders.

She says: "Europe is much more civilized. A land that
has been for thousands of years under cultivation. But
this? It's easy to believe there were Indians here
recently, or are still."

"Except for the power lines."

"Even they belong. Nothing looks real. They're like
some strange cult object from a space-age culture. It's a
landscape from a fairy tale."

"Last year, when I came back here . . ." Claire hesitates. "I immediately thought of inviting you. I had the
idea of bringing you here directly from the airport."

"A way to make up for your escape?"

"A way to enjoy your company. From a safe distance."

"That's probably as close to an apology as I'll ever
get."

"Do you see that plane tree in the distance?"

"Plane tree?" Alma has stopped walking. Now, she

looks at Claire, who is trying hard to keep a serious face.

" 'I am fortunate in not having my sandals, and as you never have any, I think that we may go along the brook and cool our feet in the water.' " Claire is having fun.

But Alma, after all, can play this game too. She, too, can quote Plato. " 'Let us turn aside,' " she says, " 'and go by the Ilissus; we will sit down at some quiet spot.' "

"You, as Socrates?"

"Would you prefer to cast me in the role of Phaedrus?"

"I'd like to be that beautiful boy wandering about barefoot outside the walls of the city, the discourse on love hidden beneath his cloak."

Alma looks at her again, shading her eyes with both hands. "You as Phaedrus! Why not? He must have been quite an androgynous beauty. Butterfly hands, a powerful neck like yours . . ."

"If you stop walking every time you have something to say it will be high noon by the time we get there."

" 'Well, then lead on,' as Socrates would say. 'And look for a place in which we can sit down.' "

Claire is still smiling. She nudges a pebble with her foot. "What did you think?"

"Our whole effort is absurd. Feminist books won't change you. Plato has nothing to say to me. Socrates drones on and on. But what is he really doing? Cruising."

"Socrates, the cruiser! I see. Could you resist anyone who courted you with a theory like that?"

"Love as divine madness! Falling in love at first sight

of beauty! No matter who the beauty is! Are you trying to convert me? Pervert me? As you know, I gave all that up a while ago."

"Did you really believe I'd never talk to you again if you didn't do your homework?"

"I read it while we were going through customs. I thought, if they give me any trouble about visas, I'll pass myself off as a European intellectual."

"Here's the place. A lofty and spreading plane tree Socrates called it, I think?"

"Don't try any of your tricks on me, Claire Heller. You can't make me into the expert on Plato. And especially not this morning . . ."

"I keep forgetting you must be tired."

The two women lean against a large pine tree. Claire has tucked up her legs and is resting her chin against her knees. Alma is sitting very straight, shading her eyes with her hand.

Alma says: "Was I talking about fatigue?"

"You had something else in mind!"

"Why Plato anyway? Why drag him in?"

"You feminists imagine you've invented the liaison between eros and the sacred. I wanted to remind you the idea was more than two thousand years old. Why throw out culture? Claim your place in it. Adapt it!"

"Adapt it? The way you and I do? Using it to hide behind? My letter didn't."

"But it was I who wrote first. I came back to see you. I invited you to visit . . ."

"Aren't you curious to know why I accepted?"

"I know. You've got something to propose. Good old intimacy again."

"Claire Heller, I'm sick to death of these unearthly passions you and Socrates keep raving about."

"I see. And you imagine I would be capable of nothing else! This, I take it, is what you've come here to tell me?"

"You know why you invited me. I know nothing for sure. I can imagine many reasons."

"Perhaps I invited you in order to find out why I wanted to invite you."

3

Noon. The two women are still sitting beneath the pine
tree.

The landscape, however, has changed. The mist has
gone out of it, leaving the hills, the trees, the grazing
cows, the small yellow flowers growing along the path,
sharply etched in the clear light.

It is cool beneath the tree. As they get up to walk on,
the sun beats down on them.

Claire Heller says: "I hate the heat."

"You never said a word in the South of France."

"I was your guest then, on good behavior."

"Is that why you left so suddenly?"

"Because of the heat, yes."

"You are still a master of the double entendre."

"Fortunately."

"For me, a great misfortune. I never know where I am.
I'm not a match for you, Claire. I feel that I'm walking
on water. It makes me dizzy."

"You are much better at it than you let on. I've been
completely unable to overcome you."

"A fight to the death?"

"Why not say, an effort at conquest in which no one
was intended to be either a victim or a victor."

"Conquest? What kind of conquest could that
be?"

"Debate? Seduction?"

"Too edgy for my taste."

"I'm ready to teach you."

"I wish you were learning from me."

"To say exactly what I mean, as you do?"

"I try. But I end up defeated. You refuse to let it be said."

Claire looks thoughtful. "Or is it simply my love of sport? I always think, if it can be said with indirection, why bother with sincerity?"

"For you, I'm still a dream, no matter that I'm actually here beside you. You're still trying to make me come true."

"Maybe I have the power?"

"Even Claire Heller can't live without making the distinction."

"I don't believe in it. That perhaps is why I am not capable of what you call intimacy. The shedding of the ritual mask? The ceremonial garment? That's what intimacy means to you? The whole point of passion is the escape from the mundane, the humdrum, the obvious, the apparent."

"Now you sneak passion in again. As if it were the same as love?"

"What's the difference?"

"I know you don't know."

"Alma Runau! Do you imagine your letter, once and for all, had explained it?"

"If knowing means I've experienced it, I admit, once again, I have not. But I can imagine the difference. I'm tired of games. Claire, I am."

"Why should I be different? Isn't it you who are trying

to change me? To adapt me to your fantasy of the politically correct companion?"

"You shouldn't read any more Socrates. Your conversation is already too seductive."

"My conversation?"

"An evasion."

"Of?"

"Whatever might happen if one didn't play."

"Which is?"

"Precisely what neither of us will ever know if we go on this way."

Claire is silent.

Alma says: "Can't you imagine something direct and therefore beautiful? Beautiful because real. Down-to-earth. A beauty one sees in the other because she has dropped her mask. And shown herself, finally."

Claire is looking at her intently. "It is a different sort of beauty, I see that."

"What do you see?"

"Something in your face I haven't seen before. In a way I, too, hardly recognize you."

"Disappointed?"

"Not at all." Claire seems to reconsider. "But you're very different from that boy who ran from Marathon. Hard to describe. Indeed, like this handful of earth. It is what it is. Fascinating, in its own way. Although I've never been curious about a handful of earth before."

"Suddenly the truth? Yet fascinating?"

Claire, averting her eyes: "Fascinating, yes. The fundamentally unknowable nature of anything other than oneself."

"Isn't that what love is about? The fascination that the unknowable other can be known?"

"Sounds like a mystery. Aren't we back in my realm?"

"Of course, a mystery. Isn't the other, in her unique reality, the only mystery?"

"Now it is you who are evading. I had the impression we were talking about you, Alma. Your beauty."

"My reality."

"Evidently, the same thing."

"A handful of earth?"

Claire, smiling to herself: "You, the proponent of beauty according to nature. Reality's beauty. I, the advocate of the beauty one confers, willingly, upon the other. What you call intimacy. It's a failure of nerve. A closing down of the child's capacity to toy with the real."

"You turn the child's acceptance of reality into a choice?"

"Children make the world beautiful by insisting it is. Then they fall into reality and never recover from their despair. Except when they become children again and invent love."

"Reality fills you with despair? I can easily believe it."

"That, my dear Alma, is not only an analysis of me."
Silence.
Claire says: "So we are alike, after all?"

"I am tired of being what I have been."

"So, it is you who have come here to convert me!"

"To reality? Not easy to imagine."

"It isn't easy to imagine of you either. In spite of your

letter. No one gets rid of her past with an ideological snap of her fingers."

"At least I am making an effort."

"By which you mean, you didn't comb your hair when the plane arrived in San Francisco? You didn't put on makeup? You didn't change your travel clothes?"

"I thought I looked beautiful enough?"

"I woke up very early to make myself as beautiful as possible for you. It was my way of letting you know how important our meeting was. I was thinking very little about reality. Very much about the pleasure of seeing you again."

"And if you hadn't tried? If you'd taken the same risk you took when you showed up in the South of France? Without illusion of any kind?"

"That time you didn't recognize me either."

"If you hadn't left, sooner or later I would have recognized you."

"Recognized me? As what?"

"You tell me."

4

The sun is low, the sky slightly overcast. Flowers, flowering shrubs, rocks and stones are burning discreetly in the long afternoon light, small lamps scattered here and there in the fields.

Alma says: "Recognize you. You of all people. You drown a relationship in a mystic bath without ever asking yourself what might be there if you opened your eyes and looked. What is it you can't bear to see?"

"The naked, unadorned human, I take it."

"Your own nakedness, handing yourself over to the other? The other's frailty, given into your hands? You don't even see the problem."

"And you manage never to notice that I, too, am vulnerable."

"It's you, Claire. You, who would never be able to face the clinging, sometimes desperate vulnerability of the other."

"Which makes me a bad risk?"

"An impossible risk."

"But you are the one talking about facing one's fears."

"I'm not talking about throwing myself off a cliff, *tu sais*."

"As Sappho was said to have done. For love of her faithless sailor boy."

"I don't believe it. But it goes along with the whole

scenario. Love's desperation, eros and death. Why is it we cannot imagine a great love that lives on?"

"A passionate love that endures." Claire sounds angry. "Sure, everyone wants that."

"Even you?"

"Of course. Yes. I do. But if it's possible, why hasn't anyone pulled it off?"

"I've told you all I know. Now I feel like I've been invited to Madame Aubernon's salon. You pick the subject, I hold forth. If I'm good enough I'll be invited to dine a second time."

"I?" Claire lifts her chin. "I'm not in the least like Madame Aubernon. I, at least, serve good food."

"Come to think of it, I am hungry."

"I thought that's what you were driving at. Where's my sweater? I've brought almonds and dried figs for hors d'oeuvres. What meal is it for you?"

"No idea. I ate several on the plane. I'll have whatever meal you're taking."

"I couldn't eat a thing. It always happens to me when I'm excited."

"I'm just the opposite. When I'm happy I eat."

"I'm glad you're happy, Alma."

"For once I'm glad you've changed the subject."

A silence.

Alma shades her eyes, stares out at the landscape, goes back to gazing at their feet. "I never thought to see Claire Heller in shoes like that."

"What's wrong with them? They're perfectly sensible."

"When you were traveling around the world you wore winged sandals."

"In Berkeley walking shoes are the height of fashion."

"I should have known."

"At least you're laughing. If you'd gone on, your Teutonic severity might have broken my heart."

"I doubt it."

"But you could, quite easily. Some of the things you say. I am stripped positively naked. But still not recognized."

"You have been asking for recognition. I for reality. No wonder we've both failed."

"Why is it so hard to recognize me? I am the way I am. Why is that so hard to grasp?"

"You don't look like the reality I've always expected."

"What do you see? What am I like? Tell me the truth."

Silence.

Alma says: "You scare me."

"But I've never understood why."

"Your seductiveness makes me feel I have to take the initiative, initiate you. And you know so little about a simple, straightforward human connection."

"I know so little about women?"

"If I have to initiate, I'll end up in the dominant role. If you know more I could be dominated. Both seem unbearable. You want the truth, Claire? I'd rather avoid it all."

"If that were true would you be here?"

"If that were true would you have waited three years? Claire, what are you scared of?"

"This ruthless tearing down of the artifice that makes reality bearable."

"You and I will never agree."

"Why should we? The minute we do we'll have nothing left to say."

"You imagine we could go on like this?"

"For ever and ever . . ."

"You, forever evasive. Never letting anyone get to you. I ask again. What are you scared of?"

"I'm desperately afraid I might wither away in the clutches of your literalness."

"I thought you were bolder."

"I thought you were less afraid of taking a risk."

"For me you are risk *par excellence*. You are still a mirage, Claire. There's too much at stake here, too much to lose."

"All these years, all these stories and letters and conversations, and you imagine I haven't told you everything I can? Surely even Alma Runau can't be that prosaic?"

"I've been very open. Why shouldn't I ask the same of you?"

"In my own way I, too, have said a lot. But that doesn't mean . . ."

". . . you would ever tell one simple fact without drowning it in ambiguity?"

"Facts are ambiguous. I cannot make myself, my life, or even the universe as simple as you would like them to be."

"Claire Heller, we can't go on like this. It gets nowhere."

"You're perfectly wrong about that!"

"If we go on like this, three weeks will pass and I'll never . . ."

". . . get to see my home. Either we'll become dinner for a mountain lion or you'll insist I drive you back to the airport for the next plane. And anyway, why only three weeks? Don't tell me you already bought your return ticket?"

"In fact, I haven't . . ."

'One simple fact, yet it could be as well a gesture of infinite trust or infernal suspicion. It could mean you are free to leave tomorrow. Or free to stay any length of time at all. How exactly shall I take it?"

"Ambiguously, as you've understood . . ."

"Between us any stopping point will be arbitrary, is that what you mean?"

"Not exactly . . ."

"Aren't you tired? Cold? There's a fog coming in, I can feel it in my bones. In an hour this place will be desolate. The wind howling, the trees bent, strange figures approaching out of the darkness on the path of the future . . ."

"I've eaten all your almonds, most of your figs, I could go on walking all night if I had to. If that would make you stop smiling."

Claire holds out her hand to Alma, who hesitates, and then does not take it. Alma says: "There's something in this provocation I like, after all. We force each other to see through each other's eyes. Push past our limits. Why not continue? The fog is coming? I can take it . . ."

"To tell you the truth, I had something in mind. You're ruining my staging, carrying on like that. It's summer here, that means by nightfall very cold. In no time at all I can have a fire going. Who knows? There might even be a wine you've never tasted. A future vintage, unimaginably delicious. Bread I've baked with my own hands. I'll play the piano for you while you look out the window at our fairy-tale city, shimmering in amber lights. Our mysterious Baghdad of the Bay. Our Aphrodite of cities, scarcely risen from mist and sea foam. Ships, distance, the idealization of distance . . . a perfect setting in which to continue . . ."

"Well, in that case, I am exhausted. And hungry."

"And cold?" Claire puts her arm protectively around Alma's shoulder.

Alma steps aside. "Continue what?"

"Won't I do as the familiar stranger?"

"Familiar, after one day?"

"Here I am, coming toward you, and what do I get?"

"I know what I get. Can your scene include a hot bath, a large towel? Don't you have anything but bread to eat?"

"Bread baked by my own hands is about all I don't have . . ."

"I see, the perfect setting to make yourself irresistible."

"You've been resisting all along. And yet you're here."

"There are things, *ma chère,* not yet decided even in your staging. What if this time I make the fast getaway?"

"You won't get far. You'll trip over our friendship." Claire extends her leg across the path. "These walking shoes are a tribute to you."

"You're telling me you've got your feet on the ground? That's news."

"As for you, you're wilder. Even playful. Hard to

believe. What a stormy letter you wrote. If you don't watch out you'll soon grow wings."

"You mean we've changed each other?"

"What else matters!"

"No final scene to your little drama? But who gets to have the last word?"

"The last word? On your mark, Alma. I'll have it if you get there first."

ABOUT THE AUTHORS

Kim Chernin has studied and written about women's lives for a decade. She is the author of four works of non-fiction—*The Obsession, In My Mother's House, The Hungry Self,* and *Reinventing Eve*—a novel, *The Flame Bearers,* and a book of poetry, *The Hunger Song.* She is a writer and private consultant in Berkeley, California.

Renate Stendhal is a journalist, translator, and editor. She was born in Germany and lived for twenty years in Paris. She now lives in Berkeley, California, where she has a writing consultation practice.